Wendell H. Jones

High School Noir

Published by: Ingram Spark

2023

High School Noir

Copyright

The characters and events in this book are fictitious. Any similarity to real persons, living or dead, is coincidental and not intended by the author.

High School Noir, Copyright 2023 by Wendell H. Jones. Manufactured in the United States of America. All rights reserved. No other part of this book may be reproduced in any form or by any electronic or mechanical means, including information storage and retrieval systems, without permission in writing from Wendell H. Jones, except by a reviewer, who may quote brief passages in a review. First edition.

ISBN: 979-8-218-13114-2

Interior layout and cover design by Donna Loyd
dmlfreelance.com

To my family,
who never doubted I could write a novel.

Table Of Contents

chapter one

"No, no. Don't leave. Stay on Mommy's lap. Look at the picture book. Listen, here's a lovely poem about us, Sweetie. It has your name in it.

Bobby Shaftoe's gone to sea.

Silver buckles on his knee;

See. He's a little teddy bear. Look how cute he's dressed, Bobby, with the silver buckles. I'll make you a sailor suit like that. You'll be the only little boy in the neighborhood with one.

He'll come back and marry me,

Just like you, Sweetie. Daddy will stay gone, Bobby, and you can go to sea, come back, and marry me.

Bonny . . .

That word means he's pretty, like you, Sweetie. Here's a big kiss from Mommy.

Ooom wah!

Bonny Bobby Shaftoe!

Oh my, this poem's making Mommy excited.

Bobby Shaftoe's bright and fair,

Combing down his yellow hair;

He's my love for evermair,

That last word must mean 'evermore.' Just like us, Bobby. Whenever you leave me—which won't be very often—you'll come right back to me. Because we love each other for evermore. We can say 'evermore' to each other, even if it doesn't rhyme, Sweetie. Evermore! Evermore! Oh my, we'll be together evermore! Just us two. How exciting!

Bonnie Bobby Shaftoe!

The end. Wasn't that an exciting poem, Sweetie! You make Mommy so happy. More happy than anything in the world. Evermore! Evermore! Can you imagine that—you and I will be together evermore. Here's a big kiss. Oom wah! Oh, oh, I almost forgot— always remember there are dangerous people out there! Yes, many people are dangerous, even some of our neighbors. Well. Why don't you go out and play now. But it's dangerous everywhere. Well. Why don't you go play with Clarkie, he's a good playmate for a three-year old like you. He takes a bath every day."

* * *

"Hi, Mrs. Shaftoe. I brought Bobby back to you. He walked up to Don and me a little while ago, like he wanted to play, but he looked scared. You know, like he always does. Anyway, Don and I were just throwing the football around, getting ready for our game Friday against Washington High. Coach says I'll be the quarterback again! Anyway, Don says, 'Clark, throw the ball to Bobby.' You know how Don always talks loud. Well, Mrs. Shaftoe, I throw the football to Bobby as gently as I could—he's just three. But I think Don scared him, talking loud. Bobby caught it, but he started to cry. Just stood there holding the ball and crying, like he wanted to play, but was scared. So here he is, Mrs. Shaftoe. We're sorry if we did anything wrong."

"Oh, Clarkie, you're a good playmate for Bobby. You're so clean. I know you take a bath every day. Bobby, what's wrong with you! Clarkie, I keep telling Bobby to go out and play. Bobby, there are some bad people out there. We never know who they are! Clarkie, I don't know why Bobby doesn't go out and play. Thank you for bringing Bobby home, Clarkie. Bye now."

"Bye, Mrs. Shaftoe. Wish us good luck against Washington High."

"Bye, Clarkie. Never mind, Bobby. Well. We never know who the bad people are. You need to go out and play more. Mommy will always dry your tears. And, look, look, Mommy has another book. You'll like this one too. It's about a sweet little birdie. Wouldn't you like a story about a sweet little birdie? Here's a big kiss from Mommy. Oom wah! Now, sit on Mommy's lap. Oh, Sweetie, look at Mommy's fingers. This always cheers you up. They're like a little birdie walking on your knee. Yes, does that tickle? Don't giggle. Don't giggle.

Once upon a midnight dreary, while I pondered, weak and weary,

Over many a quaint and curious volume of forgotten lore—

Oh hell, Bobby, we know that part. Let's just skip ahead. Do you remember this poem has my name in it? Lots of times. Lenore. Lenore. Yes, it has your Mommy's name in it—Lenore. And here comes the sweet birdie, walking up your pant leg. Does that tickle? Don't giggle. Don't giggle. Here's my favorite part!

But the Raven, sitting lonely on the placid bust, spoke only

That one word, as if his soul in that one word he did outpour.

Oh, it's so emotional and exciting, Sweetie! My soul. I mean, the birdie's soul. It's lonely. Can you imagine!

Nothing further then he uttered—not a feather then he fluttered—

Here comes the birdie. Here he comes, walking up

the inside of your leg, Sweetie.

Till I scarcely more than muttered "Other friends have flown before—"

Yes, other friends have flown before. Like your father. Thank goodness he left. Bobby, you'll leave, too, but when you come back you'll marry me.

On the morrow he will leave me, as my hopes have flown before.

But we find out the sweet black birdie doesn't leave after all, Bobby. Look, he's walked a long way up your leg. Don't giggle. Don't giggle, Bobby. Shh. Be quiet. This will be a secret between us, Sweetie.

Then the bird said "Nevermore."

After this, we can take our bath together."

* * *

This and earlier incidents caused a feeling of apprehension that dogged Shaftoe into adulthood. But of course, as an adult he could recall none of those incidents.

chapter two

Now, decades later, a machine gun *rat-tat-tat* hammered Bobby Shaftoe's body. It was the rapid-fire explosion of big-rig engine brakes. Simultaneously he heard nerve-shredding screeches of tires, and the shudder of semi-trailer bodies. In the scorching June heat and humidity, he leaped from the highway toward the far-off curb. As he leaped, he glimpsed towering 18-wheelers bounding and jackknifing toward him. So close he could touch them. Christ!

Then, he was safe on the curb. The tumult stopped. Except within his body.

His legs quivered, his heart threatened to rocket out of his chest. The pedestrian signal still read *walk*. In the hot haze of burning tire smoke, blazing Midwestern sunlight, and diesel fumes, a big rig driver leaned out his cab window and gave him the finger.

Shaftoe thought, I should have fucking anticipated this. I've seen dozens of students jump like this. My turn was bound to come. Why can't I concentrate on my surroundings!

The traffic light changed and the drivers, cursing, straightened their rigs and moved off through the potholes. He'd lost a shoe in the chaos. He found it in the gutter, flattened, ripped, and grimy. He retrieved it and tried to knock it back into shape on the curb. Then he hesitated. I can't walk around with one shoe off and one shoe on. Something reminded him of his mother reading him nursery rhymes. *Diddle-diddle* something. Those words seemed sexual. The shoe looked like shit. He squeezed his foot into it.

Feeling unsteady, High School Counselor Shaftoe stumbled the few yards to the run-down classroom building of Entonces High School, which also housed the school's counseling center. Inside, he pushed open the waist-high wooden gate and walked past the desk, unoccupied for the moment, of the counseling center clerk, which looked lonely in the middle of the large room that was once a classroom. Then he sat down, off to one side in his so-called office, really a former broom closet with dusty wooden floor, no window, and a doorframe but no door.

But there was no respite from the highway turmoil.

His desk and two chairs—all the furniture that would fit into his tiny space—vibrated from the truck route traffic. His eyes burned from tiny particles that drifted down between the pulsing florescent tubes on the ceiling. He hoped that the particles weren't asbestos. Some days the tubes seemed like strobe lights and he had headaches. And every time he looked back outside through the building's front door he saw Kenworths, Macks, and Peterbilts come raging down the highway to do their noisy, smelly, dance under the sinister traffic light.

Damn it, did other professionals have to put up with conditions like this? This was sensory overload. Psychedelic!

Psychedelic? Does anyone use that word anymore? He guessed that the current-day equivalent among his counselees might be "Clusterfuck!" But he wasn't sure. Kids' slang changed so fast.

Was there some rule that high school campuses in dying small towns like the town of Entonces had to be bisected by crumbling truck routes? How the hell did the five hundred students put up with it? Surely it interfered with their already hormone-distracted ability to concentrate. Concentrate on schoolwork, that is. Of course, their capacity to concentrate on one another wasn't impaired. Traffic pollution's a health hazard, but to the kids it seemed to have the superfluous effect of erection pills for the boys and vibrators for the girls.

God knows, neither sex needed anything extra.

And to top it off, he needed to go see varsity football coach Ed Zachary this morning. He'd put that meeting off too long already. Shaftoe anticipated an ordeal of classic proportions. But perhaps that was a baseless fear. He knew he had several of those.

Well, he thought, I've talked with Dr. Mallard about my fear of forceful men. Dr. Mallard led me to believe—Shaftoe considered his choice of words, *led me to believe,* and decided they were accurate—she led me to believe that my fear comes from a lack of experience. Father left me, and no male authority figures were present in my early life. They couldn't stand to be around my mother. But why can't I get over that fear?

No siblings. That had been lonely, but at least no sibling rivalry to linger into my adulthood.

He dreaded leaving the relative safety of his office—was *office* the right word, considering how demeaning the conditions were?—for his impending meeting with the coach. So much uncertainty. Why couldn't he get used to it; his college professors had warned him that ambiguity and lack of resolution were part of a school counselor's work.

The whole atmosphere today was unsettling. There were no bodies moving on campus. The presence of students usually had a calming effect on him, but this was the week after classes ended, the start of summer vacation—vacation for the students and teachers, that is, but not for him. The only employees on campus this summer were the coach, the principal, counseling center clerk Sweet Jillie, and himself. They were finishing up paperwork and planning the next school year. Nine weeks of this relaxed pace to look forward to.

Shaftoe was thankful that there were no messages on his answering machine.

Despite the ongoing traffic noise, the relative quiet was ominous. He thought, In the eye of the hurricane is silence. He hadn't seen the campus lawn so devoid of movement since the mandatory assembly about the state bird, flag, and flower. And even then, especially then, there were a dozen students under the bleachers, smoking, laughing, and goosing one another.

Shaftoe left his tiny vibrating office and its particle-laden air, and walked unsteadily down the diesel-scented hallway, toward the sidewalk which led to the field house. He felt his eyes blinking rapidly. He couldn't make them stop. The traffic-damaged shoe made him limp. Bad shoe! Bad shoe! Like scolding a dog. Was he going nuts?

He stepped into the oppressive heat and humidity outside the classroom building's backdoor, and heard the bang of its closing and, a split second later, the metallic click of its panic bar. He flinched. It sounded like a rifle being fired at him and reloaded. His heart had slowed down from the close call on the truck route, but it was speeding up again, just as fast, in anticipation of his meeting with Coach Zachary. Shaftoe knew his anxiety was excessive.

As he took the long hot walk through the overhanging elms, he hardly noticed their beauty. Coach Zachary's office was in the new field house, the only building with air conditioning and soundproofing. Zachary said it was the only building on campus that was up to safety code. He'd bragged that he got the money for his wall-to-wall office carpet by calling it "acoustical treatment" on a requisition to the school district.

Shaftoe shook his head and frowned. The coach was located as far from him, the students, the faculty, and the truck traffic as he could get. Out there with the lush green practice fields. In the field house named for him. Never-never land. Showed you the big money the little town of Entonces had coughed up over the years in tribute to his winning high school football teams. Coach Ed Zachary the local hero. In his new castle, The Ed Zachary Field House.

All this happy horseshit was pissing Shaftoe off, but the student body was fascinating! Traditional male and female, LGBTQ+, non-binary, gender-fluid. And every sexual preference, ethnicity, religion, income level, dress, behavior, and level of intelligence. Most of the students would never be healthier, look better, or feel sexier in their lives. But adolescence could be the best of times and the worst of times, sometimes both within the same day. Even within the same minute. That was why he'd been hired to be the school's counselor a year ago—to help the students get through it all.

For some kids, their worst of times would be unremitting, as if the torture would never end. They would be lucky to get through an hour without emotional disaster. He remembered his own times like that. As he'd told Dr. Mallard, he still had them, in memories and nightmares. But what kind of people could be more interesting to work with than high schoolers! He'd never had a job where time went so fast! Never a dull moment.

School days here certainly weren't like his own high school days. The most unexpected thing was—today the kids almost always got along with one another. Better than the adults on campus did. Certainly better than he and Coach Zachary would.

In a few seconds, he'd be talking with the coach. He was terrified that he'd lose control of himself.

chapter three

"Lying with my baby. She'll enjoy every minute . . ."

Shaftoe recognized the rock-and-roll lyrics blasting from the new field house. Who could be playing it so openly? Wouldn't Principal Orson Fluke consider the words obscene and ban the song from campus?

On the other hand, it was one of Shaftoe's favorites. Hearing it, he felt a little better. Its words, *"She's got a beautiful body, and her mama is gone,"* always set off his sexual fantasies. He wondered what the girl in the song looked like. That began to give him an erection. But then, he wondered what her mama was like. Did she read nursery rhymes and poetry? Was she dangerous? He began to wilt.

As he entered the Ed Zachary Field House, he was certain the high-decibel music was coming from Coach Zachary's office. His stomach tightened as he peeked through Zachary's open doorway into the coach's large, cool office. There were cigar butts and empty Heineken bottles on the new carpet. He saw a school-issue music player on the coach's desk. The volume seemed to make it bounce in time to the beat. Like a scene from *Fantasia.* Shaftoe thought, Can I trust my perceptions? School's out. Party time. Coach Zachary lived in his own world of arrested emotional development.

"Shaftoe, you pussy, 'decided to come to the men's world, huh?"

Christ, Zachary, Shaftoe thought, I resisted phoning you because I didn't want to hear "Can't you face me like a man." So here I am, in person, and I'm getting insulted anyway.

The coach, a big man in loose gray sweats, powerful looking despite the beginning of a beer belly, stood in the middle of his office, jerking about to the music, completely off the beat. With one hand at his crotch, he was jiggling what looked like a pleated grey and blue cheerleader skirt and a pair of white, panty-like, cheerleader briefs. With his other hand he waved a school pompom.

That made Shaftoe wonder if Zachary had a passkey to the girls' lockers. Was he opening their lockers and snooping? There was something creepy about the guy. Shaftoe found it hard to focus on what he had come to Zachary's office to accomplish.

It occurred to Shaftoe to comment on the contrast

between the coach's greeting and his behavior. But he knew that wouldn't fly. Instead, "Hi, Coach. How ya doin' ?"

Zachary said nothing, and continued his disgusting dance.

On the other side of Zachary was Harley Huntington, the school board president and publisher of the local paper. He was standing on a wooden chair, swaying in an uncoordinated way. He was dressed in a blue open collared button-down shirt and khaki pants, and was smiling at Zachary. Buddies, Shaftoe thought. Huntington waved a tampon in one hand, and a half-empty bottle of Heineken in the other. There were several empties and their bottle caps on the floor near his chair.

Along the far wall of the office, Principal Orson Fluke sat on a similar chair. Spine straight, chin up, legs crossed knee over knee, he was affecting a regal bearing. He wore a black pin-stripe suit and a red tie with tiny grey fish printed on it. The clothing salesman must have told Fluke that his suit and tie were a power uniform, but Fluke had tied the necktie way too short. And with his big clunky shoes he looked like a tall slim hillbilly waiting for a funeral to start.

Shaftoe looked down at his own truck-ravaged shoe. He hoped no one had noticed it. Who was he to think ill of Fluke's footwear.

"Mr. Zachary, perhaps you should stop doing that dance. You're putting your reputation at risk," Fluke said tentatively. "You know, the Bible says, 'A good name is rather to be chosen than great riches.' That's Proverbs, Chapter Twenty-two, Verse 1." Despite his stately posture and his recitation of Bible verse, Fluke's voice had no authority in it.

Zachary leered at Fluke and continued to jerk the cheerleader skirt and panties up and down. His tongue lolled out. "Shut up, Orville."

"That's *Orson,* Coach." Principal Fluke spoke softly. No one acted as if they'd heard him.

Now, for the first time, Zachary appeared to Shaftoe to be thinking, rather than on autopilot. But he kept flouncing about. Shaftoe hoped that Zachary wasn't thinking of inviting him to join in. The sooner he could get his professional duty accomplished, the better.

"Orville, how about 'Women, submit yourselves,'" Zachary said. "That's First Peter, Chapter 3. Didja hear that, Harley? First peter! Submit yourselves. Get it?" Harley Huntington grinned fondly at Zachary. Zachary turned to Orson Fluke, "Is that one of your favorite chapters, Orville?"

Shaftoe thought, the coach's voice is completely sober. Just being his gross self, and reveling in it.

Zachary sashayed toward Huntington. "A *first* peter, Harley. Just what this sweaty souvenir needs." Zachary pressed the panties up against the board president's nose.

Harley Huntington gave the intimate apparel an exaggerated sniff. He chortled. "Yeah, Ed. There *is* something I like about high school girls, but I can't put my finger on it. They won't *let* me!" He looked around as if to say, Come on, guys, we know Coach is just kidding. He began making train-whistle noises by blowing across the top of his beer bottle.

"Hey, Shaftoe, cured anyone lately?" Zachary yelped.

"Coach . . ." Why can't I stop showing him this respect, Shaftoe thought. The whole community intones the word *Coach* as if it were *King.* ". . . that's not what school counseling is about. . . ."

"Oh, yeah. I keep forgetting. You weren't hired just to listen to the girls moan about their PMS, and the boys cry about how their girlfriends won't put out."

Huntington and Zachary guffawed. To Shaftoe, the sound was both obscene and belittling.

But the coach was on a roll, suddenly full of good cheer, "Hey, Bobby, watch this! This is a good one!" He moved to the far wall where Principal Fluke was sitting silently.

"Stand up, Fluke." Fluke did as he was told. "Step away from the chair!" Zachary sounded like a law enforcement officer. "Turn your back to me." Fluke did.

Zachary glanced at Huntington and Shaftoe to be sure they were watching.

"Are we ready for a sports joke? Shaftoe, you were a wrestler in college, right?"

How the hell did Zachary know that? Shaftoe didn't like the "Gotcha" look that Zachary gave him.

Shaftoe hadn't told anyone in town about his less-than-stellar wrestling days. But he'd heard the rumor that Fluke permitted the coach to snoop through the faculty's application papers. If he snooped, he must have noticed Shaftoe's small number of college wrestling victories. But wrestling had put Shaftoe in great physical condition for an average-sized man, and he continued to work out.

Without waiting for a response from Shaftoe, Zachary put his belly against Orson Fluke's lower back. From the rear, the coach curved his right arm through Fluke's right armpit, and closed his hand on the back of Fluke's neck. "Half nelson," he said, and gave a confirming nod to his audience of two.

"Coach, let me go." It sounded like a plea, not a command.

"Be a man, Orlow."

Maintaining the first wrestling hold, Zachary then reached his left arm through Fluke's left armpit and up. Now the back of Fluke's neck was held by both of Zachary's hands. "Full nelson!"

Shaftoe didn't know why Fluke put up with this. He wondered. Coach Zachary has status in the community because of all his winning football seasons. Hell, the school board named this very field house after him; that usually didn't happen until a person died. Had the coach pulled strings to get Fluke the principalship? A principal who would never overrule Zachary. He could have used his bud, Board President Harley Huntington, to accomplish that. After all, under school law the Town of Entonces School Board outranked everyone, even the superintendent of schools. Was Ed Zachary, the local hero, the big frog in a small pond, the power behind the throne? Maybe behind every throne in town?

Shaftoe wished he were somewhere else, but he needed to convey important information.

"Pay attention, guys!" Zachary shouted. Huntington stopped making train-whistle noises. Shaftoe's mind returned to the action in the room. Coach released his wrestling hold on Fluke, and quickly stepped in front of him. Coach formed his hands into two cups just inches from Fluke's testicles, reached toward them, and gleefully yelped, "*Father* Nelson! Get it, guys? Half nelson, full nelson, *Father* Nelson!"

The action had gone from surreal to totally inappropriate. Damn, Shaftoe thought, how many ways are there to be forceful and insensitive?

Fluke had flinched. His face turned red, his ramrod posture collapsed into a round-shouldered slump, and he left the room. Some adolescent part of Shaftoe didn't know whether to smirk or break into tears. What a place to work.

There was a moment of quiet except for the lyrics *"She'll stay young forever . . ."*, and Zachary's and Huntington's giggling with their hands over their mouths. To Shaftoe, they seemed suddenly girlish.

Well, enough minutes wasted. Time for courage.

Shaftoe surprised himself with his directness. "Listen, Coach . . ." That worked—Ed Zachary's eyes met his. ". . . Could we talk in private?" By way of asking permission of the board president, Shaftoe gave a quizzical look to Huntington. He thought Huntington caught the meaning of the look, but Huntington didn't respond in any way.

"Don't be a little girl, Shaftoe. Anything you have to say, you can tell me right here, like a man!"

"Well, Coach, it's about Chip." Huntington would know that Chip is Zachary's son. Maybe now he'd give Shaftoe and Zachary some kind of sign, encouraging them to confer privately. Maybe he'd even excuse himself and leave the room.

No such luck.

Shaftoe's stomach ached. Anxiety, he thought. Zachary, you asked for this.

"Well, Mr. Zachary, your son, Chip, won't be playing quarterback for you this fall."

chapter four

Shaftoe studied Coach Zachary. The coach looked stunned, then furious. He punched Shaftoe in the chest, like a pile driver. It hurt. It hurt a lot, like a broken bone. Shaftoe hoped he didn't let it show.

"Whata you mean, Chip won't be quarterback!"

Because of the punch, Shaftoe was having trouble breathing. He wheezed, "Chip's academically ineligible, Coach."

Zachary glared at Shaftoe. "Godamit, he's gets all A's."

"Not anymore, Coach. A teacher caught him cheating on a final exam." His chest now felt like a giant toothache.

Huntington spoke. "Mr. Shaftoe, what's that teacher's name?" His voice was smooth and firm, and carried a lot of authority. Huntington's calling me

Mister, Shaftoe thought. I hope that means he's putting this on a professional level where it belongs. He chose not to answer the board president. This was a matter strictly between himself and Chip's parent, Ed Zachary.

"Yeah, Shaftoe, who was that lying pussy?"

"You'll get a letter this week, Mr. Zachary."

"Bobby, you wimp, be a man. Who was it?"

"Sorry, Coach. You get officially notified the same way as any other parent—by mail."

"Chip was cheating? That lying wussie teacher. I'll kick his ass!"

Shaftoe didn't see any reason to tell Zachary that two separate teachers had caught Chip cheating on their respective final exams. Keep this visit short. Chip would not be getting his usual straight A's. Instead, Zachary would be getting two letters, one from each teacher. After that, the coach would get Chip's spring report card, with two F's on it.

Zachary suddenly smiled. He looked proud. Shaftoe was surprised.

"That's my boy. He'll do anything to win."

Shaftoe suspected that was the truth. Chip must have been relentlessly pressured by his old man. Overkill was the coach's mode of operating. Shaftoe's chest still hurt. He was only beginning to feel as if his breath was coming normally. He said "Um-huum," to

Zachary and then chastised himself for only making that vague acknowledgement sound, like a stereotypical nondirective counselor.

"Hey! What the hell's wrong with your shoe, Bobby? It's leaving dirt on my carpet."

Shaftoe decided to ignore the shoe question. After all, he told himself, I'm here on a professional mission. Keep things on track. Get this over with.

"Well, Mr. Zachary, you can talk to the teachers involved, when you get their letters." Oops, Shaftoe realized he had just complicated his life by revealing that Chip had been caught cheating on two separate finals, not just one.

"*Two* lying bastards. I'll kick their asses!"

Shaftoe refrained from pointing out that Coach was blaming teachers, not Chip or his own high-pressure parenting. Keep it simple.

Now another tack from Zachary, "Godamit, Shaftoe, Chip holds the league scoring record. How can I keep the championship next season without Chip!"

Shaftoe shrugged and shook his head. Your problem, Coach, he thought. But he suspected that the coach's football problems went deeper than the loss of his quarterback, as gifted as Chip might be. Rather than helping all his athletes improve, had Zachary failed to prepare a back-up quarterback? Was that because he wanted Chip to be the only one, to be heavily recruited by colleges? Shaftoe decided to risk checking that out. "What about your backup quarterback?"

Zachary blinked. For an instant, he looked as if the concept was new to him. "No one's half as good as Chip. Not a third as good."

Board President Huntington stepped in again. "Surely, Mr. Shaftoe, as an experienced school counselor, you know that teachers sometimes make mistakes. I'm sure you've made some mistakes, too. Our school board will understand that. And I can see that this never gets into the newspaper."

Soft soap, and manipulative, Shaftoe thought. Huntington thinks he's showing me a way out. Shaftoe reminded himself that the Board president also owned and published the local small-town rag, *The Conqueror.* Half of its content was Entonces High School sports. A losing varsity football team in the upcoming season could cost Huntington a lot of readership, a lot of advertisers, and therefore a lot of income.

"Nope, Mr. Huntington. I don't think the teachers made a mistake."

"Chip can fix this by going to summer school!" Zachary yelped.

"Mr. Zachary, there is no summer school." Shaftoe was thinking, I'll bet the school board has diverted summer school money into your varsity football program for years now. He looked at Huntington. He thought the school board president caught the significance of the look, but his face showed no response.

Zachary reverted to type, "Shaftoe, you aren't man enough to make this stick."

Shaftoe felt his cheeks heat up. He told himself, be professional, then get out of here. "Mr. Zachary, it isn't up to me, two teachers bubbled-in 'F' on Chip's grade sheets."

"Dammit, Bobby, have you heard of an eraser! It's easy."

Huntington took a more sophisticated line. "Who sends the ineligible students' names to the state athletic commission, Mr. Shaftoe? Coach does, right?"

"Not on this, Mr. Huntington. I do."

"Oh, then we have some time to set this misunderstanding straight."

Shaftoe knew that he was about to drop a bomb. "No, Mr. Board President, Chip's F's are at the state athletic commission already."

Huntington's mouth opened a little, then closed. Veins stood out on his neck. He looked at Shaftoe and lifted a finger to his chin and tapped it. Shaftoe wondered if Huntington was aware it was his middle finger. "Damn it, Mr. Shaftoe, who authorized you to contact the commission? Does Principal Fluke know about this?"

First question first, thought Bobby, "The commission authorized me, Mr. Huntington. It's in their written policy. It authorizes the school's *custodian of records.* That's me." *Custodian,* Shaftoe thought, these two bastards better not make a joke about my broom-closet office.

Huntington asked again, "Does Principal Fluke know about this?"

Shaftoe didn't answer. He knew that it would have been less than useless for him to give Fluke a heads-up; Fluke would have run to Zachary, and Zachary to the board president.

"The school board can overturn this." It was an empty threat from Huntington.

"Sir, you might want to check with the district's legal counsel." Shaftoe doubted that Huntington would.

"Godamit, Bobby, why are you picking on my son! You got something against success?"

"Coach, you've worked here a long time. You know that every semester about a dozen kids lose their athletic eligibility; it isn't just Chip."

But Shaftoe began to feel that in the two other men's eyes he might look vulnerable. In truth, he didn't know for sure if any of this spring's other ineligible students were from varsity football or not.

"Ah ha, Bobby! Chip was the only one from varsity football, wasn't he!" Zachary had found a chink in Shaftoe's preparation for this encounter. Christ, Shaftoe reflected for the hundredth time that school year, you've got to make your preparations to parents ironclad.

"It's irrelevant, Mr. Zachary."

"Oooh. Fucking grad school word. Ir-rel-e-vant!" Zachary stretched out the syllables.

Huntington again, "Mr. Shaftoe, within the next two hours I expect you to find out exactly which students are ineligible for which sports, and get that information to my office. You're new to this district, aren't you. That means you can be dismissed at the board's discretion. We don't even need to state a reason."

What an asshole, Shaftoe thought. But he knew that Huntington had power. He also knew that he could easily and quickly get the information to Huntington's office. But would that be a good move? He had sent the list of ineligible students to the state athletic commission quickly, so he could take an irrevocable stand with Ed Zachary, but he hadn't scrutinized the list. Then he'd immediately made seeing Zachary his next priority. Was that only because he feared a Zach attack on his masculinity if he didn't tell the coach face-to-face and in advance of Zachary's receiving the letters from Chip's teachers? Well, Shaftoe told himself, that strategy hasn't eased my pain.

"Send that to my office, Counselor Shaftoe..." Harley Huntington looked at his wristwatch, "...before ten o'clock this morning. Remember who signs your paycheck."

Zachary stepped closer to Shaftoe, putting them nose to nose. Zachary's body odor, and his beer-and-cigar breath, made a foul stench. Shaftoe refused to take a step backward. He knew that Zachary would interpret that as cowardice.

"Shaftoe, you little girl. You gutless wonder. Grow some balls. Or maybe you don't need 'em. Do you even *have* a sex life?"

Coach had hit a sore spot. Shaftoe really wasn't satisfied with his intermittent, single-guy affairs. But he was working on that, wasn't he, with his psychotherapist, Dr. Mallard. His anger rose. Was coach trying to make him crumble? Shaftoe was terrified of crumbling. What would that be like? Would he shed tears? Would he slink from the room, like Fluke? Would he fire back verbally? Would he do physical battle with Zachary, get destroyed and humiliated? He hadn't come to Zachary's office to do any of those things—just to deliver a short message in a professional way. He imagined grabbing Zachary's leg behind the knee, jerking it upward, tipping him onto his back, pinning his shoulders down, and making him say "uncle." The coach was bigger, heavier, and possibly stronger, but Shaftoe thought he could get the jump on him.

Zachary wasn't stopping, "I can hurt candy asses like you! I swear it." The coach clenched his fists and leaned closer. The stench—Shaftoe began breathing through his mouth.

Shaftoe knew it would cost him his job to get physical. The coach and Huntington were making this personal. They would back each other up. Orson Fluke would be no help. And none of that would matter anyway. It was his first year with the school district, so they could fire him without stating a reason. He deliberately glowered into Zachary's eyes. He hoped his expression showed courage, but he feared that he only looked drained and sad.

Now Zachary stood with his feet spread and his hands on his hips, staring at Shaftoe. Was the coach about to laugh in his face? Shaftoe had nothing more to tell these guys. The superhero line, "My work here is done," came to his mind. Time to demonstrate it. "Look for the teachers' letters, Coach," he said, and headed for the door. He tried to walk with more self-respect than Fluke had walked.

When out of sight in the hallway, he tried to calm himself. He told himself, Take slow and deep, calming breaths. But that made his bruised chest hurt. Outside, as he passed through the overhanging elms, he felt like crying. He asked himself why. He had wanted to throw Zachary to the ground. Why should he even be wondering if Zachary was right to insult him.

He imagined a teddy bear in a sailor suit with arrows shot into it. Bad day at the zoo, he thought.

As he trudged back under the elms, toward his unsatisfactory broom closet, a rustling of leaves and a frightening snapping of wood came from overhead. There was a shriek, and Shaftoe was explosively struck on his shoulders. He crashed face first into the sidewalk.

chapter five

Oof! Damn. What happened!

Shaftoe was flat on the sidewalk, his face pinned against the hot gritty concrete. His eyes watered and he felt blood coming from his nose. Was it broken? He felt puffs of breath near his ear. The breath smelled like Spicy Nachos. He tried to sit up, but the weight on his back was too heavy. He waited for the next blow.

What the hell had struck him? Zachary must be behind this! Shaftoe used all his strength to twist at the waist. Out of the corner of his eye he glimpsed a video recorder held at arm's length, protectively above the concrete. He was sure now that it was a human body on his back, pinning him face-down into the sidewalk. But how had it happened? He hadn't heard any steps behind him, but the body had struck him full force.

As the weight slowly lifted from his back, Shaftoe

heard Coach Zachary's voice booming from the far away field house doorway, "Bobby, you punk, don't let that kid butt-fuck you on campus!" It seemed loud enough for the whole town to hear. Then came Zachary's obnoxious giggle.

Shaftoe rolled onto his back and saw his attacker, now struggling to stand up; his eyes were terror-stricken. That was not what Shaftoe expected.

"Oh, gosh! Mr. Shaftoe, I'm so sorry," a voice squeaked.

"Christ, kid, what the hell are you doing!"

Both of them struggled to their feet. The boy looked familiar, and Shaftoe felt embarrassed that he couldn't remember the kid's name. It had to be one of his counselees, Fluke had assigned him the whole school of five hundred.

"Ohmigod, Mr. Shaftoe, your nose is bleeding! Are you okay?"

Shaftoe didn't want to reveal that he didn't know the kid's name. He might have to make a report, maybe even to the police. If the kid realized that his counselor didn't know his name, he might run off. He looked at the kid's shoes. Keds. Yellow with black laces. Even if the kid ran and whipped off his shirt to muddle any identification, he wasn't likely to change his shoes. And maybe he would recognize the kid's voice. It was very adolescent, and cracked as he spoke, as if it was just beginning to change. He got a good look at the medium-height, skinny frame of his attacker, and decided it was probably a ninth-grade boy that had crushed him.

"Here, Mr. Shaftoe, take my handkerchief. It's okay, my mom just washed it. I promise."

"Thanks, kid." Shaftoe had his own, but why turn down an offer that seemed conciliatory. He took the wadded up grey handkerchief and blotted his nose. The flow of blood was heavy. He pinched the sides of his nose firmly. That had always stopped his nosebleeds in the past, even in college wrestling matches. He began breathing through his mouth.

The kid continued to stand, awe-struck. Flatfooted. It didn't seem like he was going to run. Over the kid's shoulder, Shaftoe saw Coach Zachary go back into his namesake field house, shaking his head from side to side.

"Mr. Shaftoe, don't you know me? It's me, Zeus. Ohmigod!"

Then Shaftoe remembered. The boy was Jesus Jimenez, the kid who'd told him, "I spell my name like Jesus, but it's pronounced *Hey, Zeus*. Teachers always say it wrong. Just call me Zeus."

Zeus carefully placed his video recorder down onto the grass next to the sidewalk.

"Zeus, you got some *'splainin'* to do." Shaftoe tried to sound like Desi Arnaz from the old *I Love Lucy* TV show. But because he was still pinching his nose, it sounded like he was speaking through a comb and wax paper. Why scold the kid and make him feel worse. If that happens, Zeus might clam up or lie or still run away. Immediately he felt stupid; Zeus was way too young to catch on to *'splainin'*. But Zeus looked like he *had* caught on. Shaftoe wondered if Zeus was a peculiar ninth-grade boy who watched *Lucy* reruns.

"Oh, I get it, Mr. Shaftoe—*'splainin'*—like Desi says to Lucy, huh?" Zeus appeared to relax a little. "Well, I don't know how to tell you this . . ." He paused. "You won't understand."

"Just start, Zeus. If I don't understand, I'll ask questions. Like this—Who sent you?" Shaftoe continued to fear that Coach Zachary was involved.

"Huh, Mr. Shaftoe?"

This kid was setting a Guiness Record for saying *Mr. Shaftoe* so often in a short time. Shaftoe was getting annoyed with it. "Who sent you to hurt me?"

"Ohmigod. I knew you wouldn't understand. I can't tell you." Zeus now looked both fearful and greatly embarrassed.

"What is it you can't tell me?" When he'd used that question with counselees in his office it secretly amused him, but it worked nine times out of ten.

"Gosh. Well, it's like this . . ."

Maybe the *Mr. Shaftoe's* had finally stopped. Come on kid, don't make me start you up again.

"Omigod. Well, it's like this. I know school is over now, for the summer. I know I'm not supposed to be on campus. But I have this plan to video some footage, so I can sell it to the Seniors at the end of next school year. Like a video yearbook. I wasn't going to tell anybody until I'm ready to sell it. Ohmigod, I can't believe I fell on you!"

The *Mr. Shaftoe's* had stopped, but now Shaftoe was getting irritated by the *Ohmigod's*. They sounded a little effeminate. But maybe Zeus had learned English from female elementary school teachers and had unwittingly picked up their inflection. Then Shaftoe wondered if it was Zachary that was making him construe everything as sexual. Or maybe his own past? He'd been talking with Dr. Mallard a lot about that.

He forced his attention back to the matter at hand. Why couldn't he concentrate on the present!

"Let me guess, Zeus. You were up in the tree with your video recorder running. To get footage to sell later . . ." Zeus was hanging his head, alternately clicking his tongue and sighing. Maybe he was relieved that Shaftoe was putting this violent happenstance into words for him. ". . . But why in the tree?"

"Well, Mr Shaftoe, Sir . . ."

That seemed a little too obsequious, even considering the circumstances.

". . . I wanted a high camera angle; it's more dramatic. I was going to call this segment, *Counselor Shaftoe Exits the Zachary Field House.*"

Christ, kids do strange things.

"Well, Zeus, maybe I should feel honored to be your subject, but I don't. You could've really hurt me."

"I *did* hurt you, Mr. Shaftoe. Your nose is bleeding. And look at your shoe!"

"Zeus, I've bled before. I'm a tough guy. And my shoe was already like that!" Whatever. "But, are you okay? Where do you hurt? Do you need to see a doctor? Will your camera still work?" Shaftoe realized he might be the one held accountable. He didn't want to get sued by Zeus's parents; crazier lawsuits had been directed at school employees.

"I'm fine, sir. Thank you for breaking my fall."

With what seemed to be admiration, Zeus looked into Shaftoe's eyes. The look made Shaftoe uncomfortable. This is getting ridiculous, he thought, let this goofy kid go. Zachary hadn't sent him.

"Zeus, forget about filming. Stay off campus this summer—that's for the next nine weeks. Don't go up any trees. I don't want to see you with a video recorder, anywhere, ever! Got it?"

Zeus nodded agreement.

Best to double check. "Now, repeat what I just told you, please."

"Uh, forget about filming. Stay off campus for the next nine weeks. Stay out of trees. Don't bring my video equipment to school?"

"Close. You forgot I don't want to see you with a video recorder, *anywhere, ever!*"

"Oh yeah," Zeus started over. "Forget filming. Stay off campus. Don't go up trees. You don't want to see me with a video recorder. Anywhere. Ever. Right?"

"Do I need to go to my office, print that out, and have you sign it?"

"No. No, sir. I'll remember."

"I'll expect you to."

"Are you going to tell my mother?"

Damn, I've heard that line a hundred times. Don't these kids have fathers? "Just knock off the filming, like we just agreed. Make money some other way. I'm not going to tell your mother."

"O.K. Can I go now?"

"Yes. This never happened, right?"

"Are you going to tell my parents?"

I guess he does have both parents after all, Shaftoe thought.

"What did I tell you about that, Zeus?"

"This never happened."

"And . . ."

"And you're not going to tell my parents."

"Right. Byc now," Shaftoe waved his hand to indicate dismissal, "Enjoy the rest of your summer. Be like other kids."

Zeus picked up his video recorder from the grass. He headed off campus, his head tilted to one side, gently shaking his recorder next to his ear.

Shaftoe thought, maybe I shouldn't have said, "Be like other kids," but I'm entitled to give at least one normal response to this abnormal situation. Christ. A kid in a tree, with a recorder, slamming my nose into a sidewalk, and, to Zachary's glee, the kid landed face down on my back. How crazy can things get?

As soon as this nutty workday is over, I need a drink—I'm not going to be breathing alcohol breath on any students or parents soon—and I'm going to get one.

chapter six

Shaftoe was rumpled and ached all over. He walked away from Entonces High School, very carefully across the truck-laden intersection, back to the faculty lot for his nondescript car, got in, started it on the second try, and headed for his apartment to clean up. He thought, The Wagon Wheel is the town of Entonces' notion of a restaurant and bar. Nothing in Entonces is more than five minutes' drive from anything else. Gee, I don't know what kind of clothes people wear to the Wagon Wheel. Some of my colleagues might be there, it's Monday, the first day of their summer vacation. I figure they'll dress casually.

At his apartment, he shed his wrinkled dirty clothes, took two extra-strength aspirin, showered, shaved, put on khaki pants, a blue polo shirt and loafers, and threw his traffic-destroyed shoe into his kitchen trash. One shoe off and one shoe on? No way. He threw its mate in after it, along with Zeus's bloody handkerchief. He thought, I'll buy the kid a new one. And Christ, before next school year, I'll have to spring for more shoes. He wondered if the school district would consider his loss to be in the line of duty, and buy him a pair. Not likely. He dismissed that idea. Now he wanted a little aftershave. He sprayed a bit on, from his Ancient Mariner bottle. It was just like his back-up bottle, the additional bottle that he kept in his gym locker in the Ed Zachary Field House.

Yeah, I need a drink ASAP, he told himself. He hoped he wouldn't get the cold shoulder from whatever number of teachers he might find at the Wagon Wheel. They had invited him several times to Friday happy hours, but he'd always been working late or was too exhausted. I hope they won't hold that against me now, he thought. I really need to kick back with some compatible peers. At least I hope they'll be compatible. After a year, he could attach a name to every teacher's face, but he still didn't know what they were like in their spare time.

As he drove to the Wagon Wheel, Shaftoe fantasized. Maybe Natalie Barney would be at the Wagon Wheel. If so, that would be the first really good thing of the day. He realized he only knew her as eye candy. Like him, she was new to Entonces High School, too new to have a regular classroom of her own. A traveling teacher of English—different classroom every period. But that was fine for him, because once a day he got to admire her long legs and short skirt as she pushed a cart of student workbooks, supplemental texts, and paper and pencils into the classroom near his tiny office. As she passed by one day, he saw a male student eye her and heard him softly say, "You live in a nice house, Miss." She didn't seem to hear it. The kid was right, Shaftoe thought, her body was elegant. Some days, she even bent from the waist to get materials from the bottom tray, near the wheels of the cart. There was no way that was deliberately for my benefit, he thought. But he benefited nonetheless. Ms. Barney had the kind of slim body and shapely rear that Shaftoe found exciting. Small breasts, he thought, but he reflected that it had been weeks before he'd even noticed that. Yes, Shaftoe thought, he was definitely a leg man. Face? Thin and with a goofy smile; and he liked the goofy smile.

As he entered the Wagon Wheel from the afternoon sunlight, it was too dark inside for him to see who was there.

"It's Shaftoe! The prodigal son! Jesus Christ!" came a welcoming voice from the back of the large barroom.

That sounded like Ethan Borner, the stocky teachers union rep. He liked to use Biblical references.

"Did you ask for Jesus Christ? Yes, I'm present, Mr. *Boner*!" said a boisterous, artificially fey male voice.

Shaftoe thought, that would be Kent Greef, the only self-acknowledged gay man on the faculty, deliberately mispronouncing Borner's last name to give it a phallic implication. Kent was putting on his "outrageous" act. Shaftoe'd seen it at faculty meetings.

Then a female voice, "You *pendejo,* Kent. Taking our Savior's name in vain. *Buenas tardes, Curandero Shaftoe.* Or should I say *Consejero? Curandero* means medicine man."

'Sounds like Sara Moreno, the veteran Spanish and Chemistry teacher, Shaftoe thought. Her dignity engendered respect. On a campaign to teach the rest of us a few words of Spanish. He knew that the word *pendejo* meant 'fool,' and he'd heard that it had a sexual derivation. He wondered if this afternoon would be a good time to ask Mrs. Moreno about that—as a professional matter, of course. Borner, Greef, and Moreno had the guts to behave that same spontaneous way in faculty meetings, with only the slightest connection to any business that Principal Fluke was trying to conduct. Of course, Fluke always became flustered; he didn't have a clue how to handle that kind of humor. As he navigated through the dark, brushing against empty bar stools and tables on the long walk to the back of the barroom, Shaftoe thought about how Kent Greef was one of the students' favorites. For laughs, he played on their adolescent stereotype of the outrageously gay male. Shaftoe had some concerns about Kent making jokes in class about cruising Central Avenue in the state capital, fifteen miles away, but most of Greef's students thought the jokes were hilarious. Students who had heard about the jokes and were uncomfortable with that kind of humor never signed up to take English or Trigonometry from Mr. Greef, and newcomers assigned to Greef by the school computer were quickly moved to another teacher if they asked Counselor Shaftoe for schedule changes. Shaftoe didn't have time to explore every student's attitude. He thought with amusement, why stir up grief—or in this case, *Greef.* He wondered how Kent was coming along with his efforts to get everyone to call him *Mr. Sunshine* instead of his real last name.

But, Shaftoe thought, I've seen Kent Greef when he wasn't going for laughs—those times when Kent's been maturely concerned about troubled students. He'd seen Greef take several troubled male students under his wing in the school setting. That was definitely a risk for any teacher, especially a male teacher, especially a male teacher who openly indicates he's gay. But Shaftoe had only gotten worried when one of the fathers phoned to say that if a straight man joked so frankly in class about his sex life, he'd be fired. Shaftoe had repeated the message to Greef, who said he would take his "butch pills" before he opened his mouth again. Shaftoe couldn't tell if Greef was taking the message seriously, but no further tales of cruising in Capitol City reached Shaftoe's ears.

Now his eyes were adjusting to the dark. They confirmed that he'd guessed right about the voices. He looked for Natalie Barney, but she wasn't there. He saw Borner, Greef, and Moreno together at a table. Then a couple of new, younger faculty members in a darkened booth just beyond. It was the Girls P E teacher, Miss Reynolds, tomboy cute in white tennis skirt and top. She had sun wrinkles on her face, making it hard to guess her age. She looked up, smiled, and nodded at him. Then she seemed to be forced back into conversation by her booth-mate, Mr. Monzo, who was leaning toward her and excitedly saying, "Wait. Wait. Your boyfriend wanted you to get breast implants, but you said no because . . ." Monzo was a fresh-from-college, newly married teacher who some of the students had dubbed *Mr. Gordo.* Shaftoe assumed the nickname was a play on Monzo's last name and an allusion to the slight paunch on his otherwise skinny body. Shaftoe wondered what it was like to get married right out of college and then begin working with cute women from the world at large.

Time to stop ruminating, sit down, order that double
I'm wanting, and get with the social scene, he thought.
He looked forward to more of his intelligent colleagues'
improper remarks. He grinned and said loudly, "You
teachers are all alike, sitting in dark bars and talking
dirty." Some chuckled. He nodded at all of them and
squeezed in to sit between Borner and Greef.

"Oooh, does this mean we're going steady?"
In return, Shaftoe said, "Hi, Kent. How's it going?"
He knew that Greef's exaggerated batting of eyes at
him was calculated for comic effect. Kent liked to put
people on. Everyone present had seen it before with
Greef's other faculty targets. Now, they barely laughed,
except Monzo, who guffawed. Shaftoe wondered if
drinks were affecting the young husband already. He
noted that Miss Reynolds and Monzo were in the booth
by themselves. Did that mean that Miss cute tomboy
Reynolds and Gordo Monzo had come in together? Be
realistic, Shaftoe told himself, the table was full now,
and might have been full when Reynolds and Monzo
came in. Came in together?

Everyone had a soft drink or liquor in front of
them except Shaftoe. No one came to take his order. A
typical small-town business establishment, he thought.
Even though there were no customers waiting at the
other tables, or on the bar stools, he had to walk over

to the bartender to get his drink. He brought his double bourbon and water back to the table. Yes! He felt better already. After a quick sip amidst the babble, Shaftoe found himself thinking, Damn, I've been looking at Ms. Barney's legs and ass all school year, and I don't even know if she's married, divorced, or what. I never think to look for a ring. *Ms.* could mean anything. Maybe I can find a way, without seeming obvious, to ask about her. But just the thought of asking about her made him anxious.

chapter seven

As he settled into the dimness, as the neon beer signs buzzed and blinked on the walls, Shaftoe told himself, I've only watched these teachers at a few faculty meetings. I need to put thoughts of Natalie Barney aside. I gotta remember to stay focused on cementing friendships, so I can pump the others for information I might use to do battle with Zachary. Be surreptitious. Now's the time.

He turned to Ethan Borner, the teachers union rep and the oldest teacher at the table. "Summer vacation for you, Ethan? Or do you think of it as forced unemployment every year?"

"Not a problem. Every day I'll be working out at Bekins Athletic Club."

His answer had surprised Shaftoe. "Working out? No wonder you're in good shape for an old guy."

He hoped Borner would appreciate the "old guy" ribbing. "But *Bekins* Athletic Club? Like the moving van company?"

"You got it. I've wrestled furniture into their trucks for thirty summers now. The best paying summer job in this burg. Lots of people wait 'til summer to move. You know, so their kids won't have to leave a school district while school's in session. Bekins is God's gift to my wallet." He paused and anger showed in his eyes. "You know, Zachary drained the summer school funding. No teaching opportunities there, Bobby."

Shaftoe nodded. He thought, He called me *Bobby.* That's good. Being on a first-name basis will help. And Borner has just confirmed my suspicions about Zachary's trickery. But I have to get more.

I'm a rambler and a gambler, and a long ways from home . . . Words and music came from the tinny loudspeakers in the corners of the ceiling. Shaftoe felt like the morose Western tune was a message for him.

Now Gordo Monzo, with Miss Reynolds in the darkness of their booth, distant from Shaftoe's table, was saying something more. Shaftoe strained to hear. "You do yoga, Reynolds? Downward-facing dog position? Or only when your boyfriend stands behind you?" In the gloom, Shaftoe couldn't see Miss Reynold's reaction. He wondered how she felt about Monzo's crassness. Well, the era was long gone when men would protect women teachers from rude remarks. Professional equals and all that.

But he had to get back to making friends and fishing for information.

If the people don't like me, they can leave me alone.

Christ, those lyrics were appropriate. Shaftoe felt like a stranger who might be rejected. He'd never tried to finesse information out of adults before. He'd better play his cards right.

He turned to Kent Greef. "How about you, Kent? What do you do in the summer?"

"Countess Cruise Lines again. They love me like a mother, Mr. Counselor. I'm teaching 'Literature of Scandinavia' on the *Queen of the Fjords*," he paused, with a twinkle in his eye. "Countess. *Queen.* How gay can a cruise line sound!" Greef was using the same "outrageous gay man" fake voice that Shaftoe'd heard him use to rattle Fluke at faculty meetings.

"Hard to believe," Greef continued, in his normal tone of voice, "but some people really do prefer my seminar to playing bingo, or table tennis, or sea creature trivia. And after that I'm gonna give another literature seminar on a ship to Australia. Yes, Australia—going 'down under' with the Gay Men's Cruise. Omigod, did I say *going down, gay men*, and *cruise* all in the same sentence! Omigod! Will you be telling a parent, Bobby?"

You gotta admit, the guy is witty. And he makes us laugh, and disarms anyone who might scoff at him, all at the same time. What a great coping skill. "Kent, you know I didn't tell that parent anything about you. He just phoned and I passed his message on to you."

Greef said nothing.

Oh! It's dark and a-rainin' and the moon gives no light . . .

Borner chimed in. "And you, Bobby? Making big bucks this summer while the rest of us scramble?"

"Yeah, Ethan, I'm a wage slave. That's the only reason I went into school counseling . . . to do paperwork during the summer and get those two extra months' pay checks. I'm as rich as Bill Gates now. Anyway, my union dues come out of every one of my checks. So that's more dues overall than a teacher pays." That should make a hit with the union rep. Shaftoe needed friends he could count on.

"But you're not as rich as Coach Zachary, Bobby." Borner's enunciation seemed more uncertain than it had at faculty meetings. How many drinks had the union rep had? "He gets money for every practice he holds, plus supplemental pay for being Chair of the P E Department. And Fluke—or I should say Huntington, through his puppet school board—just appointed Zachary to be 'Athletic Coordinator.' That means he schedules games. He was doing that *anyway*! But now it'll bring Coach an additional stipend. No teacher can make that kind of extra money."

Shaftoe took another sip of his drink.

My pony won't travel this dark road at night . . .

Borner looked pissed. He hissed, "That asshole!"

What a surprise! Borner hadn't used strong language at faculty meetings. Shaftoe assumed "that asshole" meant Zachary, but he also thought of Fluke and Huntington. He wanted to narrow that down. "Hey, Borner, you're talking about our professional colleague. His teams win the league championship every year." He hoped that Borner would know he was needling him.

"Oh, for sure. And with Chip coming back as quarterback, they'll do it again."

Well, that's a clue that Chip's ineligibility hasn't reached the ears of the faculty yet. Shaftoe didn't plan to tell anyone. He asked himself if he was afraid of Zachary, or just keeping a professional confidence. He prided himself on keeping confidences. He wondered how long the hot news would remain confidential, and who would eventually leak the news that a new quarterback would be needed. "A little nepotism there,

Ethan? Or is Chip really that good?" Shaftoe hadn't seen any Entonces games last year. By the time he'd caught up with his responsibilities at Entonces High, the football season was history.

"Oh, Chip's damn good, Bobby. Zachary's been grooming him since birth. He had the kid in Pop Warner football from the cradle, and put him in private schools known for their athletics. He's trying to live through his son—put huge pressure on the kid to be the best in every way—somehow Chip turned out to be a good kid despite his father. He's smart and honest."

Smart? Yes. Too honest to cheat on tests? No.

Go put up your pony and give him some hay . . .

Now Monzo appeared to be verbally messing with Miss Reynolds again. What was he saying?

"Reynolds, you see all those girls in the showers, right? Tell me, do all the blondes have carpets that match their drapes?"

Well, Reynolds would have to fight her own battles. Women teachers had to cope with teenage boys, and Reynolds would have to cope with Monzo. Shaftoe felt aroused by her good looks. And he felt a little tipsy. He wondered if it would be a mistake to have another drink. Wait—he was here to gather info about Zachary.

Sara Moreno spoke up, "Then Zachary made Chip transfer here to run up scores for his dad. And he acted as Chip's agent to recruiters from famous colleges."

Shaftoe directed a question at her, "I heard that Chip even got a mention on TV, right?"

"Yes, on ESPN. *High School Highlights* two years ago. One of those games where Coach had Chip run up the score for Entonces High. The one where Mid-Valley's coach did the right thing, Bobby. As a protest, Mid-Valley's coach took his team home at half-time."

"Wow, I hadn't heard of that one. What happened?"

"Entonces was ahead 56 to nothing at the half. Mid-Valley had played five games already that season and got their patooties kicked every time. Fifty-six to zero, and Zachary hadn't sent in any bench warmers, like any other high school coach would have done. Mid-Valley's coach did the right thing."

"Christ, Sara, what happened then? Did the league censor Zachary?" Shaftoe knew he was leading her on.

She frowned and shook her head. "The opposite. Mid-Valley had to forfeit the game. And Chip got even more notice from big college recruiters. Coach Zachary doesn't care about anything but that."

Greef interrupted, "Chip's stardom keeps sales up for the school board president's rag, the *Clunker.*" Everyone chuckled. The newspaper wasn't named the *Clunker*, it was the *Conqueror.* "And more readership means more advertising revenue for Harley Huntington." Apparently, in addition to his "outrageous gay" act, Greef had a nose for intrigue.

Mrs. Moreno said, "Then Harley Huntington has a vested interest in Chip." It wasn't a question; it was a conclusion.

Now Shaftoe felt like he had some allies. Zachary's conniving was well-known by the faculty. Why did the school authorities put up with it? The faculty looked sad. All conversation stopped. Shaftoe felt forlorn. He took another swallow of bourbon. He wished Natalie Barney was there.

Dear, take your seat by me, so long as you stay . . .

The silence was broken only by the canned music and the clinking sounds of the bartender's housekeeping. Shaftoe stared at the neon beer signs. One had gone out. He heard Monzo say to Reynolds, ". . . because he will always be facing north!" Monzo's words had nothing to do with the main conversation. On the contrary, they were the punch line of a joke that started with, "Why shouldn't a man take erection pills and iron tablets at the same time?" Christ, was Monzo telling the Girls P E teacher penis jokes now?

The bourbon in Shaftoe's glass was running low. He was thinking of going to get another one.

In the booth, Reynolds twisted away from Monzo, into the dim light, to face the others. "He's too disgusting!" she said to everyone. Her slightly husky voice matched the tomboy impression that her physique and face conveyed. To Shaftoe she looked more enticing than when he'd come in. He thought that she was commenting on Monzo's remarks to her, but she wasn't. "Enough about Zachary, he's too disgusting! Let's change the subject. Listen, what about those cheerleaders? Those girls look goood!" She stretched out the vowels in the last word, to emphasize her appreciation. The men perked up.

"No, you guys! I mean they're very . . . gymnastic!"

It seemed like Miss Reynolds thought the men were looking up the cheerleaders' skirts. Was she on target, or was she protesting too much? Maybe she was attracted to the girls herself. Stop thinking like a two-bit psychoanalyst, Shaftoe told himself, not every Girls P E teacher is a lesbian. But why did they all walk the same way? Kind of a stomp. Or maybe it was just the brand of tennis shoes they bought. Then he wondered if the events of the day, his empty stomach, and the bourbon were catching up to him.

My pony ain't hungry, he won't eat your hay . . .

"Listen, R. J. . . . ," Greef said to Reynolds.

My gosh, her name is *R. J.?* R. J. *Reynolds*, like the tobacco company?

". . . You know how those cheerleaders got on TV? KKOW-TV keeps re-running the program they performed at the State Cheerleader Championships.

Well, Zachary got that TV station to put them on, and KKOW-TV loves it because that big banner behind the cheerleaders keeps showing on the TV screen." Greef spread out his arms to indicate the banner. "KKOW-TV Sponsors Entonces Cheerleaders."

"And *Senior* Zachary gets them excused from class *a lot*," said Mrs. Moreno, "even more than the football team. They miss *a lot* of instruction, especially when they go out of town."

Sure, the cheerleaders go to all the away games, plus their own competitions.

Greef continued, "R. J., didn't you know KKOW-TV pays big bucks to sponsor those girls?"

"But, Kent, it's against amateur athletic rules for a sponsor to pay money to a high school sports team!"

Greef showed his profile, raised his chin, and Shaftoe knew he was about to use that "outrageous" voice again. "Our *exalted* school board ruled that cheerleading *isn't* a sport, R. J."

"But they go to cheerleading competitions! I see their trophies in the gym."

Greef shrugged and held up his hands in a helpless gesture.

Shaftoe was surprised that Greef had passed up the opportunity to keep talking. He decided to probe for more evidence against Zachary. "Where do the payments from KKOW-TV go?" It was a newcomer's question. He figured that it wouldn't arouse suspicion that he was pumping the teachers for information. Teachers loved to answer questions for newcomers.

Borner mumbled, "The payments go directly to the Entonces High School Education Foundation."

If you get into trouble, just write and tell me . . .

Looked like Borner was a thorough union rep, he'd done his detective work in search of more dollars to add to his members' salaries. "Oh, that's good," Shaftoe said, suspecting that it wasn't good at all.

"No, that's bad. Zachary started the Foundation himself, Bobby. The only Foundation member is Zachary. The money stops with him."

"Zachary gets his hands on all that extra money? Then we can assume it isn't used for textbooks, teachers' salaries, or to reduce class size."

Shaftoe saw Reynold's mouth form a silent *Oh*, and she blinked. It was a sexy look. The best kind of look. He wanted to spend more time around her. He looked at his empty glass. Then he realized that every teacher was looking at him with interest. He hoped that meant that they were accepting him as one of their own. He might need their support soon.

Greef jumped back in. "Do you need more evidence, anyone? Look at the King Zachary Palace . . . you know, the Ed Zachary Field House, compared to the decrepit classroom building; and his lush practice fields, compared to the bare campus lawn."

Lots of nodding.

Well, Shaftoe thought, I've got a lot more dirt on Zachary than when I came in, but maybe I don't have enough yet to do battle with him.

Monzo had stopped subjecting Reynolds to his humor, and had been listening. "Does the principal encourage good grades?"

Monzo should already know the answer; he's been here a year. If he doesn't, he's too slow a learner to be a teacher. If the average IQ of teachers is high, it must be the women teachers who are pulling it up. Shaftoe wondered if he would be thinking that way if he hadn't been drinking.

Borner answered, "Principal Orson Fluke? Of course he checks. He even walks into our classrooms and interrupts our teaching to check." Borner looked at the others. "But has he ever checked on any student who wasn't a varsity footballer?"

Did Borner have an additional bone to pick? Was he a former coach who'd been put back in the classroom for having losing teams? Or had a Huntington-Fluke-Zachary conspiracy jerked him around somehow for some other reason? Shaftoe told himself he'd have to find out.

When you get to Wyoming a letter you'll see . . .

A chill ran through Shaftoe. He thought, Those lyrics sounded ominous, but what do they portend?

Borner was eying his own empty glass as if he wanted another drink but didn't want to leave the conversation. He took a verbal leap. "Right," he said to no one in particular, "Coach just doesn't play some of the freshmen. You've heard the term 'red shirt'? Then he plays 'em their second year, when they're bigger."

This was adding up to something more sinister than red-shirting. "Wait," Shaftoe said, "Suppose those red shirts don't graduate from Entonces with their class, can Coach play them one more year, when they're even older and bigger?"

"*Compadre,* if you know the answer, why do you ask the question?" Mrs. Moreno said. She seemed to be fighting to speak in a controlled way. "He even brings in over-age, non-graduates from out of stricter states, who have an extra year to play under our state's more generous rules. And do those huge hairy grownups do any schoolwork? Never! Even the ones who speak Spanish at home are flunking my Beginning Spanish, and they drop out of school as soon as football season's over. So twice they haven't graduated—in *two* states—and now they're even older, with still no high school diploma. If Coach had known them when they were four-year-olds he would've had them wait an extra year to start Kindergarten. So they'd be bigger for high school. And the way he leers at me! He's a warped man!"

She sighed, leaned forward, and put her head on the table.

Greef added, "And his winning record helps his businesses."

Shaftoe noted the plural: business*es*.

Monzo's eyes lit up. "His businesses?" He sounded like he was interested in making money on the side. Not surprising for a married beginning teacher.

Greef answered, "Yes, the private 'football camps' he runs. For kids 8 to 19."

Shaftoe marveled at Zachary's scheming. "Kent, isn't that a way to do physical conditioning and develop players outside the jurisdiction of the state athletic commission?"

"Bobby, you're smarter than you look."

No one laughed. Zachary's unethical behavior obviously had too much impact on all the Entonces High School teachers and their students.

If I'm in your book, dear, please blot out my name.

The music ended.

What the hell would Zachary pull next? Just how underhanded could he be? Shaftoe wondered, Who will be on my side if I ultimately battle Zachary?

chapter eight

Shaftoe got another double bourbon and water from the bar and began drinking it as he walked back to the table.

Ethan Borner looked at his watch. "Well, folks, three is my limit. Gotta stay in shape for Bekins. Good talking with you, Shaftoe." He pushed back his chair and stood up. At the scraping sound, Gordo Monzo and Miss Reynolds looked over from their booth. Through the gloom, Borner headed toward the door. His head was down. Without looking back, he gave a fluttering wave over his shoulder. Shaftoe couldn't tell if Borner was indicating "'Bye, all," or "Whatever." It appeared to be understood by the others that Borner didn't necessarily expect a response.

Sara Moreno leaned across the table toward Shaftoe. "Ethan hates Coach Zachary, even though Ethan was winning the fight."

"Fight?" Shaftoe thought that perhaps Borner and Zachary had taken opposite sides on some teachers union matter.

"In the faculty lot. I was on campus early, and I saw it."

"You mean a fist fight in the teachers parking lot?" The idea of two beefy teachers duking it out at work was offensive to Shaftoe's sense of professionalism. Yet he had to know more.

Kent Greef spoke up. "Ethan pulled into a parking stall that Zachary wanted." Now Greef wasn't using his exaggerated "gay man" voice. He sounded serious. "None of the spaces are reserved! But Zachary dragged Ethan out of his car and punched him in the face. What a bastard!"

"And, Bobby, Ethan defended himself," Mrs. Moreno said. She clearly seemed to feel that the story was hers to tell. "He was beating up that *pendejo* Zachary until . . ." She stopped abruptly, put her hand in front of her mouth, and then continued, "How should I say this?"

Greef chuckled. "Sara, just say, 'until Zachary kicked Ethan in the *cojones*.'"

Shaftoe's Spanish was limited. He thought, *Cojones? Cojones?* There was a Spanish word something like that which meant rabbits. Almost without meaning to, he mouthed the question "rabbits?" silently to Greef.

Greef apparently saw the confusion on Shaftoe's face. "No, Bobby, Zachary didn't kick Ethan in his rabbits! *Rabbits* is *conejos.* I said *cojones;* that's slang for *testicles.* That chickenshit Zachary kicked Ethan in the balls! Put him down like a ton of bricks. Then Zachary told his patsy, Fluke, that Ethan had attacked him, and got Fluke to replace Ethan as basketball coach."

Shaftoe looked at Mrs. Moreno. She hadn't been laughing at his confusion about Spanish slang. She had been nodding as Greef took her off the verbal spot and finished the saga. Now she was slowly shaking her head from side to side and looking sorrowful. Shaftoe had seen that same expression on women mourning beside a casket.

"Christ, Sara, that's awful. Did Ethan tell Fluke the truth?"

"Bobby, you know how *macho* all you men are. . . . Sorry, Kent. . . ." Moreno unsuccessfully attempted a smile at Greef. She was trying to joke and lighten things up.

"No offense, Sara." Greef was playing along.

" . . . Ethan didn't want to talk about it with anyone. Such dignity. He treated the fight as if he were the loser fair and square. Only I can tell the story correctly, because I was the only one who saw it."

Shaftoe looked down at his most recent double bourbon and water. He was surprised that it was nearly gone. Shaftoe's wishful thinking of grabbing Zachary's leg, tipping him onto his back, and pinning him, came back to him with an additional head of steam.

"Listen, *profesores,* I have a husband waiting at home. I've talked too much. I hope this wasn't too upsetting. I've got to go." Mrs. Moreno headed for the door. Shaftoe thought she was walking unsteadily, but maybe it was just her high heels and the darkness in the Wagon Wheel.

The two young teachers in the booth seemed to take her departure as a cue. Gordo Monzo stood up and looked back at R. J. Reynolds, his booth mate. Was he leering? Then he looked at Shaftoe and Greef, and said, "I've got to go home. I promised my wife I'd do something with her."

"Do something with your wife, huh?" Greef had returned to his flowery tones, "Well, Mr. Monzo, don't let her start without you." Shaftoe suppressed an impulse to say, "When a woman does it, is it called Jilling off?" He realized he was tipsy.

He thought, is it my imagination, or did Monzo's ears and Reynold's face just turn red? Would the cute Girls P E teacher linger a while, then exit without arousing suspicion and meet Monzo somewhere? Had Monzo tried to say something innocuous to ease himself out, and then Greef correctly sensed an underlying meaning? As Monzo left, Shaftoe wondered, Were Monzo and Reynolds starting an affair?

Now, Greef apparently had already forgotten about the pair. He stopped affecting his mellifluous tones, "Jesus, Bobby, Sara got serious all of a sudden. Let's change the subject." Greef, Shaftoe, and R. J. Reynolds were the only patrons in the Wagon Wheel now. Shaftoe thought he saw a wicked gleam come into Greef's eye.

Greef said, "Tell me, Counselor, what's this about a student sodomizing you on campus?"

Shaftoe heard R. J. Reynolds gasp. It seemed to Shaftoe that Greef was talking very loudly. He saw the bartender's eyebrows rise at Greef's words, and the man looked at them from across the room. Reynolds looked increasingly disconcerted, mumbled something, and headed for the door. When Shaftoe turned to watch her attractive rear as her tennis skirt swung, he was pained to see that Natalie Barney had entered the building and stopped just inside the open door. Silhouetted by a streetlight, her slim form and lovely legs were unmistakable to him. She seemed to be peering into the dark as if she had recognized Greef's voice. As she began the trek past the bar, to Greef and Shaftoe's table, he could make out an astonished look on her face. Now he was sure that she had heard what Greef had just said! Sodomy? Shaftoe felt nauseated. Was it only from the bourbon on his empty stomach? He didn't think so.

Shaftoe whispered, "Kent, shut up!" but Greef was energized.

"Coach saw me in the supermarket. You know how he is. He yelled down the aisle at me. 'Hey, fancy pants, some kid came down from a tree and buggered Shaftoe's butt on campus today! Did you put one of your queer little students up to that?'"

Shaftoe glanced back at Ms. Barney's approaching and tried again to get Greef to shut up, but he was on a roll.

"You know, Bobby, Coach thinks he can shake me up with shit like that. I yelled back at him, 'Zachary, you dreamed it. Your wife told me you've been looking at porn again and you always dream that stuff afterward.' Well, Coach didn't expect that; he's not too swift. He looked around to see if anybody'd overheard what I said, then he began jumping straight up, trying to look over the tops of shelves, to see if anyone in the other aisles had heard me. You should have seen him jumping up and down. He was going nuts."

Now Ms. Barney was just a step from their table. She had a goofy grin on her face. Greef noticed her for the first time. He looked at the young woman as if she were an apparition that had instantly materialized near his shoulder. He sheepishly glanced at Shaftoe.

Shaftoe tried to act cool, as if Ms. Barney couldn't possibly have heard any of Greef's words. Shaftoe said to her, "Well, hi. Look who's here." He immediately felt that he'd made a stupid remark. Despite his agony, he realized that in her abbreviated summer dress, with bodice and undulating above-the-knee-skirt, she looked very good. He felt sexually aroused, and it felt great.

He wondered if Greef was embarrassed. Shaftoe didn't think that was possible. But Greef said nothing more, nodded at Ms. Barney, looked apologetically at Shaftoe, and left.

Now Shaftoe and Ms. Barney were alone.

She answered, "Who's here indeed, Counselor Shaftoe. It is I, Natalie Barney." The goofy grin remained. It occurred to Shaftoe that she was either eccentric or had a charming sense of humor. Maybe both.

"Glad to see you," he said. No doubt about that. "Please call me Bobby, I don't know who you're talking to when you say Counselor Shaftoe." He reflected that he'd heard guys say something like that in such situations. They had worked the words "It makes me think you're talking to my father" into it somehow. Shaftoe thought, But I have no father. Something wasn't jibing here. He tried to focus. "Sit down. May I buy you a drink?" Showing her he knew the difference between *may* and *can*. She should like that, being a teacher of English. She sat down next to him at the table. Her perfume was delicately pleasing.

"Yes, thank you. I'd like a mai tai, if you please."

A mai tai? Is this a time warp? Do they even know what a mai tai is in the town of Entonces? She definitely is eccentric, but I like eccentric young women sometimes. Can't fault her for ordering girlie. He excused himself, walked to the bartender, who seemed to eye him suspiciously, and ordered. The barman said, "A mai tai, huh?" Was there some kind of challenge in his voice? The man made the Tahitian drink, put a straw and a tiny pleated pink umbrella made of paper and toothpicks into it, handed Shaftoe the mai tai and a lacy paper doily, and said, "Is it for you?" Shaftoe ignored him, ordered his third double bourbon and water, and walked back to the table with the drinks.

"Your drink, fair lady." Christ, he was saying stupid things. He sat down next to her, and she gave him her goofy grin again. On second thought, grin wasn't the right word for it; that wasn't being fair to her. It was more like an enchanting smile. He felt fortunate to be the recipient. Somehow she was even better looking than he'd thought. He stood up to ask her to dance, tipped his chair too far and almost fell over it. Then he looked around the Wagon Wheel, heard no music, and remembered it had been turned off. He righted his chair and sat down carefully. He said nothing. Maybe she hadn't noticed his ineptitude.

She deftly moved the toothpick umbrella around in her glass, so she could use the straw. Shaftoe was bowled over by the femininity of it all. He was relieved that the formalities were over and they could stay seated and get acquainted. He was impressed that she could smile so well while using a straw. An exceptional young woman. Except for the alcoholic drinks we could be teenagers on a first date. The thought seemed ridiculous. He waited, and she said nothing. Then he remembered that he didn't know her marital status.

"So, Ms. Barney, how are things going for you and your loved ones?" He wondered if that was an okay thing to say. What little confidence he had with women seemed to be deserting him. And him a grown man. He felt ashamed. Not for the first time, he thought there was something wrong with him. He'd have to talk with Dr. Mallard some more about that.

"I'm calling you *Bobby*, please call me Natalie."

"Okay." His one-word agreement sounded inadequate to his ears.

"Hmmm," she said, "How are things going, you ask? A provocative question indeed. It might plumb unknown depths. Well, in my car, on the way over here, I was listening to a Leonard Cohen tune."

Shaftoe was ecstatic. He liked Leonard Cohen's words and music too. What a sensitive woman Natalie was turning out to be.

"I was listening to 'Suzanne,' she continued. "You know, in those lyrics is some profound shit . . . Oh, I'm sorry, Bobby, I mean . . . some profound *wisdom*."

"Thank you for correcting yourself, Natalie," he hoped she could tell he was beginning to kid her, "Being clean minded, I don't allow anyone to say shit, fuck, or goddamn around me." Well, he thought, that might help open her up.

Her laugh was loud and charming. Kind of a shriek. The bartender looked up from his glass-washing when he heard it. Then he tilted his head to one side and pounded his downside ear with his palm. It seemed to Shaftoe that the bartender was confirming Natalie's lovely laugh. She was indeed alluring.

Shaftoe watched her take the tiny pink umbrella out of her glass and begin to play with it, closing and opening it. She did it in a sensuous way. It was moist inside. He wondered if her opening it was some kind of good omen for the future of their relationship.

"Listen, Bobby, excuse me; I've got to pee."

He thought, Can I watch you? She would be very attractive peeing. But he only said, "Sure."

While she was gone, he noticed that she had finished her mai tai already. Even the pineapple slice was gone. And the cherry. But not the little umbrella. It was in the empty glass, but the umbrella was closed now. That worried him.

He was totally unprepared for what happened next. When she returned, she didn't sit down. She smiled at him, rested her hand on his shoulder, and said, "Bobby, thanks for the drink. I like your company. Maybe we can do this again soon. I just noticed the time; I have to meet someone." She fished the folded little umbrella out of her glass, tapped a few drops of liquor off it onto the doily, looked at Shaftoe, looked at the umbrella, opened it, and said, "A dear souvenir of our precious time together." She kissed him on the cheek, and headed toward the door to the parking lot, tiny open pink umbrella delicately extended at arm's length in front of her.

She moved so smoothly she reminded Shaftoe of a line from literature. Something about a weasel.

Well, he thought, this has gone exceedingly well.

As she passed the bartender on her exit walk, she looked over her shoulder seductively at Shaftoe and enticingly called out, "Maybe next time you can tell me about the kid who butt-fucked you on campus." Her voice was like a beautiful harp interlude. A magical voice like no other woman on earth. Well, maybe a tad too loud just then. The bartender glared at Shaftoe.

The exquisite scent of Natalie lingered. Shaftoe thought, Do I feel that life owes me something I've been cheated out of up till now? It occurred to him that during his time with Natalie he hadn't thought once of his problems with Coach Zachary. He wondered if he was in love.

chapter nine

Shaftoe sat alone a little longer at the Wagon Wheel. He liked the dim light and the quiet. Just the bartender and him. For the first time, he perceived that the room smelled of peanuts and beer. The aroma was tranquilizing. He liked the peace and anonymity—if a person could have anonymity in the town of Entonces. It was about time.

He watched the bartender begin to close up. He was cleaning the beer taps, wiping down the liquor bottles, taking the empty beer bottles into the back room, putting the washed glasses on racks, and counting cash from the register.

What time was it? Shaftoe looked at his watch. Only 8:00 p.m., and the place is closing? Well, this is Entonces on a Monday night. Eight is late for the tired farmers around here. The teachers are gone. Just me left, and apparently no more patrons are expected.

All of a sudden, he realized how bone tired he felt from the day's close call with the 18-wheelers, the crisis of Zachary's son being ineligible for quarterback, the pressure of controlling himself with Coach Zachary, Zachary's blow to his chest, and the physical impact of Zeus's falling from the tree. Had that all happened in just one day? Who would have believed it! And trying to be circumspect at the Wagon Wheel while probing about Zachary's conniving had added to the strain.

But then Natalie had shown up, and now everything seemed almost okay.

Nothing to do now but head for his apartment. And then what? Watch a flick on the Skinamax Channel? All the nudie cuties were starting to look alike. Well, the channel rarely showed their faces. Suddenly, he felt profoundly lonely. Why am I living alone? Is there something wrong with me?

What a change, he thought. A minute ago I felt enchanted, possibly boozily enchanted, but the alcohol hadn't caused the enchantment. He closed his eyes, envisioned Natalie Barney, and the enchanted feeling crept back over him. She'd made his world so glamorous. Words and music came to him, can't help it if I'm feeling amorous. That was the song he always thought of when he fantasized about a new woman. And he was aware—if only for a split second—that he hardly knew Natalie. Such considerations didn't matter. He felt so good.

He glanced again at the bartender. The man still seemed surly. Should that matter? Shaftoe chastised himself, Bobby, you'd like to control the attitudes of others, but no person can. That's what Dr. Mallard had said to him. Bobby knew that was true, but he didn't like the idea. He thought of the old gag, A psychotic thinks that 2 and 2 is 5; a neurotic knows that 2 and 2 is really 4, but he doesn't like it. Was he neurotic?

He stood up, caught the eye of the bartender, dropped some bills on the table, nodded at him, and said, "Thanks. So long." The bartender only glared and mumbled something under his breath.

Christ, Shaftoe thought, I put up with his insinuations, left him a tip, and still he's an asshole.

As he very carefully drove the short distance home, with one eye out for the sheriff's black and white, he thought blissfully about Natalie. Am I experiencing nirvana? I hope the feeling never ends.

Back at his apartment, he ate some leftover pizza and began watching the day's final newscast. It started at 9:00 p.m. in Entonces; farmers went to bed early. It opened with a raging fire at a teddy bear factory in Capitol City. He thought of a little teddy bear in a sailor suit, burning. He wondered if preschoolers were watching and crying. The thought made him sad. He hoped they were asleep already.

Later, as he fell into bed knowing that he would have to be up at seven to get to work at the high school, he wondered, Is Natalie single, married, or what? She didn't tell me. Is she divorced? Does she have children? One or two good-looking, smart, well-behaved little kids would be okay with me. He thought about his own history, how his parents had only produced one child and how he didn't know anything about his father. None of his ex-girlfriends had gotten pregnant by accident with him. He didn't know if he was happy about that or not. He thought, What if I'm sterile? But that wouldn't matter if I married a perfect woman like Natalie, with one or two happy, charming little kids. Maybe she's a young widow who'd had a happy marriage. A widow. That would put the kids' father out of the picture. That would be ideal.

But the image of an angry ex-husband with child visitation rights came to mind. Was the alcohol beginning to make him depressed?

He finally fell into a restless intermittent sleep.

At 3:00 a.m. his bedside cell phone rang insistently.

chapter ten

The deafening cell phone awakened Shaftoe from a dream. His mother was reaching toward him, her hand touching his belt buckle, her face larger than life. He'd had that dream before and it always made him feel small and powerless and anxious.

Clumsy from sleep and a hangover, he rolled over and reached for his phone on the nightstand. He knocked it onto the carpet. The ringing continued. Damn!

He looked at his alarm clock. The lighted display said 3:00 a.m. Christ! His eyeballs felt like they were rotating in sand. In pain, he slowly leaned out of bed, found the phone on his carpet and fumbled to get it into position so he could talk. What bastard is putting me through this at this ungodly hour! He finally manipulated the phone properly and the ringing stopped at last.

"Hello," he croaked. No sound came from the other end. Then he heard a muffled angry voice, swearing, distant from the other person's phone, and a door slamming, cutting off the cursing. Had someone dialed him, then been pushed outside in mid-tirade? A 3:00 a.m. prank by some school kids? Fuck!

He tried again, "Hello?" Silence.

Then, a frail voice, "Bob-bee?" The sound was a sob combined with . . . what? A death rattle? No, that would only happen at the instant of death. He shivered in the summer heat. Was it his mother? She often sounded like that when she called him, distraught, in the middle of the night.

"Bob-bee. I'm so sorree. Who else could I . . . ! Omigod!"

"What?" Shaftoe was now wide awake and straining to hear. The sobbing gurgle was distorting some of the words. Did the person have blood in their throat? "I can't understand you."

"It's Natalie. Barney. Natalie Barney. The teacher. Help me!"

"Christ, Natalie, what's going on there? Are you at home?" The cursing and the slamming door made Shaftoe think of an ex-husband storming out. "Did someone just leave?" Were children with Natalie?

"God no, I'm not . . . at home." The sobbing interrupted her words, but the gurgling sound was gone.

Shaftoe was still worried about Natalie's possible children. "Are you alone?"

"Yes. Finally. Bobby . . . Mr. Shaftoe . . . Sir. Oh shit. You've gotta come over here."

"Are you alright?"

"No. Unequivocally no."

"Are you in Capitol City?" He knew from the faculty address and phone list that she lived there, fifteen miles away. "What's your address? How do I get there?"

"Capitol City? Yes, I live there." Now she sounded confused and in pain. "But I'm at the Entonces Motel."

"What?" Motel? She didn't sound romantically inclined.

"Damn it, Bobby, you're a college graduate. It's simple. I need help. Ohhh, I'm a mess," her voice was a whine. "Entonces Motel. Can you get over here? Now! Room Three."

He wanted to help her, whatever was going on. "Yeah, I'm on my way. Lock the doors and windows. Turn out the lights. Put your phone on silent and take it into the bathroom with you and lock yourself in if you can. Did you dial 911?"

Shaftoe heard her phone go dead.

He pulled clothes on and ran to his car. He hit the ignition, put it in gear, and floored the accelerator. No other cars on the street at this hour. Easy to get a ticket; but he didn't care. Natalie had called him for help.

At the Entonces Motel, his headlights lit up the place. Its faded peeling sign said Newly Redecorated. The place looked old and shabby. He spotted Room Three on the ground floor, near the manager's glassed-in office. At the counter, a balding night clerk was sleeping, his head on folded forearms. Shaftoe parked out of the clerk's line of sight and walked quickly and quietly toward Room Three. His legs felt shaky. He was fearful of what he might find. Why had Natalie sounded so awful? What did she mean when she whined, "I'm a mess."? What kind of help does she need? Why isn't she in Capitol City? Who had angrily left the room? Why did her phone go dead?

Then his thoughts shifted. Am I walking into some kind of trap? Am I being set up by Coach Zachary? Is Zachary here somewhere? Will he hurt me? Shaftoe looked over his shoulder. Now that his headlights were off, the surroundings were pitch dark. What kind of harm had Zachary done to Natalie? Shaftoe wondered if he was being paranoid.

Now he was at the door to Room Three. It was closed. He didn't want to alert the night clerk by knocking. Instead, he used a dime to tap on the front window of the room. All the lights remained off, but deep inside he heard a latch move. Must be Natalie coming out of the locked bathroom. Good. Despite his shakiness, he began to feel like a hero.

He whispered, "It's me, Bobby Shaftoe," hoping his voice would carry into the room.

"Who is it?" Natalie whispered.

He repeated his name a little louder.

"Bobby, thank God. Are you alone?" Her voice wavered as if frightened, and what else? Ashamed?

Shaftoe looked over his shoulder again. "I'm alone. Are you alright?"

"No."

"Are you going to open the door?"

No answer, but Shaftoe heard the jangle of the security chain being slid from its slot, and the clunk of the deadbolt opening. In the early morning creepiness of the place, the sounds seemed very loud.

Then the door opened a crack. An eye stared out. He couldn't tell if the darkness on the skin around it was smeared make up or a bruise. He saw Natalie's hand with a comb in it. He wondered if in these dire circumstances she had hurriedly combed her hair for him. The thought pleased him.

"Natalie, you ready to go? Or maybe you need to wait for the police?"

"Let's go. With all dispatch!"

The woman did have a quaint way of communicating, even under duress. Apparently she hadn't called 911. Probably a good thing, too, given that they were both school employees, too new to the district to have job rights, and given that nothing seemed to go unnoticed in the town of Entonces.

"Okay, Natalie, the motor's running." It wasn't, but Shaftoe wanted her to know he was ready to exit quickly. Then he thought of something.

"Do you have everything? Purse, wallet, anything that could ID you?"

"Just a second. Faculty address and phone list. I used it to call you."

Shaftoe was impressed that she had her wits about her. As she turned to go get the faculty list, he was aware of a heavy fragrance—men's cologne?—that was new to him. He didn't like the smell.

Natalie quickly returned. As he held the door open for her, and she squeezed past, Shaftoe noticed that she smelled of liquor, that she indeed had a shiner forming around her left eye, that her lipstick was smeared, and her summer dress drooped off one shoulder. The back of it was unzipped to the waist. He caught a glimpse of white panties. Sexy. Well, he thought, no time to explore that. Let's get outta here.

In his car, with headlights off, they took the only exit, past the manager's office. The night clerk was standing now, looking from their car to a pad in his hand. Was he jotting something down?

"Bobby, my car is at the Wagon Wheel. Take me there and I can drive to Capitol City."

"Are you sure you can drive okay? What the hell happened?"

"Don't ask, Counselor Shaftoe. It was awful!"

"You look beat up. Shall I take you to a doctor?" At this hour, he had in mind an emergency room.

"No," then a long pause, "It was someone I knew. A friend. I thought everything would be okay." Natalie sank back into the seat and tried to close her eyes. She touched her swollen eye gingerly. "Ouch." For the first time, Shaftoe noticed dried blood on her upper lip, as if from a staunched nosebleed. He thought, A pretty woman made ugly by a man she knew. It wasn't right. He wondered if there were any women who hadn't been made ugly in some way, whether it showed or not.

He recalled Natalie at the Wagon Wheel, thanking him for the mai tai, and leaving, saying she had to meet someone.

"You'd arranged to meet this person in the parking lot of the Wagon Wheel?"

"Yes. Then my friend wanted to . . . go someplace . . . private." She was speaking softly and hesitantly. "We'd done it before. Christ, do I have to talk about this?"

"No, you don't have to talk. I'm just glad you're okay. . . . More or less."

But she seemed to need to keep talking. "We'd done it before. It was okay before." She sighed deeply.

Shaftoe was beginning to envy the guy. But I can do better with her, he thought. I sure as hell wouldn't beat her up like this.

"But this time . . . ?" he prompted.

"This time my friend wanted me to do some new things." With that, she stopped, and Shaftoe thought she was through talking for a while, but she started up again, "I didn't want to do those things."

"And . . . ?"

"When I said no, this person hit me."

"More than once?"

"More than once? Oh god, yes." For the first time, Natalie turned to look Shaftoe in the eye, as if to see how he was taking what she said. Her cheek was cut and bloodied, finger marks showed on her upper arms. Shaftoe thought, if a student looked like that, I'd have to phone the sheriff or child protective services.

"Does 'this person' have a name?"

"I can't tell you that."

Shaftoe thought of saying, What is it that you can't tell me? He'd used that line many times on the job. But now he thought of it as a cheap counselor trick. Was Coach Zachary behind this? "This is really awkward, us calling him 'this person.' Is it someone from Entonces?"

"Jesus, you ask a lot of questions, Bobby." She dabbed at her face with a lacy handkerchief. Then she looked at the hankie, now spotted with blood.

"Well . . . ?" Shaftoe said.

"Oh my God," she seemed indignant. "Let's stop talking. It's no one you know. The person's name is Charlie. Satisfied now?"

He thought for a moment. Natalie's right, I don't know anyone called Charlie. Or Charles or Chuck. Not even a Carlos. Well, Natalie was willing to take a risk for sex. Maybe that bodes well for me later. But maybe Charlie has something I don't have. Why do I always think this way? Even when a woman's just been attacked.

As Shaftoe drove to Natalie's car at the Wagon Wheel, he wondered what sex act it was that she wouldn't do. If he asked her, would she tell him?

chapter eleven

After watching Natalie shakily enter her car at the Wagon Wheel and cautiously head off toward Capitol City, Shaftoe drove to his apartment. Then, after only three hours restless sleep, he headed for Entonces High School. After all, it was Tuesday, he was expected at work by 7:30, and anyway he wanted to be on campus in case Coach Zachary tried to somehow negate his letter to the state athletic commission. He was sure that in Ed Zachary's eyes, the cause of his son Chip's ineligibility for quarterback was Shaftoe, not Chip's having failed two courses because of cheating on the finals. If he had read Coach Zachary correctly, Zachary might even want to play kill the messenger.

As he drove, glancing to his right as if Natalie were still sitting, beaten up, in the passenger seat, he thought, She might have an eccentric way of speaking sometimes, but she has guts. He didn't feel right letting her drive from the Wagon Wheel to Capitol City by herself last night. No, it wasn't really last night, it was this morning, just four hours ago. But she'd made it very clear to me that she wanted to drive home alone, even though she was in pain. Or maybe she just wanted to get away from me, no matter what.

He found himself wondering again what sex act it was that Natalie had refused to do.

Then, as Shaftoe pulled into a space in the faculty lot, he heard truck brakes, and saw Zeus, the kid who had fallen on him from the tree, crossing the dangerous intersection toward the high school. Zeus successfully dodged all trucks. Shaftoe admired the agility of youth. As the kid reached school property, Shaftoe got out and yelled across the highway, from the parking lot, "Get off campus. Go home. Go home." He felt like he was yelling at the family dog. Zeus's head jerked in the direction of Shaftoe, his mouth fell open, and his eyes got big. Shaftoe made a big motion with his arms and hands, like a baseball coach waving an outfielder away. Zeus clutched his video camera to his waist, turned quickly on his heels, tried to hide the camera with his body, and headed off campus. Damn kid, he promised me he'd stay away! And I don't need any reminders of Zachary yelling about butt-fucking.

Shaking his head in disbelief, Shaftoe locked his car, made it across the dangerous intersection, walked to the classroom building, unlocked it, and went to his broom-closet office. The display on his office phone indicated eight unanswered calls. He listened to them all. Mostly parents, hoping he would tell them that the low grades reported for their children had been an error. He put off returning the calls. His answer would be routine, "You'll have to check with the teacher who gave the grade. No, I don't phone teachers at their homes; they aren't school employees during the summer and some of them are at other jobs they get for the summer." He thought of Ethan Borner and wanted to add, *like loading furniture for Bekins.* "No, we don't give out our teachers' home phone numbers or addresses. I'll put a note with your phone number on it into that teacher's mailbox here at school, telling him your concern; but he might not see it until he gets back here in September, when school starts up again. Yes, if there's been a mistake, the teacher can submit a different grade to me then, and we'll correct it on all the records." He wished more school people would stick up for their colleagues. He suspected that some of those parents wouldn't take his telephonic hint and would directly call any teacher whose number they could find in the Entonces or Capitol City listings. If they did that, some teachers might phone him, pissed off, thinking that he had given out their number. Oh well, he thought, every job has its downside. In exchange, I get to work with the students during the regular school year, and they're fascinating.

He'd return the calls later in the day; it was only 7:50; some parents would resent being awakened.

Shaftoe's body screamed for a cup of coffee; he hadn't had time to make any, or stop along the way. He'd leave campus at break time, after Principal Fluke had observed that he was at work. 'First-year teacher in the district, can't be too careful. He'd walk to Miracle Burger, pondering their ambiguous slogan, *If it's a good burger, it's a miracle,* and order a coffee. Later, he'd phone Natalie on his cell to see if she's okay; he was looking forward to that.

Shaftoe took blank forms from shipping boxes and carried them to the device that would print transcripts of Seniors who had graduated last week. Those had to be sent to colleges right away. He anticipated that his day would be filled with setting the computer and printer to do their thing, and interruptions: phone calls, unscheduled visitors, and paperwork with Sweet Jillie, the counseling center clerk. He wanted to leave promptly at 4:00 because he had an appointment with Dr. Mallard, his psychotherapist in Capitol City. He wondered if, while there, he might drop in on Natalie. Nah, better not press my luck. Beat up like she was, she might not want to be seen.

Finally, it was 3:45. Now Shaftoe felt even more short of sleep, but he'd made some headway in his work. His calendar said that next week would be crowded with more paperwork. And meetings with Fluke—reviewing the recent school year, he assumed. He hoped that Fluke had the common sense to conduct a review, and a needs assessment for the next year. Because it was Shaftoe's first summer at Entonces High, he wasn't sure how Fluke would run the meeting. He had some suggestions to make for improving the school, but he reminded himself that trying to change the way a boss does things could cost him his job. It seemed odd to think that Coach Zachary would be more likely to engineer any such firing than Principal Fluke. Of course, the professional jargon would be "probationary contract not renewed."

Only fifteen minutes till I leave, he thought. Piece of cake. I've made it. If I don't fall asleep at the wheel, I'll get to Capitol City just in time to see Dr. Mallard. I can tell her about my dream of Mother, my rescuing Natalie—I'm looking forward to that part—and maybe we can work some more on why I feel so insecure around women I like.

His scattered thoughts were interrupted. It was Principal Fluke in Shaftoe's doorless doorway.

"Mr. Shaftoe, may I see you in my office for a moment."

Damn! If I tell him I'm in a hurry to leave, he might ask me why. He's so out of it he might put a stigma on psychotherapy, and I don't want to dodge the question by saying it's personal business. At the least, he might see me as disrespectful for not staying into unpaid time. I hope he means what he said: "for a moment."

Shaftoe left his tiny office and walked to stand between Fluke and Sweet Jillie, the neatly-groomed clerk, who was at her desk, an island in the center of the room.

"Certainly, Mr. Fluke. Sweet Jillie, I may be with Mr. Fluke for the next fifteen minutes. If so, I'll leave from his office at 4:00." Shaftoe looked to see if Fluke would pick up his reference to time. Did the principal know it was already 3:45? As Fluke stood nearby would he check his watch? No such luck.

As Fluke and he left the counseling center and approached the principal's office, Shaftoe saw Coach Zachary sitting inside with his legs crossed, facing Fluke's desk. His comfortable slouch suggested that he had been there for some time.

"Hi, Bobby," coach greeted him with a cheery grin, "you sicko."

Shaftoe nodded to him. Fluke and Shaftoe entered Fluke's office and the principal closed his door. Shaftoe stood while the principal sat down at his desk.

"Mr. Fluke, what's the topic of this meeting, please?" Shaftoe knew that his union contract gave him the right to know, beforehand, the topic of a meeting with any school administrator. And when he'd seen Coach there, he suspected that the topic would be Chip.

"Topic?" Fluke looked at Shaftoe like he'd never heard the word before.

"Fuck the topic, Bobby."

"Now, Mr. Zachary, there's no need to use that kind of language," Fluke said.

Zachary just smirked at Fluke.

Shaftoe tried again, "Yes, Mr. Fluke, could you tell me the topic for this meeting, please."

"Well . . . ," there was a pause. Fluke glanced at Zachary, ". . . just a little chat about how things are going."

"Do we need Coach Zachary for that?"

Fluke again looked at Zachary.

"Oh, hell. Orwell . . ."

"That's Orson,'"

"Oh, hell, Orson, just tell Bobby the topic is Sodomy On Campus."

Fluke looked acutely uncomfortable. His cheeks reddened.

Shaftoe said, "I'm asking to reschedule this meeting. And without Coach present . . . unless he was an active participant in the . . . what was that 's' word he used, Mr. Fluke?" He stared quizzically at the principal. He thought, at this point, I don't give a damn if Fluke doesn't like this stare, I want to see if he can say "sodomy"; he seems like the kind of guy who wouldn't say "shit" if his mouth was full of it.

"Sod . . . uh . . . me?" Fluke was whispering.

"Yeah. That's the word. Was Coach an active participant in that? If not, when we have the re-scheduled meeting, he shouldn't be at it." Shaftoe thought that he said that with a sincere, ingenuous tone. He had in mind bringing his union rep, Ethan Borner, with him to the re-scheduled meeting. Unless Borner was too busy loading furniture, or would make the case that he wasn't an employee of the school district in the summer and therefore wouldn't do any union-related duties. Oh, well, Shaftoe thought with amusement, if that happens, Fluke will just have to postpone this meeting until Ethan returns in September. Shaftoe knew his rights under the union contract, whether Fluke had read it or not. Coach didn't seem to like what he was hearing.

Fluke said, "Now, now, Mr. Shaftoe, as professionals we all have to understand one another's *positions.*"

Not bad, Mr. Fluke, Shaftoe thought. I see you

learned at least one all-purpose line in your graduate studies for the administrative credential.

But I'm on a roll, he thought. "Sounds like Coach's *position* might have been prone."

Coach leapt up. "Shaftoe, you fucking wimp."

Fluke said, "Now, Mr. Zachary, I wouldn't want to have to describe your behavior to the Superintendent."

Coach apparently decided that he had overplayed his hand. He shut up and sat down. Maybe Zachary hadn't corrupted the Superintendent yet. Shaftoe noted that Fluke knew better than to threaten Zachary with Zachary's buddy, Harley Huntington, the school board president.

Shaftoe remained standing. He decided to press his advantage. Though Fluke had given no indication that he understood Shaftoe's rights, Shaftoe said, "Thank you, Mr. Fluke, for understanding. Please, when you have the time, just jot down the topic for the future meeting of the *two* of us, and give it to Sweet Jillie. 'Just a scrap of note paper would be okay." He was pretty sure Fluke wouldn't make the topic *Sodomy on Campus,* no matter what lie Zachary had told him. And he was doubly sure that Fluke wouldn't write 'sodomy' on anything that he might hand to Sweet Jillie. Shaftoe tried to imagine a very respectful tone of voice, then he used it, "Mr. Fluke, when Jillie gives me your note with the topic, right away I can give you some dates and times I can meet with you."

Fluke blinked. He looked as if he didn't know what to say or do next. Finally he squeaked, "Sounds good, Mr.Shaftoe."

It was 4:00. Shaftoe headed for the door. Fluke stood up and took a step toward the door, to open it for him. The principal had manners.

When Fluke turned his back on Ed Zachary, Zachary scowled, raised both hands, and gave both Fluke and Shaftoe the finger.

chapter twelve

At Dr. Mallard's office, Shaftoe sat in a recliner chair. At least he assumed from the lever on the side of the chair that it reclined. He'd been coming here for many sessions, but he'd never felt enough at ease to try the lever. Recline? He couldn't picture himself relaxed enough with Dr. Mallard to recline.

Juliet Mallard, Ph.D., sat in a gigantic black leather chair, facing him. She was wearing her usual high heels and dark blazer with a knee length skirt. The ensemble looked Armani to Shaftoe. She had good legs. He wondered if she knew how distracting they were to him.

Neither of them spoke. The silence seemed to last forever.

Finally she said, "You seem a little jumpy today, Bobby." She said it softly and pleasantly, without smiling.

"Yeah, I was afraid I might be late." Shaftoe was

aware of always wanting to please Dr. Mallard. "The principal wanted to meet with me. He let me know fifteen minutes before quitting time."

Shaftoe stopped talking and smiled at Dr. Mallard, who didn't return his smile. In her gigantic chair, she swung her legs up alongside her shapely hip, and began slowly stroking them from ankle to knee.

He thought, she isn't making it any easier to decide how I want to start this hour. Really only fifty minutes. Dr. Mallard's time was expensive, and the way she caused him to elaborate on certain of his statements made the time go by very quickly. He didn't want to get behind with the problems he brought to her each week. What would happen if he got behind? Would he explode? Would he be more trouble than she could handle? Would she suggest in her persuasive way that he double up on appointments? He couldn't afford that; and anyway he didn't want to become that preoccupied with his psychotherapy. Or maybe examining his behavior, thoughts, and feelings was *supposed to* occupy his every waking moment.

He thought he would have finished his psychotherapy by now. He sometimes thought of it as his "cure" for being single and alone. Had it been a mistake to start? After all, he knew other single men his age, who, like him, were serial daters. They seemed happy; why wasn't he? "Serial daters" had a derogatory sound to it. Like "serial killers." Sick? Why did it bother him that he had broken up with so many women he liked who were, like him, eligible for marriage? Why wasn't Mallard *fixing* that?

Shaftoe heard Mallard's wall clock ticking behind him. It was placed where she could see it, but he could not. He tried to tell himself that the clock wasn't really his life ticking away. Why had everything become so ominously symbolic since he'd been coming to see her? There was a pervasive ominosity here in her office. Was ominosity a word? His stomach muscles tensed. He really didn't feel like being here today, but he might as well get started.

He told her about Chip's ineligibility and Coach Zachary's hostile response. He told her about Zeus's falling out of the tree onto him. Then he told her about what transpired in the aborted meeting in Principal Fluke's office. Though Dr. Mallard only nodded from time to time, and said nothing, Shaftoe got the feeling that she approved of how he had handled himself.

She said, "The coach sounds like he could use some psychotherapy."

Silence.

Then, "Any dreams, Bobby?"

Shaftoe almost jumped out of his skin.

"No," he lied, and immediately felt guilty. He wondered if Dr. Mallard could tell. "Well, yeah, I had one, but I want to tell you something more important that happened."

"More important than a dream?"

He didn't answer Dr. Mallard's question. But he knew exactly what she was implying. To Dr. Mallard, dreams seemed to be the most important things in the world. But he was thinking, shouldn't my behavior be just as important as my dreams? He was aware that he prided himself on his responsible behavior, his achievements, and his self-control.

"I had to rescue a colleague, a friend, from a motel!"

Dr. Mallard said nothing.

"I got a phone call from my friend in the middle of the night. Really at 3:00 a.m."

He waited for a response from Dr. Mallard. She didn't seem very interested.

Finally she spoke, "Does this friend have a name?"

She's rubbing it in that I'm avoiding something personal, Shaftoe thought. He felt humiliated.

"Yes, she does."

"Oh, a woman."

Christ, Mallard, do you have to make me feel worse, as if I deliberately kept it from you that I'm interested in a woman? Shaftoe was thinking that, but he was afraid to say it to Mallard.

Bite the bullet. Why is this so hard for me to say to Mallard? "Yes, I'm attracted to her." Well, that certainly sounded stuffy, as if my sexual thoughts and feelings are minimal.

"You're attracted to her."

Though Dr. Mallard said it in a perfectly pleasant way, Shaftoe felt that she objected to his being attracted to a woman. He was afraid to tell Mallard that he felt she objected. It all seemed so crazy. His tensed stomach began to ache. He wished he hadn't come today.

"Yes." He was watching Mallard very closely. She continued to look at him impersonally. He had to admit that she didn't have an unpleasant expression, posture, or tone of voice, even though he felt that she disapproved. Where was that feeling of her disapproval coming from? This was going nowhere. "Oh, hell. I guess you were right, my dream is more important."

"Did I say that your dream is more important than your sexual attraction to a woman?"

Shaftoe noted that Mallard had, rightly, labeled his attraction as sexual. In addition to his stomach pain, he felt like such a, such a . . . what? It was a horrible feeling. He felt small, and powerless, and afraid. He remembered Natalie's 3:00 a.m. phone call, with her tortured voice, which he had first thought was his mother's. Why did he need Mallard's encouragement to say his feelings for a woman were sexual?

"Yes. I'm sexually attracted to her. Very." To Shaftoe's own ears, his words sounded like a grudging admission. Why didn't his tone of voice reflect his pleasure?

Mallard nodded. Shaftoe thought, You'd better not smirk, bitch. He was surprised at the intensity of his frustration with her. Why was all this so difficult?

"Anyway, I went over to the motel . . . She'd phoned me from a motel. Some guy had beaten her up. He might have still been there somewhere. Maybe I saved her life." Shaftoe realized he was embellishing the story. "Well, he probably wasn't still there. Anyway, on the phone I'd told her some things she could do to keep herself safe. And it all worked out okay."

"It all worked out okay. It sounds like you really helped her."

"Yes." Somehow, his intense feelings during his adventure with Natalie seemed absolutely absent in what, to his own ears, sounded like a stilted account. Maybe that's what Mallard is disapproving of, my stilted tone of voice. Why can't I relax! He didn't want to mention being aroused by his glimpse of Natalie's bottom in her sexy underwear. He certainly didn't want to confess . . . Confess? Was he guilty of something? Why did he think any of this would be called a confession? He certainly didn't want to say right now he was wondering what sex act it was that Natalie had refused to do. He also decided not to tell Mallard his feeling of rejection when Natalie chose to drive alone the fifteen miles to her home. I feel like I'm going to throw up. What's wrong with me!

Silence and more silence. He heard the clock ticking.

Shaftoe sighed. He thought, okay Doc, you win. I'll give you what you really want. He said, "Well, the dream. You've heard it before."

Mallard nodded. Did she have a receptive look in her eyes?

"Yeah. My mother. Reaching for my belt buckle."

Neither of them spoke. Shaftoe had no memory of anything like that happening in real life. His mother's intrusive behavior only appeared in his dreams.

"How did you feel in the dream?"

Damn you. I should've known you'd ask that, Shaftoe thought. It was always the *feelings* that counted.

"I felt small . . . and powerless . . . and . . . and afraid."

They'd gone over all this before. A number of times. It always made him sweat and feel nauseated. But he was grateful to sense Mallard's approval for expressing his feelings, disabling though they were.

Then he surprised himself, "In the dream, something happened next." Well, that was new! "But I don't know what that was."

"In your dream, something happened next." Mallard was using a tone of voice that was somewhere between a question and a statement.

"Yes."

"And you don't know what that was."

"What, Doctor?" Oh my God! Shaftoe thought, I've forgotten what we've just been talking about. It's completely escaped my mind!

"In your dream, your mother reached for your belt buckle, then something happened, but you don't know what."

"Yes. I mean . . . I don't know."

In addition to his stomachache, flop sweat, and nausea, Shaftoe now felt baffled. As bad as his physical symptoms were, the bafflement was worse. Like unremitting torture.

"Doctor Mallard, what does that mean; that I think something happens next, but I don't know what it is?" He was aware that he was speaking in the present tense. He knew he was looking at Mallard expectantly.

But she was silent. Damn, the woman's putting me through hell. But she was highly recommended by people whom he knew she'd helped.

Finally, "Bobby, you want to know what that means." That odd inflection again, somewhere between a statement and a question.

"Yes."

"Whatever it means, that's where you are."

Shaftoe'd had enough. "Jesus, Doctor, I busted my gut to get here on time, I'm paying you big bucks for every minute of this, you're supposed to help people, and you say, 'Whatever it means, that's where you are.'!" He was thinking, if you were a man, I'd slug you.

He knew he was glaring at Mallard. Was she feeling sheepish? Did she realize she'd just given him some psychobabble? He couldn't tell.

His fists were clenched. He had to work so hard every time he spoke, wondering what her reaction really was. She didn't reveal much, but Shaftoe was pretty sure he was guessing right about what she felt right now. Pity.

Mallard said nothing. Her face continued to be unreadable.

Time must be running out. He felt increasing pressure to tell more to Mallard, but to tell her what? How did she cause him to feel this frightening, crushing overload? Oh, Christ, I'm on to that one, he said to himself. No one can *make* me feel anything. It's me who's making myself sick with the pressure I feel every time I'm here. I'm trying so hard! He felt like there was a dynamite stick below his belt buckle. It's not fair!

And how do I get out of this? What is it I need to

confess to Mallard? I have no major sins. I just can't seem to put into my voice the emotions I know I'm feeling. Does Mallard despise me for that?

"Bobby . . ." Mallard's voice was gentle. She was trying to get his attention. Shaftoe felt like he was slowly coming back from a distant horrible galaxy. How much time had passed? He felt like he'd achieved absolutely nothing on today's terrifying space exploration. Less than nothing. In fact, a setback to his emotional health. He felt awful. The same feeling of insignificance, weakness, and fear that had driven him to first contact Dr. Mallard months ago, but worse now. "Bobby, . . . our time is up. We can talk some more about this next week."

She smiled.

He hated her.

He became aware that he hadn't given Natalie's name to Mallard.

chapter thirteen

Shaftoe got on the elevator and took it down from Dr. Mallard's office. The elevator seemed to be filled with men and women who inhabited the professional building, wearing the clothing of upscale attorneys, M.D.s, and psychotherapists. He felt conspicuous in his polo shirt and khakis.

Christ, I'm exhausted! he thought. But it's always exhausting when I meet with Mallard. Why does it take so much energy for me to tell her anything remotely tender about who I'm sexually attracted to? And why wasn't I able to remember the end of my dream about my mother and me? He continued to feel tense and disgusted with himself.

In the lobby there was another crowd of professionals. The women were beginning to look alike. Tailored dark pants suits and skirt suits. Expensive-

looking rich-woman haircuts that were similar.
Was there some kind of dress code for Capitol City
professional women?

Shaftoe stepped out of the lobby into the late
afternoon sun and heat and thought, It's been a long
week and it's only Tuesday. Yesterday those trucks
nearly ran me over; I've got polluted air in my
office; and that annoying kid, Zeus, is back hanging
around campus! Even worse, there were those bizarre
interactions with Coach Zachary, that dangerous
asshole; and Principal Fluke, his patsy. Someone should
keep Zachary under control. Why am *I* in therapy, and
not him?

Well, he said to himself, I *did* rescue Natalie. Or is
"rescue" too grand a word? I'll think about that when I
get home. Right now I'm starving. Gotta eat.

He saw a bar and grill across the street. Maybe
it would be dark and cool in there. He needed that.
The place might be rejuvenating. He walked to it and
stepped inside. It took a moment for his eyes to adjust
to the dark.

Good. Very dark. And cool. Only a few dim shapes
of customers were scattered around. The high-backed,
dark-wood booths were mostly empty. Two guys in
business suits were the only people at the bar, sitting
together at the far end. Shaftoe took a booth along the

opposite wall, where the bartender could see him, in case there was no waitress. Right away the bartender came over with a menu.

"Good afternoon, sir. What can I get you?"

Shaftoe waved the menu aside.

"Hi. A Heineken and a double cheeseburger with Swiss, please."

"Bottle or draft?"

"Bottle."

"How would you like your double cheeseburger cooked, sir?"

"Medium." Why take a chance on under-done rare.

"That comes with coleslaw or fries."

"What?"

"Coleslaw or fries?"

"Coleslaw." Jesus, ordering was annoying. Shaftoe's stomach was growling. He was having trouble concentrating. A psychotherapy hangover, he thought. He knew what those felt like. He'd had a dozen of em: self-doubt, irritability, and apprehension. In short, brain melt and profound emotional agitation. He felt humiliated and oppressed. He wondered if he was cracking up.

"Thank you, sir. Be right back with your Heineken."

Recorded music was playing. Jazz. He liked that. Comfort food for the ears. Maybe a little too loud for the small crowd in here. Probably the management figured that the customers would stay longer and buy more with some musical cover for their conversations. It was Miles Davis, very coolly making fun of "The Surrey with the Fringe on Top." *Surrey* was usually played light and cheery. But Davis's slow, insinuating, muted trumpet made the melody sound disrespectful and sexually suggestive.

The bartender returned with Shaftoe's Heineken.

Shaftoe thought, It's okay if I drink on a week night during summer, as he took his first, most-welcome, sip. So what if I have beer on my breath at work tomorrow; no students there in the summer. When classes are in session I'm careful not to drink on a school night. Why am I thinking "school night"? Those are words my mother would use. Mother on the mind. Well, what would one expect from psychotherapy? He let out a groan.

When he took in air, he detected a pleasant scent. What was it? Mixed nuts? Sure enough, there was a small wooden bowlful on his table. The bartender must have brought it. God, I was too preoccupied to notice. He sorted out a few cashews. Crunchy and salty. The beer and the cashews went well with the wood-paneled walls and paintings of racehorses and sailboats, each painting with its own little light above it. The TV above the bar was turned off. Good, his thoughts wouldn't be disturbed. The music was a vocal now, "When I Fall in Love." Shaftoe thought, Ironic, they're playing my song. And still a little too loud. He wanted to stand up and yell at the music, You don't have to rub it in! He knew he'd never been in love. Well, that's why I decided to see Dr. Mallard. I'm too old to keep getting stuck in adolescent infatuation.

It was a long wait for the cheeseburger, but that was okay. Shaftoe wasn't really looking forward to driving back to Entonces and his empty apartment. He thought about his feeling of being stuck in therapy, *inhibited* really, when trying to express his intimate feelings. Just thinking about that provoked an intensifying tension throughout his body. Then rather suddenly, his thoughts turned completely to the Heineken. It had been unusually tasty. He waved his empty bottle; the bartender saw it and took another Heineken from the cooler. Shaftoe decided that the surroundings were indeed helping him feel better.

After the bartender brought the cheeseburger and second Heineken, Shaftoe became aware of the enticing click of high heels. A woman in a well-fitting jacket and skirt was taking her last few steps toward the bartender at his station. She gracefully perched sideways on a barstool, her knees together and her skirt slightly above them. It appeared that, without an exchange between them, the bartender was already pouring a drink for her. Straight from the bottle into a large glass. Bourbon? The lights behind the bar silhouetted her figure to her advantage. Shaftoe thought, there's something about a shapely woman in business attire that makes me want to undress her. He'd undressed a woman in a skirt suit once. It was wonderful. First the scarf . . . then the jacket . . . then — he liked the changing images moving through his memory —finally he'd removed all her clothing. Like slowly unwrapping a beautiful gift. He wanted that feeling again. He wondered if Natalie ever wore a scarf and skirt suit.

As he slowly drank and ate, Shaftoe glanced from time to time at the woman on the bar stool. She'd leaned forward and touched the bartender's arm when he'd poured her drink, and he'd given her a quick kiss on the cheek, or maybe it was an air kiss; it was too dark to tell. Her face was still turned away from Shaftoe. He couldn't have made out her features anyway at that distance in the darkness. He thought about moving to a barstool next to her, but wondered if it would be uncool to walk up to her with a cheeseburger and a beer in his hands. Anyway, he thought, guys I've overheard hustling women in bars are always better looking than me. And they always seem to be telling the woman about the great car they're about to buy, the great place they're about to move into, and the great job they're about to get.

Shaftoe's experience had been that when he'd said, "I'm a high school counselor," the hot chicks accepted another drink at his expense, but then turned away, sometimes after saying, "My school counselor didn't do shit for me." One had said, "All my counselor did was try to hit on me," before she walked away. She'd been cute, too. She'd had earrings that were shaped like tiny little green lanterns hanging from silver chains. When she moved they swung and lit up. Shaftoe remembered watching them recede from view.

Now, as some of the late afternoon patrons left, the place became quieter and he began to hear the woman at the bar, and the bartender. Was the music and distance distorting their voices? She'd downed several drinks already. Had her skirt risen higher? It looked to be mid-thigh now, as if a person could easily reach up it. The barstools on each side of her were still empty. Was she leaning closer to the bartender?

Their voices were muffled. Shaftoe could barely make out some of their words.

"Franklin, you can't shut me off. One more and I won't be so scared. You've seen me drink twice this many."

"Look, that was at my apartment. Here, I could lose the liquor license."

"License, license, la de dah. Franklin, do you think you're the only one who has a license to worry about?"

Shaftoe strained to hear. Have I heard that voice before? Is the woman one of my colleagues at the high school? What's that about a license?

"Franklin," she leaned farther across the bar, "it could be like it used to be with us." Her knees were a bit apart now.

"Look, Feather, you're the greatest, but it's time for you to go home."

"Go to hell, Franklin. You mean while I can still drive straight." Then her voice took on a lighter tone. Shaftoe wished that he could place it. "If I was twenty-eight again and this was closing time, you'd drive me to your place, like you used to."

She paused. She'd placed her hand between her knees and was slowly caressing her leg, each time stopping high up on her inner thigh. Franklin was leaning over the bar, watching. Shaftoe was getting an erection.

Then Franklin abruptly leaned away. "Only in your dreams now, Feather. Remember, Charlie got in the way."

The woman stopped stroking herself. For a moment she said nothing. Then, "And don't call me Feather! Featherdell Conratty! God, I hated that low-class name! I have a profession now, and a professional name" She paused. "And my clients are scaring me to death! But I need the money."

She quickly drained her glass.

"Franklin, you just don't get it. How about one last shot of uncondish … unconditional … positive regard. For old times' sake?"

"Huh?"

"Never mind. Fuck it." She stretched her high-heeled feet toward the floor. She seemed to be having a problem getting her bottom off the barstool. "Whoa! Why don't you get a barstool a girl can exit gracefully!" To Bobby, the woman's emotions seemed to turn on a dime. She seemed really sloshed. Of course, now her voice would be sounding different from usual, whatever that was. "And why is it getting so goddam dark in there . . . er . . . in here?"

Franklin spoke pleasantly, "Feather, everyplace looks dark when you've got your head up your ass."

"Fuck you, Franklin."

"Bye now, Feather sweetie."

She stalked toward the door, passing Shaftoe's booth. As she banged the door open, the sunlight revealed her face, eyes glaring straight ahead.

Shaftoe's mouth, full of cheeseburger, dropped open.

It was Dr. Mallard!

chapter fourteen

Still in the bar and grill, Shaftoe wondered, Is it okay that I got a hard-on looking at my therapist? It had been Dr. Mallard, showing a lot of inner thigh! And practically next door to her office, she's trying to pick up the bartender. What had he said about Charlie getting in the way? And she went from seductive to nasty to furious, all so quickly. She seemed unstable!

She's my therapist, for Christ's sake. Isn't she supposed to be emotionally healthier than I am? Shaftoe realized that he didn't know the answer to that one. Is it necessary for a person's therapist to be in good shape? Can they be an emotional basket case and still cure you?

He thought about that for a long time.

He decided to have another beer.

When Franklin, the bartender, brought it, he asked, "Is everything alright, sir?" Shaftoe thought that his tone of voice was different than if asking about the quality of food and service. He's staring at me. Damn, am I so transparent that he's worried about my mental health? Shaftoe hoped not. He thought about saying, No, godamit, my life is a mess, call 911. But he feared that the bartender would really dial the number. It crossed his mind to ask him about Dr. Mallard, but he couldn't formulate a question. Instead, Shaftoe said, "Yeah, just having a rough day."

"Well, we'll hope for better times ahead. Right?"

Shaftoe didn't answer. He thought, What do you know about how it feels to be in my shoes, asshole?

It struck Shaftoe that perhaps he was still irritable.

He had some problems drinking his fresh Heineken. The first ones, before he had recognized Dr. Mallard, had gone down easily, but now his throat felt constricted. Like he wanted to cry out in anguish. He didn't know what words he would have yelled. He thought of a story he'd read, "I Would Scream but I Have No Mouth." He continued to ponder whether Juliet Mallard—really Featherdell Conratty?—needed to be emotionally healthy to do him any good. What had she said about clients scaring her to death, but her needing the money? And if her own love life was a mess, how could she improve his?

Now the canned music was a plaintive female vocalist finishing a poignant ballad about a tragically overdue ship. Shaftoe knew how it ended: "*. . . bring my one true love.*" He found those words too painful to contemplate. He believed that his ship would never come in.

He had to get away from the music right now! Before those last words came! No point in waiting for the tab; he knew he couldn't free his mind enough to calculate a tip. With trembling fingers, he dropped more than enough bills on the table and ran out the door.

Now it was evening, and stars were beginning to show. On the drive back to his apartment in Entonces, in the moonlight the route looked blurred. It had never looked that way before. On the narrow, two-lane country highway portion, it was especially hard to concentrate. Why did they leave the fucking curbs shaped like that! He'd hit one once, it almost threw him into oncoming traffic. He leaned toward the windshield, his chest almost touching his knuckles at the wheel, his eyes blinking. His emotions continued to swirl. What did Mallard/Conratty's behavior at the bar say about her? How did Charlie, whoever he had been, cause the bartender to turn her down? Is the woman an alcoholic? Even if all the answers were unfavorable, would that mean that she isn't a good psychotherapist for me?

He didn't know how to get the questions off his mind, and next week he'd have to meet again with his boss, Principal Fluke, probably about a lie Coach Zachary had put into Fluke's ear.

Shaftoe decided to phone Ethan Borner, his union rep, right away. Would Borner agree to accompany him to his next meeting with Fluke? Was Borner even in town, or was he out of town on his summer job, completely unreachable?

When he safely reached his apartment, Shaftoe looked at his faculty address list and phoned Borner's number. He heard, "The number you've reached is out of service and there is no new number." He dialed it again. Same message.

Damn!

chapter fifteen

As he drove to work the next week, Shaftoe still hadn't reached Borner. No cell phone was listed on the faculty roster. He'd even driven to Borner's bachelor apartment. No one home, and mail piling up in his mailbox. Shaftoe phoned the Bekins office and was told that they didn't relay messages. He felt completely stymied. He didn't want to meet with Fluke without union representation, especially if Zachary would crash the meeting. Where could Borner be?

As Shaftoe parked and carefully negotiated the intersection on foot, he looked forward to seeing Sweet Jillie when he reached his office. That would be pleasant. Wait a minute! Jillie! She prepared a new faculty address and phone list every year. She was always the first one to know of any changes in a faculty member's data. Shaftoe picked up his pace.

Once he was inside the counseling center, he noticed that Jillie looked a bit sunburned. "Good morning, Mr. Shaftoe. How was your weekend?"

"It was pretty good, Jillie." That was a lie; he'd been preoccupied with what to think about Juliet Mallard, and with the still unscheduled, but no doubt upcoming, meeting with Fluke. "And yours?"

"Great. Went to the lake with my girl cousins."

So much for that. The cool lake was popular with locals, especially in the heat of the summer. But Shaftoe had something more pressing to find out.

"Say, Jillie, I've been trying to reach Ethan Borner. The info on the faculty address list hasn't helped." No need to go into detail.

"Oh, Mr. Shaftoe, that faculty list's all outdated. As soon as our paper chase settles down, I'm making a new one for the fall semester. You know, it'll be here before we know it—only seven weeks away. Just a minute, I'll see if there's any changes for Mr. Borner." She opened a drawer and took out some papers. Shaftoe watched her compare one sheet to another.

"Oh, yeah. Mr. Borner has a change coming up. Looks like he wants a cell phone listed. You want the number?"

Shaftoe felt his mind and body relax.

"Please, Jillie."

Jillie gave him the cell phone number. Shaftoe went into his office and dialed it. Borner picked up immediately.

"Ethan, where ya been? I tried to call you from the faculty list. All I got was 'There is no new number.'"

"Bobby, I had service stopped on my home phone. 'Just got a better cell phone, so why pay for both numbers."

"Oh. So where are you right now?"

"On the road the last few days. Pays extra. Bekins sent me and the driver out-of-town, so there'd be two of us to pick up loads along the way, and unload them when we reach our various destinations. Why?"

"Your mail is piling up."

"At the school? So what."

"No, I stopped by your apartment. You want me to collect it so the post office doesn't stop delivery?"

"Sure, buddy. Why not. Thanks. I'll be back in three days."

Shaftoe told him about the aborted meeting in Fluke's office, with Zachary present. So far, Shaftoe had never mentioned Zeus by name, and he didn't plan to— ever. Why besmirch an innocent kid.

Borner agreed—with relish, Shaftoe thought—to accompany him to his next meeting with Fluke—or possibly with Fluke and Zachary. Before they hung up, Borner gave Shaftoe several dates and times of day that he could be available.

And what if Fluke never gave the topic of the meeting to Sweet Jillie? Then there would be no meeting. That possibility seemed the best of all, Shaftoe thought.

Just then, Sweet Jillie walked to his doorway and handed him a slip of paper from Orson Fluke. It was folded in half. On the inside were the words, Topic of Meeting: Activities On Campus. Well, Shaftoe thought, "Activities" is more innocuous than "Sodomy." Sounds more like a routine end-of-school-year review. It allows Fluke lots of leeway, and maybe it will limit the attendees to Fluke, Borner, and myself because Entonces High School has no Activities Director.

As he'd promised, Shaftoe placed a note in Fluke's school mailbox. The note included a list of possible dates and times, all of which Borner had suggested.

Almost immediately, Fluke responded with one, and Shaftoe phoned Borner and apprised him of the meeting time and the change in topic.

Borner laughed and said, "Friend, it'll still be about sodomy unless we take control of the discussion. I know how to do that. We'll give that bastard a kick in the balls." Shaftoe knew that Borner meant Coach Zachary. He recalled Mrs. Moreno's telling him that that was what Zachary had done to Borner in the faculty parking lot.

Borner continued, "It's a bullshit charge, but my degree is in Bull Shit. It says B.S. right on it."

Shaftoe responded, "Well, mine is M.S., More of The Same. Does Fluke or Zachary have the Piled Higher and Deeper? The Ph.D.?"

Both of them laughed at the three ancient gags, common among teachers and school counselors. Shaftoe thought, That's what I need, more laughs. He knew it was true.

On the phone, he hadn't told Borner about Chip's ineligibility. He didn't know if it was a secure phone connection and he didn't want to take any chances with sensitive information.

The meeting was set for 10:00 a.m. Friday, four workdays down the road. Shaftoe thought, I'd rather get it over right away, but maybe I can use the gap to have a beer with Borner and give him the details.

On Wednesday, when Shaftoe and Borner entered the Wagon Wheel, there were only a few men in work shirts at the bar. Nursing the last drink they'd bought before happy hour ended, Shaftoe assumed. At a table, over beer, he told Borner how "a male ninth-grader" had gone up into the tree with a video cam and waited to film Shaftoe walking toward it on the sidewalk below. He didn't want to drag Zeus' name into this.

"What the hell, Shaftoe, does the kid have a crush on you?" Borner laughed, but Shaftoe didn't think the idea was funny.

Then he backtracked and told Borner how he'd verbally given Zachary the news that Chip was ineligible to play quarterback for the approaching season. Zachary must have received the two teachers' letters of bad news by now. No more need for confidentiality, but Zachary's lack of response to the letters was puzzling.

"Oh my God!" Borner said, "Now you're in for it. You don't have any job rights, and Coach hasn't forgotten about you. He'll be a bulldog. He loves that boy. He's always only wanted the best for Chip, even though he put unholy pressure on the kid to excel in every way. And I'll bet that Zachary hasn't even prepared a back-up quarterback! Chip's a model student, why the hell did he cheat!"

"Wait a minute, Ethan, whattaya mean Coach always only wanted the best for Chip? Zachary's an asshole."

"Not toward Chip, he's not. Listen, when Chip was five, Zachary found a private elementary school with strict academic standards *and* a demanding athletic program. Can you even imagine that—an *elementary* school like that! And as soon as Chip was old enough, it was Pop Warner Football. Of course the kid was already a star: physical, smarts, football environment at home; what else did he need! Then it was the same kind of junior high, private again—the tuition must have been sky high—drawing outstanding footballers from all over the state, beating everyone else their age. And you probably heard about Zachary's summer businesses: football camps, or whatever he calls them. Chip was water boy for those while he was still in diapers, and Coach slipped him into that summer program years before he was old enough. Yeah, Zachary's an asshole, but he loves that kid."

"Christ, Ethan, I didn't know all that. I've never seen Chip and Zachary interacting. A good father? I'll take your word for it."

"Listen, I hate his guts. Why would I make up anything complimentary!"

"Complimentary, yes, but maybe Zachary's pressure made Chip feel that he had to get all A's, so he cheated on two finals."

Borner's hand went to his mouth. He slowly turned his head from side to side. "Maybe. Shit. That's tragic." He paused. He lowered his hand and bit his lip. Then he gave Shaftoe a searching look and said, "Counselor, you're smarter than you look."

Tough guy, Shaftoe thought. He feels like he showed me too much, and now he's making a joke to cover it.

Shaftoe was eager to get back to his synopsis.

"Anyway, Ethan, I only went to Zachary man-to-man in his lair to tell him the bad news because I got the official word direct from Chip's teachers. It's in my job description as school counselor to notify the state athletic commission and then the parents, of who's ineligible. Coach is treating me like I caused the whole thing. I was only the messenger; but now he wants to kill the messenger." Shaftoe paused, thinking. "If anyone were to reverse this, it'd have to be the two teachers who caught Chip cheating on their finals. And during their summer unpaid time they don't even have to think about it."

"Who are they?" Borner asked. Shaftoe told him, and he responded, "Naw, they know their stuff. They'll take a stand and Fluke won't know what to do. Even if he had the guts to threaten them, neither of em need their jobs. Both their spouses are *very* well off." He paused. "That's a good thing, Bobby."

Shaftoe saw the point, but he didn't feel like it was a good thing. It looked like no one would take him off the hook.

"Anyway, this goofy kid fell out of a tree on me. He knocked me flat, face down, and he landed face down on my back. You can imagine how it looked."

"Looked! Christ, were you hurt?"

"Just a bloody nose."

"And the kid?"

Shaftoe trusted that Borner could take a ribbing, "Have you been listening to me, union rep? I said he *landed* on me."

Borner laughed. "Oh, yeah. Now I get it. You'll have to excuse me; I'm only an Advanced Placement teacher. One of the lower intellectual classes."

Another corny teacher joke. Neither of them laughed.

"And we got up, I looked back, and Zachary was standing in the field house doorway yelling something about me getting butt-fucked."

"Christ. I can't believe it. On second thought … "

"Yeah, I know. You're gonna tell me that Zachary would do anything, no matter how bizarre, to get even with me, the messenger."

"Right. So Zachary ran to our wimpy principal, Orson Fluke, talking about sodomy."

"Yep. And I'm surprised that Fluke didn't go into shock, hearing the 's' word."

"For a new guy, Bobby, you got Fluke sized up right."

"Not that it helps me any."

They each took another sip of their beers.

Borner said, "Okay, give me some more info. Under the tree, did you say anything back to Zachary?"

"No, what would have been the point?"

"Right. Good. This ninth-grade kid—did Zachary recognize him?"

"Does Zachary know any kid's name who isn't on a sports team?"

"Point well taken. No reason to drag the poor kid's name into our phony meeting."

"I agree."

The bartender looked across the room, raised his eyebrows and lifted his chin as if to ask if they wanted more beers. Borner waved his question away.

"Did the kid say anything to you?"

"Sure. Something like, Oh my gosh, Mr. Shaftoe, I didn't mean to fall on you, Mr. Shaftoe! Ohmigod! I'm so sorry. Are you hurt, Mr. Shaftoe? I didn't mean to fall on you." Shaftoe had given his best imitation. He thought it was pretty good.

"Sounds like a kid. Anything else?"

"He said, 'Look! Mr. Shaftoe, what about your shoe?'"

Borner looked baffled. He stared at Shaftoe. Finally he said, "Shoe?"

Shaftoe wished he'd never mentioned the shoe, but Borner'd asked him for more info. "Yeah. It had already been a nutty morning. I had to jump out of the way of eighteen-wheelers at the intersection. My shoe came off and they ran over it."

"Fucking intersection. Somebody's gonna get killed there someday."

"I told the kid that the shoe wasn't his fault."

"Did you say anything else to him?"

"Yeah, I asked him if he was okay. You know, broken bones, injured in any way. Was his video camera damaged?

He patted his body and didn't wince. No blood on him. I guess he got lucky. I didn't."

"Then?"

"He told me that he was filming me for something he was gonna call *A Day in the Life of Counselor Shaftoe,* or some such nonsense."

"*What?*"

"Yeah, he's a goofy ninth grader."

"Any other conversation?"

"You bet. I told him, 'This never happened.' Several times. I think he finally got it. I wanted him to stop apologizing, and forget the whole thing."

"Goddam, Shaftoe, that sure as hell could be taken the wrong way. Someone could interpret that as trying to silence a kid about sodomy. Does anyone know you said that?"

Shaftoe'd never thought about it that way. A chill struck him.

"Just the kid and me. And you, now."

"What else?"

"I reminded him that no student is supposed to be on campus during the summer. No reason to be. No summer school in session."

"Right. The money was diverted to Zachary's teams."

"I know that." Shaftoe was getting impatient.

"Anything more, Bobby?"

"Naw. . . . Oh yeah, the kid was headed back to

campus a few days later. I heard jake brakes and looked at the intersection. The trucks could have flattened his ass. I told him to go home. He tried to conceal his video cam. Then he left."

"Fucking intersection. Somebody's gonna get killed there someday . . ."

"Yeah. You already said that."

"He was coming back to film you again. And you say he doesn't have a crush on you?"

It occurred to Shaftoe that Borner's inference might be correct.

"We won't be talking about this kid at the meeting, right, Bobby." It wasn't a question. More like advice from a lawyer.

Shaftoe felt the chill return, with a vengeance.

chapter sixteen

"Mr. Shaftoe, don't you have a meeting to go to here at work?"

It was Sweet Jillie's voice, reminding him to go to Principal Fluke's office. Had he repressed the knowledge that he had to be there?

Where was Ethan Borner, the union rep? Did I give him the right day? The right time? The right place?

As he approached Fluke's office, he was relieved to see Borner heading for Fluke's door from the opposite end of the hallway. Shaftoe waved and exhaled a sigh.

"Hi, Bobby. Ready to do this?"

"Now or never, I guess. Thanks for being here, Ethan."

"No problem."

The principal's door was open. They walked in and he closed the door behind them. Shaftoe immediately saw the layout. Slouched in a chair facing Fluke's desk was Coach Zachary. Well, Shaftoe thought, not really a big surprise. He glanced at Borner, but the union rep's expression didn't reveal a thing. He hoped that it was Borner's game face and not a look of disinterest.

There were two less-comfortable-looking empty chairs, one on each side of Coach Zachary's. Shaftoe lifted one of them over Zachary's lap, coming as close to his crotch and face as possible. Never too early to start one-upmanship. He placed it next to the other empty one, so he and the union rep could sit next to each other. No reason to appear split up. Let's put on a unified appearance.

Soon everyone was seated.

Zachary scowled.

Fluke said, "Thank you, Counselor Shaftoe, for meeting with us."

Us, Shaftoe thought. The guy isn't even embarrassed to need Coach Zachary to shore him up.

Shaftoe answered, "You're welcome, Mr. Fluke. I received your note that said the topic of this meeting is . . ." He deliberately paused and looked Fluke in the eye, as if he needed help.

"Er, the topic is . . ." Orson Fluke looked pleadingly at Zachary.

"Activities on Campus, Orwell."

Fluke didn't bother to correct Zachary about his first name.

"Yes, Activities on Campus, Mr. Shaftoe."

Shaftoe asked, "Kind of a review of last year's school activities? A needs assessment of what kind of activities we might want for next year. Right?"

The principal looked at Shaftoe as if he'd just spoken Martian. Then he looked at Zachary. Zachary didn't respond. Was the coach putting Fluke on his own? That was almost unbelievable.

Fluke still didn't answer. Instead, he looked at Borner and said, "And Mr. Borner, how pleasant to see you. What brings you here?"

Shaftoe wondered if Fluke was even aware that Borner was the union rep for the faculty.

Borner used a professional tone, "Counselor Shaftoe is a faculty member and a faculty member is entitled to request that his union representative accompany him to any meeting with an administrator."

Fluke looked surprised, as if this was all news to him. "And you're Mr. Shaftoe's union rep." Shaftoe thought Fluke was trying to sound as if he wasn't surprised that Borner was at the meeting. But he wasn't fooling anybody.

Fluke looked at Borner as if he were expecting a response, but Borner didn't give any. His face continued to reveal nothing. No one spoke.

Coach Zachary looked at Fluke and made a motion

with his hands, rolling one around the other: Let's speed this up.

Fluke cleared his throat and said, "Counselor Shaftoe, let's start our review with the day of June 10, when the incident occurred under a tree over the sidewalk between the Ed Zachary Field House and the classroom building."

Shaftoe looked at Borner. No response. Apparently Borner trusted him to carry the ball. He said, "Mr. Fluke, I understood that the purpose of this meeting is to review the student activities that Entonces High School provided throughout the last school year. You mentioned June 10; but the school year ended on June 6." Out of the corner of his eye, Shaftoe saw Borner give him a nod of approval.

Zachary waved a paper in front of Shaftoe's face. "Oh, what the hell, Shaftoe. Just sign this, and we can all leave."

Shaftoe was getting angry, but he saw nothing to be gained by showing it. "I'm sorry, Mr. Fluke, maybe I misunderstood something. Is Coach Zachary chairing this meeting?"

At first, Fluke didn't say anything, then he leaned toward Shaftoe. "Mr. Shaftoe, are you unhappy in your work situation?"

Shaftoe noted the principal's tone of exquisite solicitude. He'd heard that question before, in the same tone of voice, at his previous school. It must be one of those things principals were taught to say in their graduate studies. Shaftoe's blood boiled. He'd fallen for it before. Not this time. That was then. This is now. I don't have to answer a question just because it's asked. He felt giddy at the thought. What would Christ do? No, what would Freud do? He'd meet a question with a question. "Mr. Fluke, I'm sure that your last question has to do with the topic of this meeting, Activities on Campus. Can you please help me make the connection?"

Fluke didn't have a response. Zachary kept waving the paper in front of Shaftoe's face. Shaftoe looked at Borner who gave him a surreptitious thumbs-up.

Shaftoe grabbed the paper from Zachary's hand. At least that would stop its damn fluttering. He focused his eyes on it. Its title "Encedint Report" was misspelled. Its original, computer-printed, subject line had been, Subject Of Meeting: Sawdummy On Campus. Shaftoe assumed that "Sawdummy" was Coach Zachary's misspelling of sodomy. Anyway, the word Sawdummy had been crossed out and the word "Activities" hand-printed sloppily just above it.

As Shaftoe began studying the rest of the paper, Borner spoke up. "Principal Fluke, the topic you gave to Mr. Shaftoe in your recent note to him, was

'Activities on Campus.' And just now you said that the purpose of this meeting is to review all the various activities that Entonces High School provided last school year for the student body."

Shaftoe heard all this while reading; he knew that Fluke hadn't really said that, and he admired Ethan Borner for reformulating Fluke's wording.

Borner continued, "Coach Zachary is here. If we had a Director of Student Activities at Entonces, I could understand why *that* person might be here, but we don't have one—"

Zachary interrupted. "We do now, buddy. It's me." He grinned.

Borner kept his cool, "You were duly appointed, Ed? Tell me about it." Now Borner's tone of voice was that of a skilled elementary school teacher, looking at some kindergartener's unrecognizable artwork, and tactfully saying, "Tell me about it."

Zachary looked like he couldn't wait. He leaned forward. "You betcha. My supervisor—that's Principal Orgon Fluke—duly appointed me yesterday." He sat back, gloating.

Shaftoe thought, Zachary's a bully and a horrible speller, and Fluke's his patsy, but they're diabolically devious. Out to get me.

This time, Fluke said quietly, "Ed, my name's Orson, not Orgon."

If anyone heard Fluke, it wasn't evident.

"Congratulations, Coach. Yet one more job which I'm sure you will do well. Is there supplemental pay?" Borner's sarcasm was palpable.

Coach Zachary looked at Fluke, "Is there supplemental pay?"

Fluke pursed his lips, lowered his eyelids, and barely moved his head from side to side: no.

Their talking had given Shaftoe time to scan the rest of the document that he'd grabbed out of Zachary's hand. After the lines he'd just silently read, he saw:

FACTS OF ENCEDINT

More of Zachary's inept handiwork, Shaftoe thought. Then:

To Be Completed Emedeatly

Christ, apparently Fluke hadn't even proofread this phony document created by Zachary. Unless Fluke was as bad a speller as the coach was.

More:

The employee who eicher witnesses the encedint or is soopervising at the time must complete this form. Submit it emedeatly to the Principal.

That was followed by sloppily drawn lines to write on, six boxes available to checkmark, and places at the bottom labeled "sign" and "date." The six boxes were labeled "Student," "Parent," "District Employee," "Visitor," "Vendor" and "Other," but the word "Other" had been crossed out and "Sawdummy" printed sloppily above it. A huge checkmark had already been made in the box next to the word "Sawdummy."

Other lines had been similarly crossed out and re-labeled "Schoolage District," "Schoolage Name," "Schoolage Address," "Has Schoolage Contacted Parents?," and "Was Any Schoolage Rule Violated?"

Shaftoe thought, What the hell, did Coach have some aversion to the word *School*? But why would he have such an aversion? Or maybe "schoolage" was some obscure derivation of "school," like "parsonage" was derived from "parson"? Well, there are more important things to focus on right now. Whatever. It's a bullshit form, just like this is a bullshit meeting. But I'm a first-year employee and I can be fired without cause.

Shaftoe handed the form to Borner to read, and looked Fluke in the eye. He pretended that the principal deserved his respect—no reason to give Fluke any reason to write him up for lack of professional courtesy. He pointed at the form as Borner sat reading it, and said, "Mr. Fluke, that dog won't hunt."

Fluke looked baffled; it appeared that he had never heard that expression before.

Zachary muttered "Dog? What the hell does that mean?" He looked over his shoulder at the doorway as if he expected to see a dog entering. But the door was still closed.

For the benefit of both of them, Shaftoe rephrased his statement, "What I mean, gentlemen, is that the form now in Mr. Borner's hands doesn't look official."

Borner looked at the principal and said, "Mr. Fluke, I've worked here thirty years. This appears to be a sloppy revision of a legitimate form approved by the School Board. But I'm sure that this form, in the marked-up and misspelled condition we're looking at, hasn't been approved by the Board." He held the form up so that Fluke could see it.

Fluke looked at it for a moment, then said, almost eagerly, "Hmmm. You know, Coach Zachary, I see Mr. Borner's point. I'll have to let the Entonces High School Faculty Form Committee take a look at this, when they come back in September."

Shaftoe was pretty sure that there wasn't an Entonces High School Faculty Form Committee. But until today there hadn't been any Director of Student Activities either.

How sweet it is, thought Shaftoe. Even if Fluke could find a way to dump me from his faculty, school law in this state said he'd have to do it before

September. Any Form Committee that Fluke might plan to appoint is on vacation until September.

Then Fluke uttered more words Shaftoe hadn't expected to hear, the clinchers! "This meeting stands adjourned."

Coach yelped, "But, Orson!"

Finally, the coach had gotten Fluke's name correct.

Shaftoe thought, Fluke may be a patsy, but he knows how to weasel out of a tight spot. When Borner and I called his bluff, he saw his way out and he took it, by passing the buck to a nonexistent committee. Shaftoe took the phony form from Borner's hand, folded it, and stuffed it into his own shirt pocket.

Principal Fluke stood up and looked at his wristwatch, signaling that it was time for the three faculty members to leave his office.

As Shaftoe stood up to go, Zachary whispered to him, "You haven't seen the last of me, Bobby, you punk."

But Shaftoe knew he had dodged at least one of the bullets in Zachary's arsenal.

chapter seventeen

That evening, pacing in his apartment, Shaftoe felt his anxiety rising from the meeting in Principal Fluke's office. He thought, The very idea, Coach Zachary wanting me to sign a phony document that I'd allowed a student to sodomize me. It had been a bullshit meeting, a subterfuge to let me understand that my job is in danger. Yes, my job is in danger, but that's because I reported to the state athletic commission that the coach's son is ineligible to play football.

I'm glad I asked Ethan Borner to be at the meeting; if there are any future threats, the union rep will back me up. I can count on him.

Shaftoe sat down on his sofa, sighed, and his thoughts turned to Natalie Barney.

Then it was as if he heard John Wayne whispering in his ear, A man's gotta do what a man's gotta do. Or was it Bogart who said that? Why couldn't he keep his attention focused on getting in touch with Ms.—or was it Miss? Or Mrs? Now CUT that OUT! he heard a voice saying, but the voice now sounded more like an ineffectual Jack Benny. Shaftoe thought, my God, am I developing multiple personalities?

Don't be gutless. What's the worst that can happen if I ask her out? She might laugh and tell me she's married; I always forget to look for a wedding ring. Divorced? Never married—like me? Boyfriend? Or she might have a child she'd have to stay home with, never married or not. Maybe she'd just reject my invitation; and I don't know her well enough to guess if she'd do it courteously or harshly. Well, she *is* a teacher. But I've seen all kinds of teachers.

John Wayne—or damn, was it Bogart?—prevailed. Shaftoe reached to his coffee table and picked up his faculty address and phone list. His hand trembled. His eyes blinked rapidly; his vision was blurred. He dialed.

He waited. He thought, I did rescue her from the motel. I hope she remembers that. He closed his eyes and made a silent wish; I wish she'll think of me as a hero. He heard his mother saying, "If wishes were horses, beggars would ride." That was no help.

Finally, "Hi, this is Natalie. I can't answer the phone right now, but if you'll leave your number . . ."

Shaftoe hadn't anticipated this. He thought, Damn you, Bobby. You got carried away with your romantic fantasy. People don't always answer in person. Grow up. Live in the real world. It wasn't the first time over the years that he'd said that to himself.

I'll just hang up. But what if she has caller ID? And she programmed your name and number into it? Sure, buddy—as if she even thought about you—keep on dreaming. His breathing sped up alarmingly. He felt like he was going to panic.

What would Bogart do? "Here'sh looking at yooo, schweet heart." Christ did I just now say that into her answering machine? No, I only thought it. Then, after the tone, Shaftoe heard a voice that sounded to him like Jack Benny saying "Hi, Miss . . . er, Natalie." It was Shaftoe's own voice. "This is Bob . . . Bobby . . . Shaftoe . . . from work." He'd stumbled over his own name. But, so far so good. He took a slow, deep, calming breath. Breathe in stress—breathe out peace. He continued, "Sorry you can't come to the phone, Natalie . . ." His stomach hurt.

Then, "Hi, Bobby." It was her voice, picking up.

She sounded pleasant—and something else: apprehensive? Why didn't I plan this better? He recalled the conversation they'd had at the Wagon Wheel—about Leonard Cohen. That had gone well. He felt whipsawed by his emotions.

He said, "Hi, how ya doin'?" He took another slow, deep, calming breath. He gave himself credit for making the initial move, no matter what the consequences. But what if she turns me down, and makes fun of me behind my back to the other faculty women?

"Enjoying your vacation, Natalie?"

"Yeah, so far. You know, sleeping late and stuff."

"Great, lucky you." Sleeping late? Did that mean she didn't have a child, or someone else in her bed, like a husband or a live-in boyfriend? Or even the guy who beat her up. Shaftoe felt encouraged. "I'm working at school this summer. You know, catching up on paperwork, planning ahead. Pretty soon I'll start figuring out class schedules for next year's students." He hoped he wasn't going on too much about work; he was looking for a more personal relationship than that.

"Lucky me, Bobby? No, lucky *you*. Lucky you because you get two extra paychecks." She laughed a little. Shaftoe loved her laugh; he was glad to hear it again. He laughed in return.

She went on, "Anyway, can't sleep late much longer; Friday I start clerking at Wal-Mart."

"Jeez. You deserve better than that." Score one point for me, I hope.

"Oh, you noticed." She giggled.

He loved it when a grown woman giggled. He

could almost see her narrow face, goofy smile, and cute bottom. He forgot what they were talking about.

She gave him a clue, "Well, times are tough. I worked at Wal-Mart in college—womens undergarments." She giggled again. "So they knew me and took me back for the next six weeks."

Women's undergarments! Shaftoe felt even more excited. He'd asked Dr. Mallard if he had an underwear fetish. Now he remembered her answer, "Not if there's a woman in them." That was reassuring.

He said, "Well, good luck with that." Now, what the hell does that mean, exactly? Good luck with that? "Anyway, I enjoyed talking with you at the Wagon Wheel—about Leonard Cohen songs." Establish something in common, but be subtle, not like, *You like Leonard Cohen, right? Good, then we have something in common. Now let's get naked.* Damn Dr. Mallard's soul; I *don't want* to be in better touch with my id. He wondered if Natalie had had any psychotherapy. That would be something else they might have in common.

Back to business. "I'd like to talk with you some more." Shaftoe had read that women liked to be asked out to something specific. So they could know what they'd be turning down, and talk about it later behind the guy's back? And laugh? Just do it! "Would you like to go out to dinner Wednesday evening? You live in Capitol

City, right? Would you like to go to the Fox And Hounds there?" After years of random dating, why hadn't this gotten easier?

Shaftoe heard nothing on her end of the line. He held his breath.

Then he heard, "Listen. Don't bother to drive over here . . ."

 Oh, that's bad. Here comes the turndown. Well, fuck it, there are other fish in the sea. But Shaftoe couldn't honestly picture any other fish.

Natalie went on, ". . . I'm going to be at Entonces High on Wednesday afternoon, boxing up some school supplies I bought, before somebody snitches them. No use your driving over here. We could just meet for drinks at the Wagon Wheel. I liked that place."

Shaftoe pumped one fist in a victory sign. Oh, that's *good*. On my home field, so to speak.

"You sure?" Shaftoe said. "It's not particularly classy." Some women liked to be kept on a pedestal.

"Well, I'm a classy woman, and you're a classy guy. So we can bring a little class to the place."

"For sure." Wow! Who could ask for anything more. "And thanks for the compliment." He hoped she could tell he was pleased. "What time shall I meet you there Wednesday?"

There was a moment's silence.

"Five. I'll be through at the high school by then. . . ."

"Five o'clock for sure." Shaftoe liked her directness. He'd beaten around the bush with too many women who didn't seem to know what they wanted. "I look forward to seeing you." To say the least. Boy do I look forward to seeing you.

"And I'll wear my summer frock. And my new cute shoes, with the heels."

Shaftoe thought, You mean your chase me, fuck me, make me write bad checks, shoes? But he figured he'd better not say that. Instead, he only said, "Are those your make-me-write-bad-checks shoes?"

She giggled. "I've heard that expression, and the rest of it too. And don't get any funny ideas, Shaftoe. I don't write bad checks; I'm a teacher, you know."

She sounded naughty.

"Got it." Shaftoe laughed freely. It felt good. This was fun; he wanted more of this. "No bad checks on the first date."

"You betcha, Bobby. See you Wednesday at the Wagon Wheel, five o'clock. Bye."

And she was off the phone.

Shaftoe found himself singing, "... *your first kiss...*" He'd always found those words strangely powerful and haunting.

Let's see, who would give your first kiss to you?" Well, that would have to be *your mother*! Shit, leave it to psychotherapy to ruin a perfectly good song.

chapter eighteen

On Wednesday afternoon, Shaftoe drove to the Wagon Wheel. Natalie Barney was to join him there at 5:00 for drinks.

He thought about the confrontation in Fluke's office last week. He knew from it that he could count on Ethan Borner to back him up in the future. And he looked forward to cementing his alliances with Kent Greef and Sara Moreno. Moreno seemed to be a war horse from way back; she would brook no shit. Nor would Greef, and he always put a witty spin on all the local dynamics. To bond with his allies, Shaftoe wanted to get together with them again; before the season-opening afternoon football game, followed on a Monday by the start of classes. Those were only five weeks away.

As Shaftoe pulled into the Wagon Wheel parking lot, it was 4:30. Damn, he thought, being eager is one thing, but being half an hour early when it's only a five-minute drive from my apartment is adolescent. Adolescent? Why had he chosen that word to criticize himself?

As he walked up to the entrance, he heard recorded music coming from inside. He hoped it wouldn't be too loud for him to have an intimate conversation with Natalie. Otherwise, on a weekday afternoon like this there shouldn't be too much hubbub.

Shaftoe pulled the door open, and noted the liquor and peanuts smell and the comforting dimness of the place. As he walked alongside the lengthy bar, toward the tables, his eyes began adjusting to the dark. Sure enough, there were only a few people in the room. That was good. Relative privacy.

"Hey, Counselor. Cured anyone lately?" came a shout. Then some laughter.

Oh, Christ, it was Kent Greef. And Borner and Sara Moreno providing the laughter. I want to spend time with them, but not this afternoon; this afternoon is for Natalie and me. Shaftoe saw peanut shells on their table, and nearly empty glasses. Were they about to leave? He desperately hoped so. I should have insisted Natalie and I go to Fox And Hounds in Capitol City! But how could I have insisted on that without seeming heavy-handed?

"Bobby, Bobby, don't be the Lone Ranger," Sara Moreno called out.

"Come over here," Borner added.

Well, if I can do a half hour with them, that might help my cause, Shaftoe thought. Maybe this is a good omen—an unexpected opportunity to join again with people who can take my side against Coach Zachary.

Then Shaftoe was rattled to his core! At the far end of the bar he saw a kid. It was Zeus! Or, more properly, Jesus Jiminez. What was he doing on that stepladder? And he had a camera! My God, this kid is nuts; obsessed with getting more high-angle footage of me. He'd call it *Counselor Shaftoe Meets with Colleagues* no doubt. Would he have popped up in Capitol City if I'd gone there with Natalie?

"Just a second, guys," Shaftoe called out. And he took off at a fast trot, farther down the long bar, toward the kid. "Hold it, Zeus. Stay right there! Don't run. Don't ditch that camera."

Zeus peered through the gloom. Then he looked surprised at Shaftoe's presence. He climbed down from the stepladder.

"No need to fake that surprised look, Zeus." I gotta get that camera, Shaftoe thought. It's a damn good thing Natalie isn't here already. What would Zeus have titled *that* footage, *Counselor Shaftoe Tries to Get Into Ms. Barney's Pants*? "Gimme that camera!"

"What?"

"Damn it Zeus! Remember our conversation. You need to stay away from me."

"But, but . . . Mr. Shaftoe . . ."

"No two ways about it, Zeus. Gimme that camera." Shaftoe hadn't thought through what he would do with it. Stomp on it? Tear out whatever was inside? Confiscate it? Could he do that with a kid's property?

The bartender hurried over, "Look, Mister, is there a problem here?"

"Yeah, I'm this student's school counselor, and he's invading my privacy."

"No way, Mister, this is *Gee'*-sus, he's from Gottcha."

"Hey-*Zeus,* Sir," Zeus corrected the bartender's pronunciation.

"What, kid?"

"My name's not pronounced *Gee'*-sus, Sir."

Shaftoe told them both, "Never mind." This conversation was getting way off track. "The kid is from Gottcha? Where the hell is Gottcha?"

"Mister, this kid *works for* Gottcha . . ."

"Okay. *What* the hell is Gottcha? Small town CIA?"

"What, Mister?"

Maybe the bartender had never heard of the CIA.

"Mr. Shaftoe, I work for Gottcha, after school hours . . ."

"Zeus, this isn't 'after school hours.' It's summer vacation!"

". . . and also summer vacations, Mr. Shaftoe."

"And Gottcha is . . . ?"

"Gottcha Security Services, Mr. Shaftoe. Here in Entonces. I service their security systems." "All over town," he added proudly.

Zeus handed Shaftoe a business card: *Jesus Jiminez, Associate, Gottcha Security Services. We will spy. The law will fry.*

Shaftoe looked again at the camera in Zeus's hand. Sure enough, it wasn't a home video device. It was a security camera from an empty bracket above.

He became aware of his professional colleagues staring at him. He thought, Gotta cut my losses, calm things down. He tried to relax his face into friendliness. The bartender retreated to his station.

"Okay, Zeus. Okay. I made a mistake."

Zeus looked as if he could hardly believe his ears.

"Whatsa matter, Zeus? You never heard a school person say they'd made a mistake?"

"No, Sir, Mr. Shaftoe."

Shaftoe sighed.

"You work for this company named Gottcha? That's why you're here—to service their security equipment? I didn't understand."

Again, Zeus looked surprised.

"Whatsa matter Zeus? You never heard a school person say they didn't under . . . Oh, never mind." This conversation was going nowhere.

Over his shoulder, Shaftoe noticed that Borner was walking toward them.

"Hi, Zeus. Bobby, could I help you with anything?"

This was embarrassing. "Naw, Ethan. Thanks anyway."

Zeus smirked. Shaftoe knew why. Students always thought it was otherworldly when they heard two teacher-types call each other by their first names. Shaftoe'd had enough, he looked Zeus sternly in the eye. The smirk disappeared.

Shaftoe said, "I made a mistake. I didn't understand." Both Zeus and Borner stared at him. What the hell, Shaftoe thought, is there some code of conduct that says a counselor has to fake being perfect?

A new light came into Borner's eyes, "Oh yeah, Bobby, Zeus works for Gottcha. The kid's a ninth-grade electronic genius. Probably the best repairs this place has ever had."

The bartender walked past them, taking out trash. "This kid's a friggin' genius. Best repairs this place ever had."

Shaftoe felt as if he was being tortured by an evil ccho. Let it go, he told himself. "Okay, guys. Sorry, Zeus. Glad you've got a summer job; I'm proud of you. Nothing more to see here. Let's all go back to where we were."

Shaftoe and Borner headed to the table Borner had come from. Over his shoulder, Shaftoe saw Zeus wipe the camera lens, go back up the stepladder, and quickly reattach the camera to the bracket. Then he got down, glanced toward the tables and left with the ladder, quietly.

Shaftoe and Boerner sat down at the table with Greef and Moreno. Greef was saying to Moreno, "... and he acquired superpowers of nastiness when Chip was made ineligible ..."

So the news of Chip's ineligibility had spread.

"... But now he's back to being his old self: only his usual level of nastiness." Shaftoe's ears perked up; he figured that Greef was talking about Coach Zachary.

Then Moreno looked at Shaftoe. She glanced back and forth from Shaftoe's eyes to the security camera and said something in Spanish that sounded like "*Ee'*-hoe-lay, Bobby." From her tone and expression, Shaftoe figured "*Ee'*-hoe-lay" must be Spanish for "My gosh," or something like that. He wasn't in the mood to ask for a translation.

Borner said, "Christ, Bobby, you look like you could use a drink."

Shaftoe said, "Yeah, I want a bourbon and water." He hoped his voice sounded normal.

Greef said, "Bobby, don't let it bother you what people are saying about you. We respect you anyway."

Shaftoe's first thought was that Greef was being rude about Zachary's charging him with allowing a student to sodomize him. Then he looked into Greef's face and saw that he was not talking about any incident, real or diabolically concocted. Greef was just being his usual wise-ass social self.

Shaftoe told them, "I made a mistake just now. I didn't understand. I don't want to talk about it." He didn't see how he could explain it without revealing that it was Zeus, filming from a tree, who Zachary, that vindictive liar, had seen falling on top of him. Confidentiality was important. After all, Zeus was Shaftoe's counselee—damn, all 500 kids in Entonces High were his counselees—and there was no reason to associate Zeus's name with Zachary's falsehood. Shaftoe stood up, walked to the bar, asked for a bourbon and water, and stood there while the bartender made the drink. No use being a further fool by waiting for the barkeep to come to their table to take the order, let alone bring the drink over. Shaftoe knew how this place worked. He'd been here before.

He hoped that his colleagues hadn't been talking about him while he was accosting Zeus. The tone of their murmured words hadn't sounded conspiratorial. He paid and tipped the bartender and walked toward the table, with his drink. The weight of the glass in his hand felt good. He took a sip as he walked; why wait. The aroma and the bite were reassuring.

When Shaftoe got back to the table, he heard Greef saying to Moreno, "So that's an improvement over his attitude after Bobby turned Chip in."

"Wait a minute, Kent. I didn't 'turn in' anyone."

Moreno said, "Yeah. I guess you could say Chip brought it on himself, cheating on finals like he did."

"Yeah, cheating because of his old man's pressure," Greef said, "Zachary wouldn't get off his kid's back." He waved his hand limp-wristed, mocking himself, doing his patented burlesque of a stereotype gay man. "Football is a heathen sport."

But Shaftoe reflected that Greef knew all the scores and players' names, high school, college, and pro. Greef followed football more closely than anyone he'd ever met.

"And Zachary loved that kid like you wouldn't believe," Borner said. But Shaftoe did believe it. It was just that, as a father, Zachary hadn't foreseen the effects of his relentless pressure on the boy. Chip's cheating on his finals for fear of getting less than all A's was an unintended consequence.

Shaftoe looked at Greef, "But what were you saying when I walked up, about someone's attitude improving? Were you talking about Zachary?"

Greef said, "What? Oh, yeah, we all noticed that he's changed. You know me, Bobby, I couldn't resist giving him a dig when I ran into him at Seven-Eleven.

I said, 'Coach, you're a ray of sunshine recently. Aren't you still pissed'— 'pissed' is an understatement, Bobby— 'about Chip not getting to be quarterback? Had you even trained a back-up?' I knew he hadn't— supreme overconfidence." Greef went on, "Well, first he glared at me, then he gave me this shit-eating smile. He said 'Not to worry, Mr. Fancy Pants'—he likes to call me that, Bobby. Then Coach started over, 'Not to worry, Kent.' Kent? I couldn't believe my ears; now it was 'Kent,' as if he'd changed his form of address to give me some respect. Anyway, 'Kent, I'm taking care of that.' And he walked away. Jauntily, I must say."

Shaftoe felt a chill cross his shoulders. "Kent, what did Zachary mean by, 'I'm taking care of that'?"

Greef said, "Bobby, I'm an English and Trig teacher, not a mind reader. I don't know what he meant."

The others joined in, hunching their shoulders and raising their hands, palms up, in bafflement.

"Does Zachary have pull with the state athletic commission? Can he get them to reverse their decision that Chip is ineligible?" Shaftoe asked.

Again, shrugs of shoulders.

Just then Natalie Barney walked in. After a moment, she saw the teachers looking at her and gave a comic twirl to show off her summer frock and sexy shoes. Her legs looked even better than Bobby had remembered.

"Hi, Bobby." She smiled her goofy smile. "Hi, guys. You live here?"

Shaftoe's tablemates looked surprised to see her here in Entonces, let alone at the Wagon Wheel. To Shaftoe, that confirmed that they too thought she was a classy young woman. He was happy.

There was a tentative chorus of, "Hi, er, Natalie." That "er" told Shaftoe that she wasn't one of his colleagues' in-crowd. He was happy about that too. Maybe they would catch on and leave him and Natalie here in peace. Or not.

As Natalie approached their table, Greef leaned toward Shaftoe and whispered, "If I were to change teams, I'd go after that."

Change teams? Shaftoe didn't think Kent was talking about football. He said, "But ... ?"

"Bobby, come off it," Greef said, "I'm gay, not blind."

chapter nineteen

Natalie sat down on the same side of the table as Shaftoe, squeezing in next to him. Her light-weight summer dress crept up above her knees, which she demurely placed together. She had good legs and squarish knees. Shaftoe had always liked squarish knees. Perfect. She turned toward him, looked him in the eyes, and smiled.

The others watched them. Were they catching on? Would they leave soon?

A throbbing musical beat began thumping out of the speakers on the walls. It was an old honky-tonk tunc.

. . . He gave her things that she was needin'.

Shaftoe liked the sexual innuendo in the lyrics, and the beat was driving and lurching. Natalie, Moreno, and Greef stood up and began dancing, each with no one in particular. Borner stayed seated at the table. Natalie incorporated a charming flounce. Moreno appeared to be doing a salsa step. Greef was gyrating the most of all, with an in-your-face girly effect; Shaftoe couldn't tell if he was putting them on. The bartender stopped washing a glass and watched.

Shaftoe wanted to join them, but he didn't. Despite being coordinated in his wrestling days, he had always felt a disabling awkwardness on the dance floor. He decided to get a second drink, and one for Natalie. He stood up, caught Natalie's eye as she danced, nodded toward the bar, raised his eyebrows questioningly at her, and mimed holding a drink. She caught on, and mouthed "Long Island iced tea."

At the bar, Shaftoe ordered Natalie's drink and another bourbon and water for himself. Then he turned to watch his three colleagues dance. Maybe he would feel like it after another drink.

The recorded song went into more of its many verses. Natalie, Moreno, and Greef were really shaking it up. Especially Greef.

"Here's your drinks, Mister."

It was the same bartender as last week. Now Shaftoe noticed he had a crew cut and a tattoo on his forearm. It was a picture of a cherry, and underneath it were the words *Here's mine, where's yours?*

Shaftoe's thoughts came back to the drinks. "Oh. Yeah. Thanks." As he began pulling paper money from his billfold he noticed three drinks, not two, at his elbow. He pointed at a very pink one. "This pink drink's someone else's order."

The bartender scowled, then sneered. "No, pal. Your girly buddy's drinking greyhounds. I made this extra one just for him. It's a surprise. On the house."

A free drink for Kent Greef? Something wasn't right. Shaftoe knew the ingredients of greyhounds. "But it's very pink."

"Yeah. Pink. I used food coloring." The bartender jerked his head toward Greef, who was facing them, doing a bump and grind now. "Very pink. For your queer pal. Fags like pink."

Shaftoe bristled. "Dump it, bartender. Unless you want to drink it yourself." Shaftoe glared. He started to put his money back into his billfold. The bartender watched, sizing up Shaftoe and the disappearing money. He looked angry, started to open his mouth, hesitated, then shut it. His shoulders slumped. He poured the pink drink down the sink.

"You're a schmart guy," Shaftoe said. He thought, Oh, Christ, I'm drifting into a Bogart accent; a bad one. He put his money completely back into his billfold. He picked up his and Natalie's drinks. "And thanks for these two. They're on the house also, right?" Shaftoe turned before the bartender said anything, and walked back to the table with the drinks. He felt proud. Justice had been done that night at the Wagon Wheel. Like a gunfight at the O.K. Corral, right? But that wasn't the right metaphor, because Bogart hadn't been at the O.K. Corral. *Virginia City. The Oklahoma Kid.* He tried to remember what Bogart looked like in western gear.

Now everyone was sitting. He gave Natalie her drink and sat down between her and Greef.

Natalie said "Whew, I need this," and laughed. She looked completely fresh. She was magic. Moreno's hair was hanging damply over her forehead; she stood and headed for the ladies room. Greef was trying to catch his breath. He leaned toward Shaftoe.

"Thanks ... Bobby," he whispered. "I saw that . . . pink drink . . .'It will get . . . better'? I used to tell . . . gay students that. . . . But no, it . . . never stops. That bastard. But I could have . . . taken care of him."

Shaftoe shook his head, not looking at Greef. "You shouldn't have to. That kind of happy horseshit should never have started. Ever."

"I owe . . . you, Bobby."

"Forget it," Shaftoe said quietly. He glanced at the bartender, who was busy ignoring their table. But now that things were calming down, Shaftoe took a second to think strategically. If I need him later, I hope this all means that Greef will back me up against Zachary.

chapter twenty

In the low light of the Wagon Wheel, Shaftoe said to Natalie, "I thought they'd never leave."

He saw her eyes sparkle. And she laughed. He knew she'd seen Moreno, Borner, and Greef leave the Wagon Wheel as soon as the throbbing music had faded away.

"Borner didn't dance, did he?" Natalie said.

"Well, he's the union rep. He's got his dignity to maintain. He might want to run for higher office."

She laughed again. Apparently she agreed there was nothing dignified about working at Entonces High School, and knew that being an aging union rep never led to higher office.

It was exciting to be alone with Natalie sitting next to him, with drinks, and with only a few strangers here and there in the gloom. Shaftoe looked at her and she smiled. He felt happy.

"You like to dance," he said.

"Oh, you're so observatory."

He liked how she played with that last word. Her voice sounded a little giddy, and he was pretty sure it wasn't from the effects of one drink.

"Would that be the *Naval* Observatory?"

"Oh, did you observe my navel? Did you like it?"

Was she flirting? Whatever it was, Shaftoe liked it. He wanted more. He was feeling giddy himself. The giddiness of freedom. Yes, he did feel surprisingly free with her. "Your dancing, in that cool dress . . . With you, is it 'more flounce to the ounce'?"

"You noticed! I didn't know you cared."

She *was* teasing, and in a way he liked. "And my dress is indeed cool. In every possible way."

Shaftoe didn't know a thing about fabrics, but the dress was blue and yellow, with lace, and it clung to her breasts at the top. It was thin material, just the warm evening breeze from the open door to the street rippled the flared bottom. She took the skirt in hand and swished it up quickly, midway between her beautiful squarish knees and her hips. Shaftoe liked what he had just seen so briefly.

"Wow. May I call you Miss Glimpse?"

She laughed. Tonight her laugh was like wind chimes on the first day of spring. She tilted her head, and batted her eyes in a comical way, then smiled her goofy, perfect, smile. He felt smitten. He thought of the pop psychology question, When is thinking of someone night and day not classified as an obsession? Answer: When you're in love. He heard a voice somewhere singing "Night and day, you are the one." Then he felt scared.

"Miss Glimpse, do your male students like it when you flounce that dress?" Then he thought of the main thing he and his psychoanalyst, Dr. Mallard, were exploring. Oh my God, am I so insecure that I say inappropriate things to break up potential love relationships? He held his breath. He watched Natalie closely. He saw her astonishment.

"Mr. Shaftoe, I'm surprised at you, making that remark to a respectable English teacher. A female teacher sexually teasing an adolescent male student would be most inappropriate. Unethical even. My students are precious to me."

She seemed indignant. Shaftoe thought, Yes, I've blown it. Again. How many times will this happen during the rest of my life? He was aware that he was cringing. He felt ashamed.

"No, Bobby, I don't have the conjugation of verbs tattooed on my thighs. And I only wore this dress to class once. Then I saw all the teen-age hard-ons I was causing. The boys' laps looked like a dozen tents were being pitched. I'm told that can hurt in tight pants.

I figured the boys were forgetting everything in my lessons. I never wore this dress to work again."

Her indignant pose gave ways to peals of her wind-chime laughter.

I've been had, Shaftoe thought, and in a perfectly charming way. I didn't know whether to shit or go blind. Could being jerked around be a fun thing?

"Christ, Ms. Barney. I thought you were about to storm out. I apologize. I'm glad you have a sense of humor. I got back as good as I gave, and I deserved it."

"Forget it, Professor Shaftoe. I was flirting with you. It made you nervous. I take that as a compliment."

How many years of psychotherapy before I'm out of the woods? he wondered. And was it even working? Was it progress that he was giving some reflection to his anxiety, rather than just vowing cluelessly never to be a klutz again? But why did reflection make his stomach churn? He needed to curtail those thoughts. This wasn't the time or place. The Wagon Wheel wasn't a psych lab, and Natalie wasn't the stimulus in some goddamn experiment.

Finally he said, "Yes, you couldn't be more right. I'm embarrassed."

"No need to be." Natalie smiled.

Maybe all wasn't lost. "You're a magical woman. You must enchant men all the time." He hoped she liked his tone of voice.

In the dim light, she slowly picked up her drink, lowered her eyes, and took a sip. A big sip. Did a trace of sadness cross her face?

"Oh, yes. I enchant men all the time. . . . Or not."

A good time to change the subject, I don't want to make her sad. "So . . . how did you wind up at Entonces High?" Too late, Shaftoe realized that his tone of voice wasn't neutral. It implied that working at Entonces High suggested a tainted past.

Natalie's eyes jerked upward. "No. Not fair. You first!"

There was a new sound in her voice. A pleading. She wasn't joking. Jesus, did she slip into an insecure mode sometimes, too? Just like him? Well, he could show her the same latitude she'd shown him.

Shaftoe looked at her closely for any clue that might be coming. "Okay . . ." he took a sip of his drink. It splashed a little onto his face. Not cool. But she could take him or leave him, including what he was about to tell her. He would try to make a long story short. Start over. Use a topic sentence. "Well . . ." Just spit it out! "Where I used to work . . ." He sighed. "I tackled a kid at graduation. The administrators and the board of ed didn't like it."

Abruptly, Natalie set her drink down on the table. Her lips formed a circle, as if to whistle. No sound came out. Her lips closed. She looked intently, unblinking, at Shaftoe. Somewhat like Dr. Mallard had done so often. It made him nervous every time.

"Bobby, you . . . tackled a kid . . . during the commencement ceremony?"

"Yep. Tackled him."

"Everyone in caps and gowns?"

"Yep. Baby go boom. In cap and gown."

"Gee, Bobby. I can see how that might get you in trouble."

"Yeah. Wound up at Entonces. Truck route through the campus. Diesel fumes. Vindictive coach, who can't stand the word *school*." He remembered how Zachary had repeatedly scratched out the word school and printed *schoolage* on the phony document accusing him of sodomy. "Five hundred counselees."

"What?"

"Five hundred counselees. Whole damn school. On my best days, I try to shortchange every kid equally. That's fair to all genders, races, and religions. Just keeping my head above water."

She looked concerned. "I've watched you work. You get a lot done in a short time."

"Thanks." That was the most recognition he'd received in the year he'd been at Entonces. "That's a great compliment. And it means a lot coming from you." He hoped she saw that he respected her perceptions.

She said, "Well, our jobs aren't exactly Hollywood Bowl, with thousands of loving fans storming the stage for autographs."

"Though many students do ask for our signatures at the start of the semester."

"Oh, yes. On class-change slips."

Shaftoe knew that he was smiling ruefully. Natalie was, too. Maybe the greatest signal of bonding that school people could give one another.

"But you love your work, Bobby. Just like I do. It can be fun. And gratifying, sometimes. It's important work."

She was serious. Not a time to joke, he thought. He hoped his eyes weren't misting up at her words. "Yep. Exactly."

"But, 'tackled a kid at graduation'? 'Baby go boom'?"

"Oh, how can I keep this short. I don't want to bore you." Was he just dodging a difficult subject? Well, plunge in. Not exactly what he had in mind with Natalie when he thought of plunging in. Now cut that out! Back to the long story made short. If she wants more details, she can ask. "At my previous school, a kid rented a cap and gown on his own. He crashed the graduation ceremony. He was in line in the wings, about to walk across the stage, when I recognized him. A jerk. He wasn't supposed to be there. He hadn't earned a diploma. It pissed me off. I tackled him." Shaftoe thought, Any questions?

"Boom?"

"Yeah. He hit the floor hard. The administrators and school board were on stage. They could see into the wings. They heard the noise and saw that I had him pinned. Trouble."

"Christ, Shaftoe. Either a kid falls out of a tree and lands on you at Entonces . . . "

Damn.

" . . . or you land on a kid at your old school, in front of your bosses. Why are you so physical?" She grinned and Shaftoe noticed that one of her front teeth was longer than the others. It was lovely.

"Yes, I am physical. I was a college wrestler. . . . " He thought he'd slip that in, maybe Natalie would be impressed. " . . . Let's Get Physical. Physical." He figured she'd heard the song. He winked at her. In the dim light, did he see her cheeks color for a moment, or was it just the reflection on her skin from the red neon in the beer signs on the wall? He returned to his story. "So, I was told 'We understand that you're unhappy in your work situation. Would you like to look for employment elsewhere?' They knew that was bullshit. I loved that job."

"Sure. Just a way to ease you out, for no good reason."

"Yeah. I was still a new person, not there long enough to earn any job rights. But they didn't want to say, 'You're fired,' and be afraid I'd get a lawyer."

"A lawyer. Word would spread to other districts, and whether you won your case or not, no one would hire you."

Shaftoe nodded. "Right. No district wants to hire someone who brings lawsuits."

"Bring lawsuits, fuck . . . "

Shaftoe was surprised at her vehemence. She finished, "Lawsuit or not, any teacher who rocks the boat."

"Yep. And I figured that they would write a decent recommendation for me so that the next place would take me off their hands. Then I applied to Entonces. It was the least bad of several places."

"Got it. Me too."

"Natalie, did you say 'me too'? *You* tackled a kid at a graduation ceremony, too?" He hoped she would like the joke.

Natalie comically turned up a corner of her mouth and shook her head slowly as if in disbelief.
"No, Sherlock. How'd you graduate college?"

They both laughed.

She said, "When I said 'Me too,' I meant that I was eased out too. And Entonces was hiring."

"Few applicants. Low salary schedule."

"Right, Bobby. Too much money diverted to Coach Zachary and his program. And what about his son, Chip, being ineligible? A nice kid. Why'd he cheat on finals?"

More evidence that the gossip was out. It had reached Natalie's ears even though she was on vacation at home in Capitol City. Bad news travels fast.

Shaftoe noticed that neither of them was touching their drinks.

"Yeah, good kid. But his dad pressured him to be perfect. He didn't need to cheat to make A's. And a super quarterback. What a tragedy for Chip. He can't play his Senior year. So no college recruiters will be seeing him. And no scholarships for a cheater. Jesus, can we not talk about it?"

"Not talk about it?" she asked.

Her words reminded him of Dr. Mallard. Answering a question with a question. Recently, Mallard annoyed him more and more. Sometimes it seemed as if Mallard was accusing him of something she wouldn't spell out. But he was here with Natalie, not Mallard.

He said, "Yeah, because I was obligated to report all the ineligible kids to the state athletic commission. Of course I put Chip's name on the list, same as all the others."

"A legal obligation. You had no choice."

"Right. I'm the school's Custodian of Records." Would that impress her?

"You're the What . . . of What?"

They both laughed at how the title sounded.

Custodian. Shaftoe thought of a person with a broom. It meant nothing. Just one more headache for a counselor, with no extra pay.

"You heard me." Shaftoe smiled. Another point of understanding. He was feeling giddy again. Happy momentarily. "And now, Zachary's anticipating his first-ever losing season. He blames me."

"Kill the messenger. And Zachary trained no back-up quarterback, of course."

"Of course. He's arrogant."

"And an asshole, Bobby. You should see the way he leers at me."

Shaftoe resisted giving her a fake leer. That wouldn't be funny to Natalie. Instead, he said, "An asshole, yes. Word chosen by vote of the teachers."

Natalie smiled. "Can I still get an absentee ballot? I guess I missed that faculty meeting."

"You don't miss a thing, Ms. Barney."

She looked pleased. "Thanks. It's 'Miss.' Better yet, 'Natalie'."

"Got it. Natalie. Now your turn."

"What?"

"Remember? You said, 'Bobby, your story first. Then mine.'"

"I don't remember that."

"Unethical! And I know that you are ethical. You told me so."

"My turn? I don't know if I can do this. My story has unladylike imagery."

Shaftoe was amused by her terminology. She had to be kidding, after her graphic description of the effect she had on high school boys.

"Unladylike imagery? I like that. I'm having it engraved on my tombstone: Here lies a man who dug unladylike imagery."

His attempt at humor didn't work.

"No, really. I don't know if I can tell you this."

"Try me. Please."

"Oh, this is embarrassing." She took a deep breath and dove in, as if she were afraid of losing her courage. "My previous school district's rent-a-cop saw me bare-assed, taking a leak in the Pusey Secret Garden." She covered her face with her hands. "Oh, my God, I don't want to think about it."

What was that word she'd said? It sounded like *Pew'-see*. "I know that feeling."

"Bobby! *You* were caught taking a leak in the Pusey Secret Garden, too?"

This was an absurd conversation. But fun. Shaftoe said, "I see what you mean by unladylike imagery. Taking a WHAT in the WHAT?" Now he was kidding *her.*

"The words you just said, Bobby . . . they serve me right." She smiled. "You just got even, didn't you."

"I tried to be gentle."

"Sometimes I don't like it gentle." She paused.

Shaftoe saw her cheeks color again. He wondered if they were both thinking of the night she phoned him to rescue her, half-undressed and beaten up, from the motel room. Did she like her sex rough? Shaftoe took them both off the hook, "But you were saying . . . About the Pew'-see . . . something."

"Yes, Bobby. And thanks for pronouncing it correctly. One must enunciate carefully when saying that word around males of any age. Just so you'll know, Dr. Pusey, a former principal at my old school, eventually became the president of a prestigious university."

"Dr. Pusey?" The very idea. "With a name like that, he must have been a masochist to want to work with adolescents."

"Whatever. Anyway, the board of ed wanted to name the school Pusey High. But someone had second thoughts. They finally put his name on the school's ugly, perpetually dying, little closet of a garden."

"The Pusey Secret Garden." Natalie was right. It was hard to say that with a straight face. "And the rent-a-cop saw you bare-assed taking a leak in the Pusey Secret Garden."

"God, Bobby, do you have to talk that way. It sounds so crude and cheap."

Was she kidding him again? "But you said it that way."

She put on an innocent, big-eyed Betty Boop face. "Oh, yeah. I did."

She was adorable.

"My classroom was right next to the PSG—that's what we women teachers called the garden when we'd had enough of being careful with the pronunciation. And I was working late. Too late. Is it alright if I go on?"

"You're wondering if it's alright if you go on?"

"Stop that!"

"Sorry." Had she been hanging out with psychotherapists?

"Well, all of a sudden I realized I had to pee, right away!" Natalie looked distressed at the memory. "They lock up the restrooms as soon as the kids go home. So the PSG was the closest private place."

"No problem, you thought."

She glared at Shaftoe. He knew he'd have to give up paraphrasing things she said.

"I can't tell you the rest."

"Okay." Slowly, deliberately, Shaftoe picked up his drink to take a sip. He looked toward the neon beer signs on the wall. He knew from experience with counselees that sometimes if he stopped encouraging them to talk, it seemed to free them to go on anyway. He waited.

Bingo.

"Well, I dashed into the PSG, quickly saw a spot where nothing had grown for years—you know, I'm a conservationist—and squatted."

Shaftoe imagined that. In his imagination Natalie looked elegant squatting in the dirt.

She went on. "The rent-a-cop, a cute guy, must have heard the water running. Anyway, he showed up right away."

"A misdemeanor: Health and Safety Code, Section P, squatting to urinate in any dying garden named Pusey. I'm familiar with that Code."

"Go to hell. No. But he thought it was all so funny, he couldn't help blabbing. The story reached my bosses' ears. God knows who else might have heard it."

"And the incident in the PSG made them ask you to leave?"

"Sort of. That's what they said."

There was more?

Now Natalie's face tightened. She gave Shaftoe a searching look. Then, she seemed to take on a more distant attitude. He didn't want that. This getting acquainted had all been going so well.

"Look, Bobby, you're a nice guy. Well-dressed. In good shape. Smart and quick. I saw what you did about that insulting pink drink. That was heroic."

"Things like that shouldn't happen."

"Well, it had special meaning for me." Her eyes took on a far-away look, then they came back to the present. She squeezed Shaftoe's arm. He felt her affection for him.

She hesitated, as if the next words were hard to say. "I like you. Maybe someday I'll have the courage, or integrity, or something—to tell you the rest of this."

chapter twenty one

Shaftoe had several more dates with Natalie during the next two weeks. Dinner in Capitol City at the Fleur-de-Lis, more up-scale than the Wagon Wheel; no neon beer signs on the walls, no smart-ass bartender mixing a bright pink greyhound. A musical at the lavish new State Performing Arts Pavilion. And a movie premier; a bit of a light-weight chick flick, Shaftoe thought, but Natalie loved it, and it definitely put her in a romantic mood when they returned to her apartment and one thing led to another. It was the best lovemaking Shaftoe had ever experienced. He'd always felt nervous getting into bed with a new woman, but Natalie was different. This was more than recreational sex, mutual consent, or friends with benefits. This was more profound than infatuation. He'd grown to adore Natalie. He wanted to be sure he wasn't kidding himself, but his heart was convincing him, this is incipient love!

And the best part was, despite idolizing Natalie, he wasn't nervous. In fact, he heard violins in his head, and a voice singing, "When I'm near you . . . fears dissolve." He liked that. The words were true when he was with Natalie. Up to now, he'd only thought of the words as being corny and impossible to achieve. Now he was becoming convinced otherwise.

At 5:00 o'clock the day after the chick flick premier and the perfect love-making, he sat in his apartment, still in his confident, romantic mood from his night at Natalie's place. He could still hear the violins and the voice singing. He knew he'd never been happier in his life.

Then he thought of his mother. Was the voice singing in his head his mother's? Hell no, his mother had a voice like a crow! Immediately he thought of another black bird. It was called a . . . what? A what? A raven.

A raven. Hmm. In Dr. Mallard's office the last few times, I thought of a raven. I always have the feeling it's linked to something important. But I can't ever recall the time or place it's linked to. Then Dr. Mallard seems to imply that I'm guilty of something I can't remember. How does she do that without moving a muscle or making a sound!

He was aware that at those times he thought of her as Dr. Mallard The Bitch.

Mallard. Christ! I've got an appointment with her

at 6:00 today. Okay. Okay. I can still make it from my apartment to her office in time.

A half-hour later, in Capitol City, Shaftoe sat in Mallard's waiting room, looking at a wall hanging of a ferocious samurai warrior. Does the samurai suggest something about Mallard? Is she the right therapist for me? Maybe, to resolve my anxiety about forceful males like Zachary, I'd do better with a male therapist. On the other hand, to resolve my hang-up with women, maybe I'd better stick with Mallard. What if my therapy doesn't work? Well, there are lots of men my age who've never achieved a permanent love relationship, right?

But he knew that he was just kidding himself with that excuse, he had wised up to it even before finding Mallard; and anyway, he knew what he wanted in his life, and it wasn't what lots of male losers his age had failed to achieve. He noted his use of "losers" and "failed" in his thoughts; that seemed very uncharitable, especially if he was destined to be one of them. That possibility filled him with fear. Or was it self-loathing? Maybe he was permanently more messed up than any of them, no matter how good a therapist Dr. Mallard might be. Was he incurable?

Mallard sometimes subtly encouraged him to talk about his love life, or lack thereof. Was she just being voyeuristic? Isn't that what all psychotherapists were doing—just peeking into other people's secrets? He remembered spying on her in the dark bar and grill. But should it be called "spying"? He hadn't known she'd be there, and didn't even know it was her until she flung the door open to leave. She seemed drunk. Let's see; I watched her . . . watched her doing what? Trying to pick up the bartender. She'd apparently had a relationship with him before. Yes, for sure coming on to him, and him turning her down because of some other guy who'd come between them. Named . . . what? Marley? Charlton? Harley? No, Harley was the name of Coach Zachary's crony, the newspaper owner who always glorified Zachary and his teams. But it was some first name like that. Then the bartender rebuffed Dr. Mallard, saying something like "Marley"—was that the right name?—"kept getting in the way." Then Mallard stormed out. Yes, stormed out, furious and drunk, without noticing me.

Shaftoe glanced again at the samurai. It still looked menacing. Oh well, maybe a person could have a messed-up private life like Mallard and still be a competent therapist. He'd read research suggesting that there were therapists like that. That sure as hell had better be true. If not, with my messed-up history with women, I shouldn't even be a high school counselor. Sometimes he thought he'd taken too many college courses, and read too much research, for his own good. He wondered if he could have made more progress in therapy if that were different.

"Bobby, it's time to start now."

Christ, it was Dr. Mallard, peering into her waiting room, addressing him as if she'd been standing there for some time. I've been so fucking preoccupied with myself that I didn't know she was standing here. How much else in life have I been missing? Fifty percent? Seventy-five percent? If I'm missing important things, I wouldn't even know that, would I?

A more rational voice inside him said, maybe you're just *awful-izing*. Dr. Mallard had taught him that word. She said a lot of people awfulized, but it was a good thing to stop doing. When she'd said, "A lot of people do that," it had helped him feel normal temporarily. He valued that "normal" feeling. Maybe she was the best therapist for him after all.

He realized that he should have stood up by now. He rose from his chair.

"Oh, uh. Hi, Dr. Mallard. How are you?" He felt stupid; maybe she could sense that he'd been thinking about whether she was the best therapist for him. And— oh my god—maybe she knows I saw her in the bar and grill. He certainly didn't want to mention that to her.

She simply smiled, and nodded toward the door into her private office. He hated when that happened. It was her cue to him that this wasn't a social occasion, and that she would not be talking very much, if at all, for the next fifty minutes

Mallard sat down in her huge chair. Shaftoe sat down in the recliner, stared at the busts of philosophers that decorated her office, and tried to get comfortable. It always took a few minutes, until he was engrossed in telling Mallard about the events of his life since his last appointment. Mallard always waited, impassively, but he nonetheless felt that she was silently judging him harshly. Once he had brought that up to her, "Dr. Mallard,"—she had never invited him to call her Juliet—"sometimes I feel that you're judging me harshly." All he'd gotten in return was, "Bobby, sometimes you feel that I'm judging you harshly?" When he'd answered, "Yes," she nodded and said "Uh-huh." Then silence again. He hated her when she was like that. Like a sphinx. He'd never gotten used to it.

But today would be different. He was eager to tell her how great the time in bed had been with Natalie. Damn, what should I call it? Sexual intercourse? That sounded stilted. Fucking? That sounded inappropriate; Mallard wasn't some twenty-something chick. Lovemaking? Shaftoe heard the violins and the voice singing, "Lover . . . when I'm near you . . . fears dissolve." But he wasn't sure that this was love-to-stay.

The feeling was certainly more complete, confidence-building, and inspirational than he'd ever felt; but he wasn't sure he had the capacity for love yet. With Mallard, maybe he should use the term "incipient love." But that sounded really stupid.

And anyway, Natalie hadn't told him exactly how she felt about him. Satisfying love was supposed to be mutual, wasn't it?

Well, just start talking, no matter how it comes out.

"Uh, Dr. Mallard, since I saw you last, something really important happened. I don't know if I can find the right words to get it across to you."

"The right words, Bobby?"

Juliet Mallard The Bitch. "Damn it, Dr. Mallard, will you stop repeating what I say! It isn't necessary with me."

"You think it's not necessary . . ."

Shaftoe was full of anger toward her. He didn't know how that would play out. Would there be a huge implosion and he would just go "poof" and disappear forever? If he survived his own rage, would Mallard fire him—abandon him as a client? He wasn't sure he could live through that.

". . . because something has changed since our last meeting," she finished.

His feelings about her did a 180. He thought, bless your heart. You're making this easier for me to talk about. "Yes, I might be . . . that is, starting to be . . . Well, maybe I'm . . . falling in love." His heart was racing, and not in a good way. Why was this so hard to talk about? He hadn't even gotten to the sexual intercourse . . . fucking . . . lovemaking . . . part yet.

Mallard looked at him more intently. "You said, maybe you're falling in love?" She gently smiled a little. Or was it a smirk? Did she believe him or not? He was afraid to ask her. Anyway, it was for him to decide if he was in love, not her.

"Well, yeah. This woman I've been dating recently . . . and I . . . ," he felt like what should have been a simple sentence was falling apart, "finally went to bed." *Went to bed* seemed like such a euphemism; and his own voice, to his ears, sounded like an anxious teenager.

Mallard just sat in her chair. His relationship with Mallard had never been one of equals. Mallard held all the cards; as if she could read his mind—or his feelings—and didn't approve of what she saw.

Well, nothing to do but blurt out this new step in his relationship with Natalie, no matter what judgment Dr. Mallard might make. He wished that Mallard could simply hear the voice in his head singing, When I'm near you . . . fears dissolve. Anyway, no matter what, maybe Mallard would be pleased with his progress. He was. He felt himself smiling. He wondered if he was starry-eyed. Was it okay to be like this right now?

He was surprised to hear himself say, "Listen. It was great!"

chapter twenty two

Shaftoe continued telling Juliet Mallard about his perfect experience with "this woman I've been dating recently," whose name he preferred not to tell her.

"Well, Dr. Mallard, we were sitting next to each other on the sofa at her place. Just sipping a little wine and talking. Our minds are so much alike; we understood each other immediately. I respect her completely."

Mallard nodded. Her expression didn't change, and she said nothing.

"She was wearing a short skirt and white blouse. And she kind of twisted to face me. Then she raised her glass to her mouth. Her lips were open a little, and she looked at me and smiled. So I wondered, was she coming on to me?

Then she leaned forward and put her wine glass on the coffee table in front of me. As she sat back, it was easy for me to put my arm around her. Her breast was against my side."

Mallard said, "It's good that you were assertive, Bobby."

Mallard was talking as if this were his first sexual experience. He wished she would shut up.

"I just held her there. Then we looked into each other's eyes and I kissed her and she kissed me right back. Big time! Then, just like we'd been lovers for a long time, she swung her leg over my lap and sort of rolled into me."

Now Shaftoe began to feel uncomfortable. Telling these details to Mallard, a woman who might be judging him, wasn't easy. After all, stuff like this was usually heard in locker rooms. He knew, from his days as a college wrestler.

"Well, my dick . . . er, penis . . . was getting really hard." He glanced at Mallard. He was grateful that she hadn't said, It's okay to say dick, Bobby. "I knew she could feel it against her. Next thing I know, her arms were around my neck and her hair was brushing my cheek. Her perfume smelled terrific! I could hear her breathing near my ear. Everything felt perfect!"

Mallard's eyes looked sparkly. Happy. He'd never seen them like that.

"Well, she was lying half across my body, like we were two teenagers making out in a parked car. She was showing off every curve. That made it easy for me to stroke her hip. It fit my hand perfectly."

Shaftoe paused. "Too many body parts, Doctor Mallard? Is it confusing?"

"No. Go on."

Mallard's voice sounded breathy. Was there more color in her cheeks?

"Then I scooted my hips forward on the sofa, with her riding along. She was exactly the weight I like, and she felt like butter melting. She's a very affectionate woman, Dr. Mallard. It crossed my mind that maybe she likes me."

Mallard said, "The sexy, exciting feelings seemed mutual."

"Yes!"

"Go on."

"And from all the squirming, her skirt was halfway up her thighs. I've seen that much leg with other women, but with her it was super arousing."

Mallard was squirming in her chair.

Shaftoe thought, am I making Dr. Mallard uncomfortable, talking this way? But she'd said, Go on. "Well, something new and totally special was happening in my emotions. She moved a little more and her skirt slid higher. I didn't even wonder if she would stop me if I went farther. It all seemed so right. I can't remember ever feeling that fulfilled. Then she allowed my hand a little room between her thighs, so I guessed what I was doing was alright with her. It was like unwrapping a beautiful gift. Everything was perfect."

Mallard's eyes and body seemed luminous. Did she want to hear more? Shaftoe was no longer concerned about his choice of words. "Well, now lacy white panties were peeking out. They were lovely. I wondered if she'd bought them just for me. So I said, Oh my, what have we here? Well, Doctor, she giggled. Not as if I'd said something wimpy, but like she loved to hear it."

Shaftoe knew he was on a roll. Talking like this didn't usually come so easily to him.

"There's nothing in the world like a grown woman's giggle! I thought, Oh baby, you know what I like."

"Bobby, you were having a rare and wonderful experience. I'm proud of you."

Dr. Mallard curled her legs up onto her chair. Same as last week, and it was equally sexy. She slowly began stroking her leg from calf to thigh. She unbuttoned the top buttons of her blouse. Her cheeks had definitely colored. Her eyelids flickered. A murmur came from her throat, and she tilted her head to one side and brushed her hair off her forehead with her fingertips. That wasn't her usual office behavior.

"Bobby . . ." Her voice was soft, with a little quiver in it. She was breathing fast and audibly. She looked at him through half-closed eyes. Bedroom eyes, he thought. "Bobby," she whispered, ". . . does this woman have a name?"

Oh my God. What does that question imply? Was I describing Natalie impersonally, like an object? "Yes, she has a name. Her name is Natalie Barney."

Juliet Mallard stiffened. Her eyes blinked rapidly. She stopped stroking her leg. The blush left her cheeks. Shaftoe could have sworn she turned pale. She tried to get back into her sphinxlike psychotherapist mode, but it wasn't coming back.

She said, "Nat . . ."

"Natalie."

"Nat-a-lee?" The name seemed to be hard for Mallard to get out of her mouth.

"Yes. And then we . . ."

But now Dr. Juliet Mallard seemed all business. "Wait a minute, Bobby. I don't think you're developing a capacity to love, after all . . ."

"But . . ."

Mallard looked at him sternly. "You know, Elie Wiesel said, 'Human beings were not born to be alone. God alone is alone. Illness is not being able to fall in love.'"

Shaftoe felt his jaw drop. He felt as if everything he was composed of was gone. He thought, Mallard really lowered the boom on me. Hammering me with a holocaust survivor *and God* to tell me my capacity to love is a sick zero. Harsh! Beyond harsh. Cruel!

"Yes, Bobby. Not being able to love is a serious illness. And that girl . . . Nat . . . Nat . . . ," Mallard croaked. She gave up trying to say the rest of the name. She was talking more than usual. "That . . . that . . . *teacher.* She isn't right for you."

"But . . . it all felt so . . . ."

Now Mallard looked very grave. "You'll have to give her up."

"What!"

"You have to give her up."

"Give her up? But you were so encouraging a minute ago!"

"I made a mistake. I diagnosed you wrong. We have a lot more work to do. Yes. Oh yes, we do. A *lot* of work." Now she was talking fast. "What you told me today sounded like you weren't fully involved, Bobby." She paused. "As if you were only watching."

What the fuck!

Dr. Mallard looked at her watch. One of her cues: the session was over. "We can talk some more about your problem next time. About all the work you still have to do." She stood up.

Shaftoe thought that her professional good-bye smile was forced.

She looked at her watch again.

Shaftoe became aware of her clock behind him, ticking off the minutes. He felt completely defeated. *The bitch clearly wants me to leave. Right now.* He stood up and headed for the door. As he stepped into the hall, feelings of weakness, anxiety, and apprehension struck him full force.

In the parking structure, he felt nauseated and gagged. *Why?* he asked himself. *Because I'm nuts?*

He leaned against his car for a moment. Then, as he got in, Mallard's scornful words, "that *teacher*," came back to him.

Wait! Jesus Christ! How'd Mallard know that Natalie's a teacher? I know I never told her that!

chapter twenty three

On the two-lane highway back to Entonces, Shaftoe drove erratically. Eighteen wheelers honked at him. Fuck them. He pounded the steering wheel as his eyes clouded over with tears. He didn't know if they were tears of devastation because Dr. Mallard had told him he was still emotionally crippled, or of anger because she'd told him to give up Natalie. Mallard—the bitch had taken him completely by surprise. He felt like a homeless man without a dog.

His bowels and stomach hinted that before the day was over he might simultaneously suffer diarrhea and vomiting. Like food poisoning; but of course it was his reaction to what Mallard had said. He didn't want to spew in his car. He'd never be able to get the smell out. Like a decomposing corpse, it would become part of the upholstery. Pull over at the next service station. No.

Wait! Dammit, I can't take the time; I've got to get back to the high school right away. Tonight's the Entonces Roundup—only four weeks until classes start. The Roundup, for incoming students and their parents, is in the Ed Zachary Fieldhouse—in fifteen minutes.

I gotta be there, Shaftoe thought. Can't stop now to empty my bowels and try to puke. I gotta be there; I'm on the agenda to brief the potential new students and their parents on graduation requirements. And I gotta tell them about the school's obligation to report suspected child abuse. That's important. The kids need to know who they can turn to. And my getting the word out might stop some out-of-control parents from kicking the shit out of their sons and daughters. Then he thought of Coach Zachary; that bastard highjacked the microphone from me last year, and hogged the rest of the time to honor his football players. Yeah, Zachary the local hero, championship teams for years! At that Round Up, the parents gave Principal Fluke and me no applause, but they went wild when Zachary did his number at the podium.

Shaftoe drove on, despite more warning signals from his stomach and bowels. Zachary! And ineffective Principal Fluke, under Zachary's thumb. And the town's school board president and newspaper owner, Harley Huntington, glorifying Zachary in print. It was like a conspiracy.

Why were there more horses' asses than horses?

Trucks kept giving Shaftoe ear-splitting blasts of their air horns. He thought of his close call last month when he leaped out of the truck route. Death by eighteen-wheeler. Is that my destiny?

Teary-eyed, he drove on.

Finally, with no time to stop at a john, Shaftoe ran from his car directly to the field house and onto its basketball court. He was already three minutes late. He joined Zachary and Fluke at center court. They sat on folding chairs facing the bleachers which were filling with latecomers. A few men were wearing varsity letter jackets from years ago, but the crowd was mostly mothers with their incoming ninth-grade boys and girls. Some of the women had brought pompoms.

Five minutes late, Fluke stepped to the portable podium, set up halfway between the tipoff circle and the bleachers, and picked up a hand microphone. After some fumbling, he switched it on. "Welcome. Please join me in the flag salute," he said in his stilted voice. The distortion caused by the loudspeakers in the echoing building made him sound like a voice from a crypt. Then came the annoying sound of hundreds of shuffling feet as the audience stood up, and Fluke began spinning around, looking first left, then right, then turning his back to the audience to check the wall behind him. For their part, the audience was looking each direction, as Fluke did.

To Shaftoe, in his sad, pissed off, nauseated condition, the spinning seemed surreal. Were Fluke and the parents having some kind of group seizure?

Then Zachary stood up and grabbed the mic out of Fluke's hand, pushed him away from the podium, and took over. His laughter was amplified, "Dammit, Fluke, you forgot to put up the flag. Well, folks, just put your hand over your heart, and face that basketball hoop," Zachary pointed at it dramatically, like Babe Ruth predicting a home run, "and repeat after me . . . I pledge our regions to the flag . . ." The audience repeated it exactly.

Zachary continued to botch up the words to the pledge of allegiance. The audience didn't seem to care. They revered their leader. If Coach were mouthing the Communist Manifesto the town would follow. And Huntington would print it as a positive event.

Shaftoe wished he had a better attitude.

Fluke had remained standing after Zachary pushed him away. As Zachary moved back to his folding chair, he tossed the mic to Fluke, who caught it awkwardly. Shaftoe thought, he almost muffed it, like a little boy whose father never played catch with him.

Shaftoe barely heard Fluke's words to the audience. In his mind he was hearing the voice of

Dr. Mallard saying, "Natalie . . . that . . . that . . . *teacher.* She isn't right for you. You have to give her up." Could he give Natalie up in order to progress in therapy? And why should he! He wanted to question Mallard right now, but he'd have to phone her for an extra appointment or wait until his next regular one. His bowels and stomach rumbled.

As Fluke droned on, Shaftoe forced himself to think about what he was going to say to the audience. First, I'll give a brief summary of the state graduation requirements. Very brief. Before I upchuck.

Then he thought about his second topic, his state's Suspected Child Abuse Reporting Law. The law required such an immediate and ill-founded reaction from any school employee that he thought of it as the "hear a rumor, pick up the phone law." Yep, and it forbade the employee from investigating; law enforcement officers and social workers would do that part. Simple: If any school employee suspected a child was being abused, even if they'd only heard a rumor, they had to just pick up the phone and report it to a State hotline, then put the same story on the State-provided form and mail it in.

Thinking about that law always gave him two feelings—apprehension, and admiration. Apprehension, because it was a severe law, requiring a knee-jerk reaction, and there were major penalties prescribed for any employee who failed to report, or made an error in their procedure. And admiration, because the law protected children, discouraged out-of-control adults, and required that people who were expert—law enforcement officers or social workers—do the investigating.

He'd filed a dozen Suspected Child Abuse Reports over the years. Some students had begged him not to report that they were being abused by their parent; but he pointed out to them that after they moved away from home the investigating agencies would protect their younger brothers and sisters. That sometimes won the victim over. If not, Shaftoe filed the report anyway.

He'd been cursed by parents for following the law, and some threatened him with police and lawyers. He'd quietly told them the professional equivalent of, "Bring 'em on." So far, his work had been bulletproof.

Now Fluke, his distorted, sepulchral, voice echoing around the court, was calling him to the podium.

It was Shaftoe's turn. The hand mic was lying atop the podium. He shut it off. He'd forego the creepy amplification. He introduced himself to the crowd. They blinked when he told them his title, School Counselor. He remembered the people he'd met, whose initial response when he'd told them his profession was, "My school counselor didn't do shit for me."

Well, he wasn't that kind of counselor. He was proud of the good work he was doing.

He delivered his brief summary of the state graduation requirements. Then he asked the audience if there were any questions about those. There were no questions. At Entonces High, parents and students rarely cared about graduation requirements until a kid's senior year.

Now, on to his second topic, Suspected Child Abuse Reporting. He knew from past experience that the crowd didn't want to hear all his thoughts about that. So he just told them that there was a law, that any school employee was required to report suspicions, that law enforcement officers or social workers would investigate, and that the intention was to help any abused student. He specified that the kinds of abuse were physical, emotional, sexual, and neglect.

As he was bringing his abbreviated presentation to a close, he heard Zachary say, "Bobby, this is boring. Stop talking." Shaftoe thought of turning his back to the audience and, using his body as a screen, giving Zachary the finger, but he didn't do it. He thought, am I being professional, cowardly, or am I afraid I'll physically attack Zachary once I take the first step? One thing I know, I don't want to lose this job. Tackling that kid, the graduation-crasher, cost me my last one.

Now, most of the people in the bleachers weren't paying attention. Probably the incoming ninth-grade boys were preoccupied with fears of being bullied by the upper classmen. Some of the girls were intently peering at their smart phones. Were they playing Mario Brothers, or possibly texting, maybe even texting others who were right there in the bleachers? The parents seemed to be in a stupor. Maybe they were hoping that Zachary would start his sideshow soon.

Shaftoe thought, time to conclude my part. He assured the audience that Entonces High would love, nurture, and protect their students. He said that each student was precious to him, as he knew their students were precious to them. He checked the audience's faces again. No discernable response. He sat down.

Now it was Zachary's turn. The coach stood, marched to the podium, and picked up the mic amid applause. Shaftoe continued to feel awful, emotionally and physically. The hangover from Mallard's words was torturing him more than the nausea. He'd never felt more hellish emotional pain. He felt permanently disabled. He wondered if an abused child had the sensations that he was feeling. No wonder some kids couldn't concentrate in school. Child abuse—what an incapacitating secret to bear!

The pep band, that Zachary had no doubt coerced into coming in during their summer vacation, played the Entonces High School fight song. Of course, most of the parents and new students didn't know the words. That didn't stop Zachary from singing them into the mic and scrambling them. After the first line, the incoming kids' attention drifted away again.

Then the cheerleaders, looking super cute in their sweaters, bobby sox, and pleated skirts, leapt about. That got everyone's attention. Zachary was a master showman. Shaftoe looked at the cheerleaders. He wondered which one's underthings he'd watched Zachary fling about when he went to give the coach the bad news about Chip.

Finally, Zachary shut off the mic and laid it on the podium. In a commanding, resonant voice, he began presenting his varsity football starters for the upcoming season. They were seated on the first row of the bleachers, wearing blue jeans, tennis shoes, and mesh summer football jerseys without pads. When Zachary called each name, the player stood and ran eagerly to him, while the audience cheered. So far, the starters had all been at Entonces High School last year, and their names were familiar to Shaftoe. Zachary was saving until last the incoming ones. Those were transferring in from other states. They were usually over-age bruisers. Over-age for their home states, but having one more year of eligibility for the state Entonces was located in. Different states, different regulations. And yes, they would inaccurately be called "students." They had been good athletes in their home states, but poor students—so they still needed to repeat their Senior year, and they would spend it at Entonces while using, on Zachary's team, their newly-bestowed remaining year of eligibility. Truthfully, most would disappear as soon as football season was over. Few would graduate from Entonces or any high school, anywhere. Ever. That was not why Zachary recruited them to Entonces.

Nothing new about that. Zachary'd been importing over-age jocks for years. One reason he had championship football teams. But could Zachary win without his son Chip?

Then Shaftoe broke away from his preoccupations, to wonder who the coach was going to announce as replacement quarterback. In his arrogance, Zachary'd trained no one to back up Chip. And Chip was now ineligible. Shaftoe looked around. Chip wasn't in the gym. Shaftoe couldn't blame him. He watched Zachary begin to introduce the last of his first string for the upcoming season—the over-age ringers. Their faces were new, but so far Shaftoe recognized all their names; their transfer papers, including transcripts from their home states, had crossed his desk recently. Except for one.

Now there was just one ringer left on the first row of the bleachers, and Zachary intoned, as the player stood up to run to him, "And this season's quarterback . . . with an excellent record in athletics . . . will be . . ." The kid was tall, slim, and well-muscled. Like the earlier ringers this evening, he looked older than a typical twelfth grader.

The coach paused for dramatic effect, "Felix Anthony Skoo . . . ," what the hell was that last word Zachary said? It sounded like he'd said, "Skoo." Suddenly the coach had a strange look on his face; his mouth puckered, he cringed a little, and looked askance at Shaftoe. He'd never seen that look on Zachary before. What did it mean?

Zachary appeared to regroup, then he added the kid's last name, "Blanchard." The audience cheered wildly as the young man, hearing his last name, ran obediently toward Zachary. "Skoo"—whatever that meant—was quick on his feet, and his face beamed as if he were anticipating stardom. As he got closer, Shaftoe caught a whiff of tobacco aroma. The kid is a smoker. Whatever. The town trusts Zachary, which means they'll trust Felix Anthony "Skoo" Blanchard to win for them.

Shaftoe thought, that kid's the only ringer whose transfer papers haven't crossed my desk. Why do I have paperwork on every ringer but him?

There was something familiar about the name Blanchard. Why? Why? Of course . . . there'd been a hallowed football player in the past with a name something like that. Maybe this new kid was a descendent of the original Blanchard. And he picked up the nickname "Skoo" somehow. That was confusing. Shaftoe didn't want to think about it.

Then the meeting was over.

Shaftoe felt as if diarrhea and vomit were imminent. He stood up and stepped smartly toward the locker room. He and Zachary reached the door to it at the same time. Sick as he felt, Shaftoe knew that the best way to deal with Zachary was to take the initiative. He pushed the door open for the coach.

"Christ, Coach, I thought you'd be shaking hands with your fans."

"Right, Bobby, I'm going back out there. But I gotta piss."

"Got it. Nice show out there, Coach. The town loves you."

"I know."

Shaftoe was trying to hold everything in. They stepped into the locker room.

"Say, Bobby . . . let's let bygones be bygones."

That was unexpected! But Coach didn't offer his hand, and Shaftoe chose not to offer his. He felt that he didn't have time before puking, and he needed to say something important, right now. "Your new quarterback . . . this kid 'Skoo' . . ."

Zachary spun toward him. His fists were clenched. "I didn't say 'Skoo,' you dumb shit. Ya got a hearing problem? His name is Blanchard."

That was just like Zachary; in Zachary's book a strong offense was the best defense. Shaftoe didn't have time for it. "Listen, Coach, Skoo's transfer papers are the only ones that haven't crossed my desk. He's not eligible to play until we get them."

Zachary acted more hostile each time Shaftoe said, "Skoo." What was that about? Now Zachary was stomping toward a urinal, cursing, and Shaftoe was at the closest toilet stall, punching the door open.

"Bobby, check your fuckin' inbox! That's what you're paid for—paperwork."

"I did, Ed. Everyone's records are in. Except Skoo Banchard's."

Shaftoe was in the stall now, dropping his pants and boxer shorts.

Zachary shouted, "He's going to play. Don't even think about Sk . . . about . . . about . . . Blanchard, or your ass is grass. I'll see to that!"

In the toilet stall, Shaftoe sat down just in time. Disgusting stuff exploded from both ends. He heard Zachary laughing at his distress.

chapter twenty four

Shaftoe heard Zachary's footsteps, outside the closed door of the toilet stall, become increasingly distant. The coach was leaving the locker room.

It was several minutes more before Shaftoe felt confident that he was through purging. Pulling up his shorts and trousers, he stood up and flushed the toilet. As he left the toilet stall, he stepped carefully around his vomit on the floor. Let Zachary find someone to mop this up, he thought, it's his damn gold-plated field house. He was grateful that there was no splatter on his shoes or clothes. Thank God for small favors. The smell he'd made was putrid. It seemed to fill the huge, tiled locker room, even with its state-of-the-art ventilating system.

He thought, My God, I need to get this stench off me. Right now. Right here. I don't want to contaminate my car or my apartment. He looked around. Clean folded towels on a rack, soap and shampoo in dispensers in the shower stalls. He went to his locker, no need to get out the razor or shaving cream. And after a shower, a spritz from his back-up Ancient Mariner aftershave might mask the stink that had penetrated his bones. He hoped there was enough left in the spray bottle. He opened his locker door and took his Ancient Mariner off the shelf at the top. No problem; the bottle was half full.

He eyed the shower stall that was closest to his locker. As he walked toward it, he picked up a towel from the rack. He set the towel, his Ancient Mariner, and his watch on a sink counter facing the shower. He stripped, putting his clothes and shoes on the counter too. Then, he looked in the mirror. The face staring back had dark circles under its worried-looking eyes and its skin was a ghastly gray. His legs felt shaky.

Naked, Shaftoe walked toward the shower stall. The floor tiles were slippery. That puzzled him. All the money spent on this field house, and the floor was slippery.

He was looking forward to soaking under the hot spray. This would be the only good part of a foul evening that had started with Mallard's saying, "That . . . that . . . *teacher*. She isn't right for you. You have to give her up." He reproached himself for feeling self-pity. After all, there were bigger problems in the world. Time to toughen up. A saying came to mind. He couldn't remember where he'd heard it, Two tears in a bucket, mother fuckit.

Yes, Dr. Mallard's opinion was not an insurmountable problem. He was eager to contact her, to confront her. But he feared the confrontation. In the past, he'd gotten nowhere by challenging the usually sphinx-like psychotherapist.

But for now, he craved quiet and privacy.

He stepped into the shower and pulled the curtain shut. Just as he reached to rotate the shower lever toward "on," he heard shoes rapidly slapping the locker room floor, moving toward him. Then, a little girl's delighted screech. It echoed impressively. She giggled softly and screeched again. Again, a corresponding echo. And a giggle.

What the hell? Is a little girl running and playing in the men's locker room? It was deserted when I closed the curtain.

Inside the shower stall, Shaftoe clutched the curtain to his chest. I can't let this little girl see me naked, he thought. With his other hand he moved the rings from which the curtain hung, just enough to create an opening near the top corner, the shape of a triangle ending under his chin. He peeked through the opening.

Sure enough, he saw a little girl, virtually a toddler, running back and forth in the open space just outside his shower curtain, between the shower and the sink counter. She was wearing a frilly pink party dress with a big white bow at the waist, and was towing a yellow balloon on a string. It had multi-colored streamers and a cartoon of a cute puppy. She was screeching and giggling, apparently delighted to hear her echo. So carefree. Just having fun.

Christ, where was the stupid adult who'd let her come in here?

Shaftoe tensed as he saw the little girl notice his face, the only part of him that he'd left visible, peering through the triangular opening he'd made in the shower curtain. She stopped running and turned toward him and stared. Then a surprised smile crept over her face and she giggled. He supposed it did look funny to her; a man's face peering out. Something like a game of peekaboo. She covered her eyes with her hands for a moment, then still smiling, fanned them away from her face, and tilted her head. She looked at Shaftoe expectantly, as if waiting for him to act out his part of peekaboo.

Then she began spinning in place, arms outstretched, skirt swirling, balloon and streamers making a jerky circle above her head.

She's gotta get outa here, Shaftoe thought. Continuing to clutch the shower curtain to his chest, he curved his other arm around the side of the curtain and motioned toward the exit, saying to the little girl, "Go back, go back."

But she kept on spinning, faster and faster.

Then, looking dizzy, she began to lose her balance.

Shaftoe knew that the tile floor was slippery and hard. He winced.

Falling, she lost her grip on the balloon string, and the balloon began to float upward.

She hit the floor hard. On her hip.

She sobbed loudly. Shaftoe saw the balloon float lazily toward the ceiling, bump it, and wobble there, streamers and string dangling.

Then she awkwardly staggered upright, still weeping, and ran clutching her hip, toward the exit to the hallway.

On the ceiling, the cute puppy balloon looked abandoned, sad, and lonely.

As the little girl disappeared, Shaftoe heard a woman's voice, in the hallway, mumuring indistinctly, in comforting tones.

Thank goodness, that's over, he thought. I've kept the shower curtain closed since before I heard her footsteps, except for the little triangle that I made at the top corner so I could peek out and check the situation.

Now, judging from the silence, everyone had left the building. Nothing more can happen. Success. Peace and quiet. I deserve it. Finally. He wondered how late it was. Could he get locked in? He decided to hurry. Again he reached for the faucet lever.

Then he heard Zachary's voice in the hallway, "Oh my goodness, lady. We got a pedal-file in there!"

chapter twenty five

"Shaftoe, get outta there, you pedal-file!"

"Can't, Coach. I'm naked."

"Grab a fu . . ."

Was Zachary about to say "fuckin' towel"? The woman and the little girl must be in the hallway with him.

Zachary revised his wording. "Grab a f . . . f . . . folded towel. I'm comin' in, you pervert."

Shaftoe heard footsteps coming toward him. Was Zachary bringing the woman and child in with him? Shaftoe dashed from the shower, swept his towel from the sink counter, and whipped it around his waist. Zachary was now face-to-face with him, and took him in tow by the bicep, toward the hallway.

"Dammit, Zachary, let loose!" Shaftoe struggled, but the coach's grip was too strong; it was hurting Shaftoe's arm.

"Cut the cursing, short eyes. There's a woman and child out there." With his free hand, Zachary gestured toward the hallway.

Shaftoe noticed that Zachary had suddenly become an advocate of clean speech.

"No way I'm going out there in a towel, Coach."

"Guess again, Mister pedal-file. I gottcha now. I'm striking while the iron is hot. I knew it all along. You got a thing for children. Little girls, not just teen-age boys."

"Coach, this is another of your bullshit accusations, and you know it."

But Shaftoe was worried. Coach knew about the "hear a rumor, pick up the phone" suspected child abuse reporting law. All the faculty did. Shaftoe had trained them himself. He could imagine Zachary making a phony phone call and following up with a phony written report. He could see the elements that Zachary could twist into an accusation. But what had Shaftoe done that warranted such intimidation from Zachary?

"We'll see, Bobby. We'll see." The coach's eyes were gleaming, and it didn't look like a gleam of righteousness, it looked more like a gleam of malice. Shaftoe knew the look, he'd seen malice in the coach's eyes before.

Zachary dragged Shaftoe, clutching the towel at his waist, into the hallway.

"Lady, we got him this time—red-handed!"

Shaftoe didn't like the implication of "we" and "this time." It sounded like Coach was telling the woman that her help had been invaluable, and that for some time people had been trying to catch Shaftoe in the act. Zachary was playing his cards right so far, and Shaftoe suspected that the coach had even more powerful cards he could play. The woman looked as if she didn't understand anything Zachary was saying. The coach had picked a prime rube.

Shaftoe felt a chill. This wasn't looking good.

Shaftoe's experience was, the more that was said by an accused, whether he was innocent or not, the easier it was for his words to be twisted later. He decided to remain silent for the time being.

"Little girl, little girl . . ." Why did some men use that phrase, instead of asking a child her name? ". . . have you seen this child molester before?" Zachary's attempt to be non-threatening came across more like Godzilla. The woman looked baffled.

The girl was still clutching her hip, but no longer shedding tears. She gave Shaftoe a look of recognition and smiled the trusting smile he'd seen before. Then she covered her eyes with her hands, fanned them away from her face, giggled, and said to him, "Peek . . . "

Shaftoe's chill suddenly ran hot. He feared what was coming next.

"Ah ha, lady. That's what they all do. Get the kid to play a little game. Some game!" Zachary looked at Shaftoe, "How low can you get, you *bast* . . . You *bad* counselor."

Shaftoe thought, Coach isn't a very good actor, but this isn't funny. There's too much at stake—my job; my reputation, especially with Natalie; my credentials. Hell—my freedom from prison!

"Lady, we don't know what else this criminal has done to your daughter . . ."

"Sir . . . pardon . . .?" The woman had a supplicating smile. "*Gram* . . . daughter." No wonder she had looked baffled. Judging by her way of speaking, maybe she barely understood English.

Coach was on a roll, "Yes, lady. Your daughter is grand. Check for bruises." With his free hand, Coach whacked his own hip, screwed up his face and said, "Owie, lady. Owie?"

Apparently the woman knew "Owie?" In another language she said something to the girl, and the girl turned her back to grandma and delicately lifted her little party dress. She carefully put a fingertip to her hip, looked over her shoulder at grandma, nodded her head, and said, "Owie."

"See, lady. That's where he grabbed her. That'll be a bruise soon. Evidence! Oh, I wish I had a camera."

Shaftoe stared at Zachary, wondering if the Coach's desire to take a picture of the girl with her skirt up indicated some motive beyond threatening to record so-called evidence.

Suddenly, the little girl looked as if something worrisome was crossing her mind. She looked at Shaftoe. "Doggie?" she asked.

Zachary's eyebrows went up and his eyes grew large. He looked as if the girl's word had given him a new idea. He smirked at Shaftoe. "A dog?" he said.

Shaftoe could keep silent no longer. "Coach, don't go there. Don't even think it. That's vile! Keep your mouth shut. These are two nice people you're jerking around. She said 'Doggie?' to ask about a balloon with a cartoon of a puppy on it. She left it in there when she was spinning around and fell on her side."

Shaftoe was ready to slug Zachary. Maybe Zachary realized that. The coach said nothing. Shaftoe thought, Time for me to take charge.

To the lady and girl, Shaftoe said, "You're both nice people. You didn't do anything wrong. Thank you for helping us with our problem." He gestured toward Zachary, and then toward himself. "The problem is between him and me. Sorry I'm only wearing a towel." He tried to smile. "You can go now." He nodded toward the door to the parking lot, at the end of the hallway.

Shaftoe pulled his arm away from Zachary's grip. Zachary opened his mouth, as if to say something, then shut it. Grandma took the girl's hand and made a step toward the door to the parking lot.

The little girl tugged against her grandmother's lead. She seemed to be reluctant to leave. She still looked worried. She tried to pull grandma back toward the entrance to the locker room. With her other hand, she pointed into it. She said, "Bee-yoon?"

Shaftoe heard the plaintive tone in the girl's voice. He thought of the cute cartoon puppy on the balloon. The little dog had seemed so sad and alone when he'd last seen it, gently bumping against the ceiling, drifting back and forth in response to the ventilating system breeze, string and streamers dangling. The little girl looked even sadder and lonelier, to be separated from the balloon. Shaftoe hoped tears weren't forming in his eyes. He said, "Mr. Zachary, go in there and get the girl's balloon, so they can take it home with them. It's special to her."

The coach looked stunned. Then angry. Shaftoe wondered what Zachary would do. Then a softer look came into the coach's eyes, and he trotted into the locker room, came back with the balloon, and—leaning forward—silently and gently handed it to the little girl. Shaftoe reminded himself that Zachary had been an attentive, loving, father to Chip, even as he pressured his son onto a perfectionist path that caused him to cheat on tests he might have aced.

Grandma and granddaughter nodded their thanks to the coach. Shaftoe gestured toward the parking lot again, and they promptly left the building.

When they were gone, Zachary hissed, "Bobby, you prick, get your goddam clothes on, we've got something to settle, in my office."

chapter twenty six

"No way I'm going to your office, Coach. I'm tired of wearing this damn towel. It's been a long day. I'm getting dressed and going home."

"Oh no, pal. I'm gonna stick to you like superglue. You're a friggin' fright risk."

"I think that's *flight* risk, Ed. And this isn't court, and you're not a judge."

"Oooh. Oooh. Getting all smart ass on me? Listen, Shaftoe, I'm about to make more trouble for you than a judge ever could! You're a pedal-file, you sick fuck, and I'm takin' a statement from you, for my Child Abuse Report."

Shaftoe ignored Zachary, and headed back into the locker room for his clothes. Zachary trailed after.

"Coach, haven't you had enough jollies for one day? Ya gonna get turned on again by watching me get dressed?"

"Fuck you, Bobby. If you split now, how's that gonna look on my report—fleeing the scene of the crime, evading a citizen's arrest."

Shaftoe didn't know if Zachary had a leg to stand on. But it was clear that Coach was trying to frame him, and leaving now might make things look worse.

At the sink counter, Zachary watched Shaftoe closely as he dropped the towel and got dressed. The smell of vomit and diarrhea was still in Shaftoe's nostrils, maybe on his clothing. He reached for his bottle of Ancient Mariner, but it wasn't there. Had he not set it on the sink counter earlier? Whatever. For now, he just wanted to call Zachary's bluff and go home.

Now, Coach gestured toward the other end of the fieldhouse, "Let's go. My office."

Where the hell was the Ancient Mariner? Maybe in my locker. Shaftoe pointed toward it. "Wait, I've gotta go to my locker."

"Whatsa matter, Bobby, your panties still in there?"

"Fuck you, Coach." Bobby said no more, walked to his locker, opened its door, and looked at the shelf at the top. Damn, no bottle of Ancient Mariner. I'll just have to still stink. He shut the locker door. "Let's get this bullshit meeting over with."

In Zachary's office, the coach spoke first. "You're a disgrace to the profession, Shaftoe. Imagine, the whole town trusting you with their kids, and now you do this. But I saw through you all along. It was me who caught you last month, letting that kid . . . whatzisname . . . bugger you on campus." He put a "Nailed you now!" expression on his face.

Shaftoe wasn't about to volunteer that the kid who'd fallen onto him from a tree was a ninth-grader named Zeus, and that he'd been up there innocently filming Shaftoe, probably because he thought Shaftoe was everything he wanted to be when he grew up. And now this irony; because of the little girl, Shaftoe was open to being framed with a false child abuse report. The child abuse was all in Zachary's head, and it seemed obvious that the coach was about to go beyond his previous intimidation. Yeah, in Coach's mind, framing Shaftoe was what a good father would do for his now-ineligible son. But why now? Chip's ineligible status was a done deal.

"Bobby, let's cut to the chase. Let's nip this in the butt. You can go over this with a fine toothcomb, but I've got you cold. All the evidence."

"Coach, you've got no evidence. I was in a shower stall. About to take a shower. The curtain was closed. A little girl ran into the locker room, spun around, got dizzy, and fell down. That's how she got the bruise. That's why she was crying."

"They all say that, short eyes."

"Go to hell, Zachary. You've got it in for me because of Chip."

At the mention of his son, Zachary's "nailed you" expression changed. His face sagged. His eyes looked moist and unfocused. Shaftoe thought, My God, he looks legitimately hurt. Is he about to shed tears? For an instant Shaftoe felt sorry for Zachary. He thought, He's a misguided man, but he loves his kid even though he ruined his kid by pushing him for perfection in all things. But this is no time to back down. "Ed, your warped mind saw an opportunity to crucify me, and you're taking it."

"Yeah, that's why I was . . . am . . . a championship coach. I see my opportunities and I jump on them— quick. Like a cat on a mouse."

Was that an admission that all of Zachary's threats were lies? If he filed a false report, would anyone who read it care enough to figure that out? Even if law enforcement or social workers couldn't substantiate it, would that make any difference to Shaftoe's doomed career? Shaftoe remembered that at his apartment, he had a clipping from the *Capitol City Press*—a grim message—in his desk. No picture, but it read,

EX-TEACHER FACES MOLEST CHARGES

Silas Casebeer, a teacher at Cobaine Elementary School is facing charges of molesting a 7-year-old student. He was removed from his job upon the arrest Friday. The investigation is continuing. If convicted, Casebeer would face a prison term of between 15 and 30 years, a $250,000 fine, registration as a sex offender, public listing as such on the internet, and a lifetime term of supervised release.

No trial, no conviction yet, if ever, and already that guy's life is ruined. Shaftoe was afraid the same thing was about to happen to him.

"Mighty quiet, Counselor. Cat got your tongue? Oh, I'll bet you're wishing that wussy poem was true. That poem all you faggity counselors learn in grad school. 'I do my thing and you do your thing . . . and if we find each other, it's beautiful.' Well, my motto is '. . . and if we find each other, you're fucked!'" Zachary's cackle echoed in the empty building.

Suddenly, Shaftoe was thinking, Damn, I've misread Zachary. He just quoted an obscure aphorism by an old-time psychotherapist. A tender, if lofty, saying. And Zachary is deep and dismissive enough to convert it into his own mantra: *Be on top at all times.* I've underestimated him. This man is more dangerous to me than I'd thought. I knew he was shrewd, but I'd thought he was only shrewd about football. His mispronouncing and misspelling of words fooled me. He's a diabolical mastermind in disguise.

Shaftoe's thoughts raced. He was aware of sweat on his palms. Can Zachary see right into me? Is he a step ahead of me now? Will he always be? Do we both know I'm a goner? Am I about to be toyed with and destroyed—like a mouse by a cat?

Zachary barged ahead. "Here's what'll be in my report. . ." He picked up a form from his desk. It was headed, in large type, Submit A Copy Of This Form To The Department of Justice (DOJ).

Shaftoe recognized the form. It was his state's Suspected Child Abuse Report. Sure enough, it was as if Zachary was reading Shaftoe's mind. "Recognize this form, pal? You gave one to every faculty member when you trained us. Soon it's gonna have your name all over it, like shit on toilet paper." Zachary laughed. "Counselor, you're hoisted by your own peter!"

Shaftoe knew that the word at the end of the saying was "petard" not "peter." He was surprised that Zachary knew the phrase in any form—he wasn't sure himself what "petard" meant—but he reminded himself that Zachary was continuing to reveal a more sophisticated mind than Shaftoe had been giving him credit for.

Zachary waved the form in front of Shaftoe's nose. Shaftoe tried to grab it away, but Zachary was fast for a big man. Zachary laughed.

"So here we go, Counselor. Thanks to you I know how to do this strictly by the book. After I make the phone call, this form should boogie your name straight to the local authorities and to the Department of Justice."

Zachary began to read parts of the form aloud, interspersing his own comments, *"Part A: Reporting Party.* Easy. . . me! *Did the Reporting Party Witness The Incident?* . . . then two little boxes: *Yes. No."*

Shaftoe stood his ground, "Coach, no one witnessed the 'incident,' because it didn't happen. There was no child abuse. You lose!"

"Nice try, Bobby, but I remember how you trained us: You said the report has to go in, no matter which box I check. 'Hear a rumor, pick up the phone,' you told us. And we both know I've got lots more than a rumor. I'm gonna follow the rules."

Damn, Shaftoe thought.

"Part B: Agency You Are Notifying. Oh my, whadda ya know. In our county that's the Sheriff's Station. Deputy Suzanne Zachary—I mean Deputy Suzanne Zachary Bobbitt—will be picking up the phone, and receiving a copy of this form after that."

Christ! Who the hell is Suzanne Zachary Bobbitt?

"I know what you're thinking, Shaftoe. Nope, she's not a relative of mine."

The malicious gleam in the coach's eyes, and his ill-controlled gloat seemed to give the lie to his disclaimer.

"Just a coincidence, right, Coach?"

"Ya got that right. And it wouldn't matter if she was a relative, would it, Bobby."

Again, Zachary understood the law. Shaftoe had trained the faculty well.

Shaftoe felt exhausted. He watched an image materialize before his eyes. It took his breath away. He felt his chest constrict. Then the smell of death seemed to be in the air. He thought, Am I hallucinating? No, the image was from a very real news photo he'd seen. It was a picture of a little concrete tunnel, built by the state highway commission. It ran under a highway outside of town. A well-intentioned project. Well-intentioned like the Suspected Child Abuse Reporting Law. The tunnel was to allow small, innocent animals to travel safely under the highway, rather than wind up as roadkill. The accompanying news report pointed out one problem. An unintended consequence. In no time, at the far end of the tunnel, large vicious creatures began waiting to devour their small, cuddly brethren.

Shaftoe couldn't shake the image from his mind. Why was it distracting him now? He needed to concentrate on the trap that Ed Zachary had waiting for him.

Then Shaftoe knew why the image had such staying power. The state's well-intentioned Suspected Child Abuse Reporting Law was the tunnel. Shaftoe saw himself as the small, innocent animal going through the tunnel. And Zachary was a large, vicious creature about to pounce and devour him. Shaftoe's stomach heaved. There was nothing in it, or he would have vomited. Dry heaves began.

He cursed himself for his idealism. Wanting to be a school counselor. *Now my moments of high resolve have led to this.* Right now, he didn't know which he detested more, his misguided idealism, or Zachary's power to destroy him.

Zachary watched Shaftoe, and looked happy. He said, *"Part C: Victim. Name."* He hesitated, then said, "The rest will be easy. . . . *Photos Taken?* Damn, Bobby, I said I wished I'd had a camera. 'could have got a nice shot of the bruise you made on that girl's ass."

Shaftoe felt almost too weak to comment. He struggled to say, "She fell. She was innocently playing in the locker room. Yelling to hear her echo. Spinning around with her balloon on a string. She got dizzy and fell on her hip. The fall made the bruise."

"Yeah, yeah, fella. Sure."

Shaftoe thought, *why am I defending myself to Coach?* He realized, *If this goes to court, and I talk this way, it'll sound like I'm guilty.*

"Type of abuse (check one or more). Physical. Mental. Sexual. Neglect. Other (Specify). Well, Bobby, no use discussing this. We both know which one I'm marking. After all, screams . . ."

"Dammit. She was just yelling, to hear her echo. It was fun to her."

"Fun? Crying?"

"She fell on the tile floor. It hurt. She cried and ran out to her grandmother."

"Have you no shame, Shaftoe? What about the dog?"

"Zachary, ya got a dirty mind. You know there was no dog. She was trying to tell you she'd left her balloon in there. It had a cartoon picture of a puppy on it. You know that, you bastard! You went in and brought it out for her." Finally, Shaftoe was accosting his large predator.

"That's what you say, pal. But after this report goes to the Sheriff's Deputy, who's gonna believe you?"

Shaftoe hoped that the coach was wrong about that. He challenged Zachary. "What's the victim's name?"

Zachary's jaw dropped. He looked as if he'd overlooked something. Then he appeared to regroup. "Oh, no, you don't! I don't have to tell you her name, and I'm not going to. I'll only have to put it in the report."

A ray of hope. From what Shaftoe'd observed on the scene, and Coach's reaction now, was it possible that Zachary didn't know the name of the alleged "victim"?

"Coach, I want a copy of that damn report as soon as you've filled it in! You don't know her name, do you!"

The coach's voice took on a sanctimonious tone, "These reports are confidential. To protect the victim . . ."

". . . the alleged victim."

". . . to protect the victim. You don't get a copy, Shaftoe. If I gave you a copy, you might try to contact her. That's jury tampering."

How could Zachary be so smart and seem so ignorant at the same time? Dealing with that combination was infuriating! "Coach, contacting an alleged victim isn't 'jury tampering,' damn it."

"Fuck it, Bobby. You know what I mean. Anyway . . ." Zachary looked at the bottom of the form, "it says right here *this report must be filed even if incomplete.*"

Shaftoe saw the futility of saying more.

"D: Involved Parties. Well, Shaftoe, we know whose name is gonna be all over this section." Coach smirked. "And last, but not least, *E: Incident Information. Narrative Description.* Ooo, big words— nar-ra-tive des-crip-tion. Let's see, I can write, Naked counselor, alone in locker room after school hours, playing peekaboo to entice toddle. Screams, crying, bruise, victim's mention of dog." Zachary made a sound that rattled Shaftoe; it sounded like a giggle. The coach went on, *"Similar or Past Incidents Involving*

The Suspect: Oh, yeah, Bobby, that time I caught you face down on the walkway, and you'd let that kid get on top to bugger you. And we mustn't forget the vomit and diarrhea in the locker room. Evidence. That puke and runny shit came out of you involuntarily when you realized what horrible things you'd done to that little girl. Then you were filled with remorts and egrets." Zachary doubled over with laughter. Had he deliberately mispronounced "remorse" and "regrets"? Did he know "egrets" were birds? Was Zachary aware that his fake story line was ack basswards; that the vomit and diarrhea preceded, not followed, all the so-called incriminating items; that when they entered the locker room together Zachary had stood at the urinal and laughed at Shaftoe spewing in the toilet stall?

Shaftoe wanted to kick Zachary in the balls, but he didn't have the energy. Coach smiled at him. "Bobby, you've had a long day. You look awful. Go home."

chapter twenty seven

As he drove to his apartment, Shaftoe thought, I need a bottle of bourbon. But he knew that the town of Entonces had rolled up its sidewalks already, even the bars and liquor stores were closed. Why were the streetlights blinking? But it was his tired eyes opening and closing. Thank God it was a short drive, and tomorrow was Saturday. When he reached his apartment and made it to his bed, he collapsed onto it. Out like a light—fully clothed.

He dreamed he was a little teddy bear in a sailor suit peeking out of a tunnel built as a route to survival. There was a vicious predator waiting to rip him apart. The little bear knew he would be devoured.

Shaftoe awoke, trembling. It was the middle of the night. With difficulty he returned to sleep, but the dream kept recurring and waking him up. Each time the predator seemed more horrific and the little bear more terrified. He would lose everything.

Later, Shaftoe roused to a noonday sun burning into his bedroom. He was totally unrested. The nightmare still dominated his feelings. He staggered out of bed, stripped, threw his wrinkled clothing on the bedroom floor, and showered. The shower will help me feel better, he thought. But it didn't. He dried off. Naked, he went into his tiny kitchen and made a mug of coffee. That didn't help either. The dream was still with him. He felt as if his innards were being clawed from his body. Sitting with his half-empty mug, at his bare outdated kitchen table, he looked at his wall clock. It showed 1:00 p.m. What could he do, right now, to save himself from Zachary's lies? There had to be something he could do, but he didn't know what. Would he be needing character witnesses?

He phoned Ethan Borner, and told him of Zachary's threatened child abuse report.

"Me?" Borner said. "Be a character witness for you? Sorry, Bobby. After years of atonement, I'm finally teaching the AP courses that Zachary told Fluke to keep me away from. Bright kids. They like me. I don't have to dumb down the material. I don't want to cross Zachary again. He'd go to Fluke and I'd be back where I started."

"But, Ethan, you can get me union backing. You're the union rep. Hell, in Entonces, you *are* Mr. Union."

"Nope, Bobby. Can't stick up for you. I did my battle with Zachary years ago, in the parking lot, and got my balls kicked. Anyway, have you ever heard of a teachers' union going to bat for a member accused of child abuse? No way, it doesn't fit in with 'We only want what's best for the students.' Bad public image for the union. You're on your own."

Shaftoe felt angry and disheartened. Some friend. And what was he paying his union dues for? "Sleep on it, Ethan. I'll get back to you." But he didn't see how he'd sway Ethan's decision. He feared he'd need a better strategy.

He phoned Kent Greef.

"Are you kidding, Bobby? I'm the last person you want for a character witness. The fools in this town already think all gay men are child molesters. I'm not getting close to any situation where that's a factor. And me, a gay man, testifying for you, a single man? Single guys are among the usual suspects too. I'd like to help you, Bobby, but it would be the kiss of death for you. Maybe for both of us."

"But Kent, most child molesters aren't gay. You know that. Some are married men with children."

"Bobby, what counts isn't what you know and what I know. What counts is what these local yokels think *they* know."

"I get your point, but please think it over."

Another turndown. Shaftoe felt awful and he knew that lack of breakfast wasn't the cause of it.

His lukewarm coffee no longer tasted right. Okay, okay, who are my other new friends?

He called Sarah Moreno.

"Character witness? How seriously do you think I'd be taken? Anyone around here would think, Of course, she's just a sweet, naïve—read 'naïve' as 'ignorant,' Bobby—Hispanic woman. Raised to go to church, to have lots of children, and to acquiesce to any male asking her for help. If it crossed a jury's mind that I earned a master's degree on my own, they'd switch to, Oh, she's uppity, rising above her culture, thinks she's a man."

"But, Sara, that kind of thinking went out years ago."

"Not in Entonces."

It was no use.

Shit! Borner, Greef, and now Moreno—all the people he'd counted on had copped out.

He phoned R. J. Reynolds, the cute, sun-wrinkled, cheerleader coach. He didn't know her very well, but maybe he'd made a good impression. She was the last person he could think of who might vouch for him. He didn't want to drag Natalie into this.

No one answered Miss Reynolds's phone. He decided to disconnect without leaving a message.

He'd only been awake two hours and already he felt like death warmed over.

Stymied. Nothing more he could do right now. Damn!

What about a lawyer? But he didn't know any lawyers. Anyway, would a lawyer take his case at this stage of the game—possibly no report phoned in and mailed in yet by Zachary. Was Zachary withholding it to intensify the threat of blackmail?

And did Shaftoe have the money to pay a lawyer to follow this through? What case could a lawyer make for him, anyway? Zachary's a school employee, and the law gives huge protections to school employees who file Suspected Child Abuse reports. So Zachary's in the clear even if law enforcement finds that the report is unsubstantiated. The only crime Zachary could be charged with might be "knowingly filing a false report," but given the circumstances, how could that be proved? The deck was stacked against Shaftoe, lawyer or no.

Calm down, Bobby, Shaftoe thought, you're panicking and getting way ahead of what you need to do.

But he wasn't sure what he needed to do.

Wait a minute. He tried to put himself in Zachary's shoes, disgusting as that felt. Okay . . . Chip's ineligibility is a done deal. Zachary knows I don't have the power to reverse a decision of the state athletic commission. So why is he upping the ante by filling in phony information on a child abuse report and holding it over my head? Shaftoe felt a cold sweat breaking out. Damn. Zachary wants to keep me intimidated. There must be an issue in addition to Chip. Another issue—an ongoing one—on Zachary's calendar. What the hell could it be? Let's see. . . Chip's out of the picture, Zachary has his brand new, older but legal, replacement quarterback—that "Skoo" kid, the smoker. Oh, shit. His transfer papers still haven't arrived, and only two weeks until the first football game! Shaftoe knew he'd have to send for them again. Why was he so damned conscientious.

He realized he'd been about to kick himself around. For being conscientious? Damn. Stinkin' thinkin' Dr. Mallard would say. Conscientiousness had to be the name of the game if you're a school counselor.

When all else fails, free associate. His mind ran wild. Skoo? Scooby Doo? A dog in cartoons? What was "Skoo" the new quarterback's full name? Felix Anthony something. At the back-to-school meeting on the basketball court, after saying "Skoo," Zachary had corrected himself, along with a glance at Shaftoe and a strange look, and announced "Felix Anthony Blanchard." Was it a guilty look? Was the coach capable of feeling guilt?

Felix Anthony Blanchard. How was the word "Skoo" derived from the name Felix Anthony

Blanchard? Neither that first name, middle name, nor last name sounded like "Skoo."

Shaftoe questioned the words in his train of thought. Loose associations? Racing thoughts? Word salad? Was he going nuts? Then he cursed himself for having wasted time with those word associations. This ruminating was doing no good. But he felt hopeful, as if his kaleidoscopic thoughts had started him on the right path. A path to getting himself out of the jam he was in. But he didn't see where the path was leading.

He needed a break. He needed to do something normal and healthy.

Surprise! Words to a jazz vocal came to mind.

. . . You were made for love. . . .

Good! Another date in Capitol City with Natalie was coming up. He picked up his phone and called her.

Her phone rang. He felt the pleasant glow of anticipation spread through him. Her phone rang again. He waited for her voice to answer or for her recorded incarnation to speak. It never did.

Finally, he disconnected.

What the hell? He took some slow, deep, calming breaths. But they didn't help. He felt stupid. He pressed her numbers again, more carefully.

Same infuriating result! Nothing.

Damn. Borner, Greef, and Moreno—all the people he had counted on—had abandoned him. And now, the worst of all, he couldn't reach Natalie.

It must be his telephone service provider letting him down. Well, fuck his telephone service provider. He'd try again later.

But he had to keep working on his life—now! Next problem? That would be Dr. Mallard. Why had she said, "You'll have to give up *that teacher.*"? All he'd given Mallard was Natalie's name, not her occupation.

So many impossible questions. Shaftoe became aware he'd been holding his breath. Now he couldn't decide whether to breathe or not. Would his lungs burst? Would he scream in agony? Hurt, fear, confusion, and anger. Double plus fuck! He knew he was in bad emotional shape.

He rang up Mallard.

"Dr. Mallard is out of the office. If this is an emergency, call 911 or go to your nearest hospital emergency room."

Damn. Mallard had never pulled that before. Was that recorded message supposed to be comforting? Why hadn't she at least referred him to a colleague by name and phone number? Cold.

He called Natalie again. Ringing. Ringing. Then nothing.

It was a bitch finding the phone number of his

telephone service provider. He phoned and asked about Natalie's number.

"That number is still in service, Sir."

Now Shaftoe was worried. He felt ridiculous sitting at his kitchen table naked with cold coffee. Where might Natalie be? Well, of course, dumb ass! At her summer job in the women's undergarments section of Wal-Mart. Why hadn't he thought of that before. Maybe the answering-machine function on her phone was just broken.

He walked to the sink, rinsed out his coffee mug, and set it down in the stained enamel basin. He dressed quickly, went to his car, and began the drive on the two-lane highway to Capitol City and Wal-Mart. Taking action was good. He didn't know where it would lead, but he felt a little better already. Thoughts of Natalie always had a magical effect on him. The jazz vocal resumed in his brain.

. . . Every note . . .

A few miles down the highway, tiny raindrops fell onto his windshield. He let them accumulate, then set his wipers on the lowest speed. The blades moved perfectly. All clear. No problem.

He thought of seeing Natalie soon. He pictured her wearing the pleated skirt he liked so much, and her white blouse with the buttons that were easy to open. Smiling. Eyes twinkling. Glad to see him. Wanting him to touch her. Amid all his problems, he began to feel relaxed and happy.

. . . a lover's kiss. . . .

But now the sky darkened, thunder crashed, and lightning flashed. Exciting. Even energizing. Nothing to worry about. Then rainwater began pounding his car as he drove, and wind rocked it. A Midwestern cloudburst. He couldn't see more than eight feet. An eighteen-wheeler passed him going the other way; a typhoon of dirty water from its wheels enveloped Shaftoe's car. He flipped his wipers onto high. Ah . . . now that was better; now he could see.

Then, what the hell! The frantic wiper blade on his side flew off and clattered across his roof and then his trunk. Now he couldn't see the road. He turned on his headlights. They only created a glare. Nothing to do but keep on driving. This was an emergency, he needed the comfort of Natalie, he needed it desperately. He opened his window. Rain blew into his face and across his chest and lap. He had to at least see the edge of the road. He took a deep breath and stuck his head out the window.

Finally, after twenty minutes in the downpour, Shaftoe drove into the parking lot of the Capitol City

Wal-Mart. He got as close to the building's entrance as he could, but he was already soaked.

Inside the store he went into the men's restroom—to the mirror above the wash basins. He looked like shit. With paper towels he dried his face and pressed his hair straight down all around his head, as if with a squeegee. He tried to press some water off his clothes. But they still felt saturated, including his underwear. He stripped to his skin. He considered crouching under the electric hand dryer with his clothes spread around him but feared that he might be arrested for practicing some kind of fetish. He was in a Wal-Mart but didn't have the money to buy a complete change of clothes. He set his soaked undershirt and boxer shorts aside and put his outer clothing back on. Ah—that was better; more air was circulating next to his skin.

Then, with his wet underwear wadded in each hand he exited the men's room and bought a cheap translucent Wal-Mart raincoat—it looked like latex—folded into a pouch that said Pocket Size. Yeah, pocket-size if you're the Jolly Green Giant. He unfolded the raincoat, put it on—it was snug—and threw the pouch into a trash receptacle; he knew that it would be impossible to ever squeeze the raincoat back into it. He stuffed his seeping shorts into one raincoat pocket and his soggy undershirt into the other.

Soon he was standing in front of the Wal-Mart brassiere display, a stranger in a strange land. There were hundreds of bras, but where was Natalie? In his mind, the singing resumed. He heard—

. . . memories in a moo-light . . .

Moo light? He thought of a cow. He smiled. He was feeling much better. Almost confident. Taking action had helped him a lot.

While he waited for a clerk to show up, his thoughts wandered. Natalie would look delicious in that skimpy pink bra with matching panties. He'd always liked the underwear-look on women. He thought of Natalie's lovely smallish breasts and her adorable squarish knees.

No employee was in sight. Just when Shaftoe was about to give up, a clerk appeared. As she looked at him, a smirk came to her lips. He glanced at himself in a mirror. Oh my God, in the snug translucent latex raincoat, with his wet hair plastered straight down all around his head, he looked like a penis in a condom. And it was clear that there was waterlogged underwear in his raincoat pockets.

"Er . . . Natalie?"

"No, Sir"—the clerk pronounced Sir as if it meant *you clown*— "my name is *not* Natalie." She pointed to her name tag.

"No, no. I meant I'm looking for Natalie." Time was wasting.

"Natalie didn't come to work today, Sir." Again, that disrespectful pronunciation of the last word.

"What?"

"I wish she had shown up. I'm damn tired of running from department to department, Sir."

Shaftoe didn't feel that he owed her a Thank You for giving him bad news. He sprinted to the customer service desk. A young male employee greeted him, stared at his condom-like appearance and smirked.

Shaftoe said, "Don't even think it, buddy."

Now the clerk's eyes bulged. He had spotted the oozing underwear limply dangling from Shaftoe's pockets.

"What can you tell me about an employee here, Natalie Barney?"

The young man tried to moderate his facial expression. He typed on a computer keyboard. "Ms. Barney didn't come to work today. That's all I can tell you, Sir." This time, Sir sounded more like *you pervert.*

"I know that. I was just standing over there in women's undergar . . ." Customers turned and looked at Shaftoe. He decided not to finish the sentence.

"Personnel matters are confidential, Sir . . ."

Shaftoe felt as if his soul was being crushed. He groaned. Another dead end. He was on his own.

Discouraged, he walked toward the exit. To hell with buying a replacement windshield wiper. He didn't have the time to find the right one and stand in the rain with no tools, trying to fit it on. His search for Natalie was more important.

Then he was outta there. He ran through the rain to his car, and drove with his head out the window, toward Natalie's apartment building. Thank God it was a short distance. No wiper blade on his side, but at least this time the rain could soak him no further, because he had the raincoat on.

chapter twenty eight

As he drove on surface streets through the storm and late afternoon darkness, Shaftoe let out a long-held breath. He thought of Natalie and the words of a different song. " ... *I fall too ...* "

Yeah, Bobby, he thought, you've done it again. You fell in love with Natalie and now she's gone. She's giving you the old heave-ho, and without even a goodbye. He'd thought better of her. Damn!

Well, that was the reason he was going to Dr. Mallard, wasn't it? One busted relationship after another. Why did that keep happening to him? But Mallard had told him there were no accidents in human affairs. So it must be his own damn fault. Again. How did he keep causing it to happen? ". . . *I've been well schooled . . .* "

Schooled? "Skoo"? School transcripts? Damn. This was no time to think about a measly small-town quarterback problem. Had Natalie really dumped him? It didn't seem like her to simply disappear. Christ, maybe Zachary had found out they were a couple, and now he'd kidnapped her as part of his revenge? Was Zachary that evil? Was he holding Natalie hostage right now?

Gotta find her.

As Shaftoe sped toward Natalie's apartment building, he shook his head in dismay. Yes, I've been fooled in the past—by one love after another. No . . . not fooled by them. It was my own sick self spoiling things every time.

He felt like sobbing. His stomach rumbled from lack of food, but he had to drive on.

He knew it was up to him to confront Zachary, whether the coach had abducted Natalie or had done even worse to her. Now was the time to get to the truth. Had the coach really taken her? Or, awful as that seemed, was thinking that way just less painful than facing up to Natalie's dumping him?

Finally he spotted her apartment building. But it didn't look like the cheery place he'd been to before. Maybe it was just the effect of the threatening weather and the ominous gloom, but the Polynesian motif that he'd once found so exotic now seemed cheap. Tall artificial palm trees arched over the main gate. Fake torches with no flames, and giant carvings of Tiki gods were scattered about the skimpy strip of lawn in the front. They were like gargoyles, grotesque and somehow inappropriate.

Yes, grotesque and inappropriate. Like Ms. Schwartz, the librarian at his old school, when she'd donned a grass skirt at her retirement party, hula'd, and sung "Princess Poo-Poo-Ly Has Plenty Papaya And She Likes To Give It Away."

Shaftoe slapped himself. Why couldn't he keep his mind on finding Natalie!

At Natalie's building he pulled to the curb and shut off the engine. He made sure the car windows were closed. No point in letting the car fill up with rainwater. He didn't want Natalie to see him with his rain-soaked underwear in his pockets; he spread out his shorts and undershirt on the passenger-side floorboards. Maybe they would dry.

He opened his car door. His raincoat made it easy to slide out.

Now to enter the building and confront the hideous specter that he feared was waiting for him. He was aware that he was romanticizing his mission and needed to stick to reality, but what was the reality?

He entered the looming building through its massive stone archway. Next came the tunnel-like walkway with its endless banks of mailboxes, looking dark and foreboding. All one- and two- bedroom furnished units, some hidden away, as if deliberately. He thought, Were

there secret passageways? There must be hundreds of
lonely, transient survivors of life barely existing in here.
Did they have insatiable desires? Were they undergoing a
protracted emotional torture? Maybe he belonged in that
category too. Why would Natalie live in such a building?

As Shaftoe rapidly walked up stairwells, along
corridors, around corners, and through successive
archways, he realized that there were few windows in
the place. Like a prison. Once inside the compound, the
real world disappeared.

After a minute, he knew he was lost. He retraced
his steps and took a different route. Crashes of thunder
rattled the passageways. Now he was deeply within the
labyrinth. His empty stomach growled and his knees
felt weak.

He remembered that Natalie's apartment was near
an oversized wall sconce with iron orchids. Shakily he
trotted on.

Finally, there they were, the iron orchids, looking like
a macabre decoration designed by a lunatic. And there
was Natalie's apartment. Thank God.

Standing in the passageway, Shaftoe peered through
a slit where Natalie's drapes had failed to close. Yep,
there were the couch and two chairs in her living room,
probably just like the couch and two chairs in the hundreds
of other furnished apartments in this lonely mausoleum.

He tried her door. Locked. He tapped on her window with a coin, just as he'd done when he rescued Natalie from the motel. Maybe if Natalie was inside, alive, and not gagged and bound hand and foot, she would remember the sound and know that it was him and it was safe to come into view.

Nothing.

With a feeling of futility, he knocked on the door.

Nothing. At best, maybe she was in the shower and couldn't hear him. His sense of foreboding eliminated any pleasure from what he would normally have pictured in his imagination.

As Shaftoe waited, he thought of what might be going on in this ghastly place. Secrets, wanton unnatural urges, ritual and sadistic tortures, rapes, homicides, investigations, evidence in trash bins, DNA, arrests, perjury, and acquittals. Yes, damn it, acquittals. Blame the victim. Why are these gruesome thoughts in my mind?

He felt that he had descended into the netherworld.

Natalie wasn't going to appear. Where was she?

Frightened and chilled, Shaftoe began the long eerie walk back to his car. He walked unsteadily, quaking, glancing back over his shoulder, imagining that a woman had been humiliated, brutally degraded, terrorized, tortured, and defiled. Made to surrender her humanity.

Then she had been killed. He thought the unthinkable; he feared it had been Natalie.

What action could he take next? All avenues seemed closed and barricaded.

He felt terrified, as if by a predator. But it was his own emotions that threatened his survival. Too many, too strong and too unregulated. And they were turning him inside out.

He felt weighted down by abandonment, betrayal, self-blame, and hatred. Abandoned by Borner, Greef, and Moreno. He'd thought they would support him against Zachary. Betrayed by Natalie? Or self-blame for driving Natalie away—but he hadn't done that, had he? And hatred for Zachary. Christ, could the coach really be behind her disappearance?

This shouldn't be happening to him. He recognized his self-righteous indignation. What a waste of time, self-righteous indignation. Don't get mad, get even! Yes, his emotions were threatening his survival. But he also felt more like the man of action he'd always wanted to be.

In his turmoil, he realized that there was one more person who owed him an explanation. One more target for him to aim for, right here in Capitol City, right now!

Time to take the bull by the horns. Or rather, the Mallard by the horns. Her cruel words to him still burned.

But right now, he felt as if the predator was about to grab him. He began running down more stairwells, tunneling through more corridors, sprinting around corners and through successive archways; back past the never-ending banks of mailboxes, and finally—outside in the darkness and driving swirling rain! He remembered feeling panicked like that when he was six and his mother sent him at midnight to the back of their lot to lock the garage door.

Finally, back in his car, his lungs felt like they were being clawed from his chest. He fought to catch his breath. He was afraid to look back at the brooding building with its hideous Tiki gods.

Gotta get farther away.

Shaftoe started the engine, turned on his headlights and his one functioning wiper. He stuck his head into the punishing rain for a second to see better, and carefully pulled away from the curb. It was then he was bathed in pulsing red and blue lights. Christ!

He angled back to the curb, turned off his engine, and placed both hands atop his steering wheel where law enforcement could see them. The last thing he needed was a cop afraid his prey might reach for a weapon.

An officer exited the patrol car. In the lightning flashes Shaftoe saw it was a woman. She was wearing heavy-looking shiny yellow police rain gear. Rainwater cascaded down it.

She looked annoyed. Well, she'd have to stand in the rain to talk to him. But he heard a more respectful tone of voice, if forced, than he'd heard at Wal-Mart. "Do you know why I stopped you, Sir?"

Because she'd seen him running pell-mell from an evil building under the cover of darkness? Because she'd noticed his obscene raincoat? Because she'd seen him stick his head out the car window, into the rain, and that looked suspicious too? He decided to play it safe, "No, Officer . . ." he looked at the woman's name tag. *Armadillo* it read. ". . . er, Officer Ar-ma-DILL-oh."

The officer's eyes narrowed. She looked like she was plagued by some recurring problem. "Ar-ma-DILL-oh, did you say? Like the animal? Like roadkill? I get that a lot. My name's Spanish. It's pronounced Ar-ma-DEE-yo, Sir." This time the "Sir" had an icy edge to it.

Shaftoe felt his face redden. "Of course, officer. Sorry."

"Please show me your driver's license and vehicle registration."

Christ. Why this, now! Stopping him from rushing to Mallard's office. But at least the officer's routine was familiar. Let's get this over with. "May I reach for my wallet, and get my registration out of the glove box?"

"Yes, sir. Keep your hands where I can see them."

He handed Officer Armadillo the documents. She stood in the rain and tilted the two papers to read them better with her flashlight. She studied them, then handed them back to him.

"Mr. Step-toe . . ." Shaftoe wondered if she was mispronouncing his name on purpose, to get even. ". . . you're missing your driver's-side windshield wiper. I'm writing you a warning ticket for faulty equipment."

"Yes, officer. I just lost it, on the way over here."

The officer said nothing, began writing the ticket. This was taking too long. Shaftoe needed to get to Mallard's office right away. He should have made Mallard pay for her cruel words at the time she said them. Time was passing.

Finally the officer handed him the ticket. He stuffed it above his sun visor. She closed her ticket pad. "Get that wiper repaired right away and send proof within five days to the address on the ticket. Other instructions are on the back."

He resisted saying thank you. "Okay. Anything else, Officer Arma*deey*o?"

The officer gave him a look that Shaftoe took to mean Nice try with my name, buddy, but too late.

It was then that she seemed to notice his shorts and undershirt spread out on the passenger-side floorboards. "Wearing no underwear, and you like to run around in the dark in a raincoat, huh. Do you keep the raincoat buttoned at all times when out in public?"

Shaftoe said nothing.

Officer Armadillo appeared to think for a moment, as if wondering what additional offense she might charge him with. "I don't want to see you in this neighborhood again, Mr. Flash-toe." Then she looked upward at the falling rain, shook her head woefully, quickly ducked back into her patrol car, shut off her disco lights, checked her mirrors, and drove slowly away. Had she given him the finger as she disappeared?

chapter twenty nine

Through the now-decreasing rain Shaftoe drove to the office of Dr. Juliet Mallard, psychotherapist. He parked in the garage under her professional building and took the elevator up to her office.

Her door was locked and a note in computer-generated typeface was on it.

SORRY, I'M TEMPORARILY UNAVAILABLE. IF YOU ARE HAVING AN EMERGENCY, DIAL 911 OR GO TO THE NEAREST HOSPITAL EMERGENCY ROOM.

Below that, was her hand-written signature. Shaftoe thought, My god, she has a sloppy signature.

The first initial, *J.,* then an unreadable middle name followed by *Mallard, Ph.D.*

Shaftoe thought, *J.* for Juliet. That's the name I know her by, Juliet. But what is that middle name?

Char . . . connected to what looked like just a wavy line. Charmayne? Charlotte? The last part of the middle name was indecipherable. Charlene? Whatever. Why should I care about her middle name.

Another damn door locked and barricaded. Shaftoe slumped, turned, and headed back toward his car.

But in the underground parking garage, he didn't get into his car. He needed to think about today, and he needed a drink and something to eat. He remembered the dark comfort of the bar and grill across the street. He left his car locked where it was, walked up a stairwell, and exited to the sidewalk in front of Dr. Mallard's building. The streetlights were on, and a light drizzle continued. It was only a few steps to the bar and grill.

Now he was inside, damp shirt and pants under the raincoat, at the same dark booth he'd sat in a few days before. This time, with a double cheeseburger and a bourbon in front of him, he remembered how the canned music had sounded when he'd been there before. Miles Davis had been sensuously playing "The Surrey with the Fringe on Top." Now, a male voice sang a mournful lament, *". . . drown my sorrows."*

In a short time, another bourbon was in front of Shaftoe, then another. How many had there been? He was thinking of Natalie *". . . to drive me to tragedy."*

The music was slow, with dirge-like harmonies and complicated tear-jerking lyrics. Shaftoe thought he knew who wrote it, but he wasn't sure. After today, he wasn't sure of anything. "*. . . I decay with the others . . .*"

Shaftoe felt hopeless. Into his roiling soul another emotion came crowding. He became aware he was feeling sorry for himself. He thought of his life as a bleeding wound that would not heal. Would the bleeding stop because he willed it to? Not likely; willpower only went so far. Where was the Escape key for his kind of life—to limit the destruction?

He was also feeling drunk. And tired out. He thought, I dreamed I was a tailpipe, and I woke up exhausted. He felt a corner of his mouth turn up in a wry grimace. But he didn't find his own bizarre gag funny.

Then, the memory of seeing Dr. Mallard in this same bar and grill, tipsy on a bar stool, her skirt creeping ever higher, came back to him. He remembered the bartender's words to her as he turned down her advances. The bartender had said to her, "Charlie got in the way."

Oh my God . . . *Charlie!*

Shaftoe jumped up, threw some bills on the table, and ran to his car. He knew he had to go to the motel in Entonces where he'd rescued Natalie. Rescued her from *whom*? Back then, she'd reluctantly told him. From *Charlie!*

chapter thirty

As Shaftoe drove back to the town of Entonces, he thought, *Charlie!* Now I have something to go on! In an instant, the effects of exhaustion and of bourbon were replaced as if by the caffeine of a dozen espressos.

But who *was* Charlie? That guy really got around: he'd beaten up Natalie just before she'd phoned Shaftoe to rescue her from the Entonces Motel. And, later, the very thought of Charlie had scared a bartender into giving up his sex life with Juliet Mallard.

And today Mallard had abandoned Shaftoe. Just a recorded message on her office phone, and a note with her sloppy signature on her office door, referring her clients to . . . to whom? Not to an alternate psychotherapist, just to "911 or your nearest hospital emergency room, if this is an emergency." Cold.

Natalie had dumped him without even that much

consideration. Now his only clue to what had become of her might be at the motel.

He had only wanted to keep his love affair with Natalie alive, and for Zachary's vicious harassment to stop. But, Christ, now he had to put Zachary's phony child abuse accusation on hold, and play detective to find Natalie. Damn, was it too much to imagine that Zachary had kidnapped her? Shaftoe could hardly believe what fate had dealt him. He had never wanted to be a detective, but circumstances were forcing him to act on the only information he'd stumbled across—just the name Charlie—that might help him find Natalie. Him—a detective? What if the demands of this new role would be too much for him to handle?

At least now he had in mind a plan of action. His tortured mix of debilitating emotions was being replaced by a sliver of hope.

But his body cried out for rest. He stopped by his apartment for a shower, breakfast cereal topped with water—he'd sniffed his expired milk carton and it was gross—and finally, a little sleep.

In the early morning, on Sunday, after several hours he awoke and put on no-iron pants, tennis shoes, a white t-shirt, and an unbuttoned short-sleeved shirt printed with Disney characters. The clothes were part of his plan. His mother had given him that shirt for Easter.

He'd never worn it; did she think he was three years old? Disneyland, The Magic Kingdom, The Happiest Place On Earth. Had he ever lived in a magic kingdom, a happy place, even in childhood?

The sun had just risen. No more rain. He donned sunglasses and slapped a baseball cap onto his head—an unwanted cap he'd been sent when he renewed a magazine subscription. He never wore headgear; but all the better to complete his ersatz disguise. Entonces was a small town and he didn't want anyone to recognize him this morning. Can't be too careful while being a detective. Oh yeah, and a folded interstate highway map for a prop. He'd grab one from his car when he got in it.

He left his apartment, walked to his incomplete vehicle—he could replace the missing windshield wiper later, what he was about to do now was more important—and headed for the Entonces Motel.

He'd carefully chosen the direction from which to approach the motel. He wanted to stop out of sight of it, not drive past it or into its parking lot. As he drove toward it, he saw its faded sign— *Newly Redecorated.* He recalled Natalie's bloody face, bruises beginning to form on her body, her dress askew at the shoulder, and the back of it unzipped. His throat tightened as he pictured her tear-stained cheeks, and the fear still in her eyes. She and he were barely acquainted then and yet she'd phoned him to get her out of there. He'd felt favored. He wondered again what sex act she'd refused to take part in with Charlie.

Shaftoe pulled to the curb, well short of any security cameras the motel might have. He pulled the bill of his baseball cap down toward his sunglasses and grabbed his folded highway map from the glove compartment. As he walked toward the front office of the motel he tried to peer into it. What he hoped to see inside the office—was it there? It was hard to tell through the big dirty window of the place. Then, *yes.* Good, a break at last. There it was—a security camera, mounted on the ceiling high above the check-in counter, pointed toward cars entering and leaving the driveway. Now, would his luck hold out? Was there a gummed sticker on the security camera? If so, it must be on the far side. He saw that he'd have to enter the office to look for the sticker. Maybe he would even have to talk to a clerk in order to get the information on it.

Now, through the glass of the office door, he saw an emaciated stubble-faced employee enter from a room behind the check-in counter. The man snuffed out a cigarette, shuffled to his position behind the counter, and looked at him. Through the glass, the clerk made a half-hearted attempt to fake a welcoming smile. Shaftoe nodded at him, to acknowledge the effort.

Shaftoe decided to be friendly—and obsequious. He'd had practice being obsequious over the years. He'd needed to be, in order to get jobs and keep jobs, including his current one. He needed the clerk's help.

He proceeded toward the door, keeping as far from the driveway as possible, hoping he was out of sight of what appeared to be the only camera the place had in front. Can't be too careful. He pretended to cough, did the Dracula move, arm in front of his face, further concealing it from any security camera, just in case. Now he was at the door, pulled it open, and stepped inside. That should do it, the camera was definitely pointed to focus on the driveway, not at him.

Once inside, he took the Dracula pose again, and faked another cough. Convince the clerk. He reached the counter, with the clerk on the other side, and tried to look as if he were about to ask a question.

"Hi," Shaftoe chose to speak in a quiet voice and tried for a non-threatening smile and manner. He'd learned to do that in his counselor training. "What's your lowest price for me, the wife, and two kids please?" He jerked his head toward the street, as if his imaginary family were in a car down the street, out of sight. Then he added, in as proud and unsophisticated a tone as he could muster, "We went to Disneyland last week. We took a lot of pictures." With his highway map and Disney garb, he hoped he was passing as a tourist, as a good family man with limited funds.

"Gee, Sir, I'll bet those pictures will give your family wonderful memories for the rest of their lives." The clerk sounded more tired than interested, but he'd given it a good try. Maybe he was finishing a night shift.

"Yeah, we can't do enough for our children, right?"

The clerk looked as if the phrase "our children" was a new one to him. Oh well, Shaftoe only wanted to say enough to seem real, get what he came for, and leave. He wasn't surprised that the clerk was only standing still now, looking blankly at him, not offering any further service.

"Uh . . . about the rate. For a room . . . for four?"

The clerk's drooping eyelids opened. Had he been about to fall asleep standing up? Well, whatever. He quoted Shaftoe a price. Shaftoe repeated it in a noncommittal tone of voice, as if he were about to exit and check out the next motel down the road.

Then Shaftoe deliberately pursed his lips, looked up, and craned his neck to get a partial look at the far side of the security camera. "That's a security camera, right? What's that sticker on your side say?" He deliberately squinted, "It say *Lotsa?*"

The clerk studied his side of the camera as if he had a reading problem. His lips moved silently. Then, "It

says *Gotta.* That's the name of our security service."
The clerk didn't seem at all sure the gummed sticker
said *Gotta.* Shaftoe craned farther, still looking up, now
leaning over the counter, breathing into the clerk's face.
The clerk backed up. Now Shaftoe could see that the
word on the sticker was *Gotcha.* Just what he'd hoped
for. He straightened up and looked at the clerk. The
clerk said nothing, probably hoping that Shaftoe would
shut up and leave.

With his folded map, Shaftoe pointed toward the
camera. "How's that thing work?"

The clerk sighed, moved his head from side to side
as if thinking, What a hick. He took a deep breath, let
the breath out, and answered. "It takes pictures. A kid
comes in every week. He puts in a new disc. Then it
takes more pictures."

Shaftoe fixed his best, *I'm trying to understand
technology* expression on his face and waited.

Finally the clerk said, "That's all she wrote, mister."
He glanced at a clock on the wall.

"Wow. Cool. Thanks."

With that, Shaftoe walked off the premises and
down the block. He got in his car, tossed the baseball
cap onto the passenger seat, wriggled out of his
Disney shirt, threw it onto the cap, made a U-turn,
and drove away. Step One, completed. He felt good.

What did Sir Walter Scott write in the seventeen-hundreds? "Breathes there the man, with soul so dead, who never to himself hath said, I faked that clerk out of his jock!"? No, that wasn't quite it.

On his drive back to his apartment, Shaftoe stuffed the cap and the Disney shirt into a Goodwill collection box. It had been a month since he rescued Natalie, stranded at that motel after she was beaten up by Charlie.

Now Shaftoe knew who he was going to contact next. Step Two coming up. It was a long shot. He'd have to play his hand carefully.

chapter thirty one

Eventually the weekend was over, and it was Monday, 7:00 a.m. At his apartment, Shaftoe shaved and put on casual summer clothes for work. Nothing more he could do until after work today to solve the mystery of who Charlie might be. Until then he needed to be at his office at the high school, check his mail and messages there, put in some time tweaking the fall master schedule of classes, and tell Sweet Jillie that she was doing a good job with the summer paperwork. Fall classes would start in two weeks. Maybe she would tell him that Felix Anthony "Skoo" Blanchard's transfer papers had finally arrived. Time was running out before the first football game of the new season. State athletic commission rules allowed the game to be on the Friday afternoon three days before classes started.

As he reached for his Ancient Mariner aftershave, he remembered his back-up bottle in the Ed Zachary

Field House. But how had that bottle disappeared? For sure, it had gone missing from the sink counter there the day the little girl ran into the men's shower room and Zachary framed him. But he couldn't imagine how stealing a spray bottle of Ancient Mariner could be related to Zachary's treachery.

After parking his car at the school, he carefully crossed the highway, entered the counseling center, pushed open the waist-high wooden gate at the end of the counter; and as he walked toward his cramped office, appreciatively noted the large open space surrounding the desk of Sweet Jillie. Kind of a roomy buffer zone of quiet. Well, all the students at the school needed the semi-privacy—if not the excess coziness—of his doorless office when they told him highly personal things.

Jillie was wearing a white short-sleeved blouse with an open collar, a plaid skirt, bobby socks and penny loafers. Today she had a ponytail. Shaftoe thought she was a little too old for the garb, but she looked cute.

"Hi, Sweet Jillie. How's it goin'?"

She smiled. "Hi, Mr. Shaftoe, still enjoying your summer?" Her voice was respectful and melodious.

If she only knew.

She continued, "Without students all over, entertaining us and asking us questions, I feel like I've come to work at the wrong place. And I bet they miss you, too. They love you."

It was easy to see how she'd picked up the nickname Sweet Jillie. On the other hand, maybe that was the name on her birth certificate. Shaftoe'd come to think of her name as if it were one word, *Sweetjillie*. Well, he'd come across stranger names.

"Wow, thanks for the compliment. Yeah, in the summer, it's kind of like an office job, isn't it? Not as much fun without all the kids around." He didn't want to tell her anything about his personal life, especially his problems. He was glad that she'd never asked. He was the school's counselor, not her, though he suspected that some students might have confided more in her than in him. He knew that she kept a supply of tampons and sanitary napkins under the counter. He'd heard her whisper a question once to a girl who stepped to the counter with a concerned look, "Do you want the plug or the pad?" Well, why shouldn't Sweet Jillie talk in the language of the students. No problem. He knew of schools where the confidant of choice was the janitor. Kids knew who to turn to. Shaftoe was happy that so many turned to him.

"Anything I should know about, Jillie?"

"No, just the usual. Glad we put the grades of our graduated seniors into the computer the week after their finals, 'cause now I've sent their transcripts to colleges to finish their applications. Then, I computer-printed all the seniors' report cards and mailed them to their homes."

So now, Coach Zachary had received, in report card form, the two F's that were the result of his son Chip's cheating.

"And I've printed the report cards of last year's Ninth-, Tenth-, and Eleventh-Graders, and mailed them, too."

"Perfect, Sweet Jillie."

"Too bad we're the only high school in town, and we don't have summer classes."

Shaftoe resisted remarking that Entonces always invested their money in Coach Zachary's athletic program instead of having a summer school.

She paused for a moment as if trying to remember something more. "Oh, of course, now I've stored all the grades in the computer. And I've started a file for every kid who'll be coming here for the first time. You know, the entering Ninth Graders, and the few transfers-in."

"Good. You're always on top of things. Thank you."

"You're welcome." Sweet Jillie looked as if his thank you meant a lot to her. He wondered if anyone else thanked her. He rarely heard thank you's in this place.

He was about to walk on into his office when she said, "Oh, Mr. Shaftoe, the papers of that kid transferring in—that you asked me to watch for? That boy—Blan-something?"

"Blanchard. His papers finally came in?"

"What?"

"You were about to say, Blanchard's transfer papers finally came in, right?" Shaftoe took a deep breath, exhaled, and started to relax.

"On, no. Sorry, Mr. Shaftoe, I was about to tell you—still, nothing's come in about him."

"Damn." Then he remembered that she didn't like to hear swearing, "Oh, sorry, Sweet Jillie, didn't mean to swear. Look, when you have a chance today, please phone Coach Zachary and check on the name and address of the high school the Blanchard kid is coming from. It'll be out of state." Shaftoe often worded requests that way to her, politely, he thought, yet letting her know he wanted his request fulfilled by a definite time. She would know from experience that he would check with her before the end of his workday.

Shaftoe remembered Blanchard from the back-to-school meeting on the basketball court last month. As expected, he looked older, bigger, and stronger than the regular varsity players at Entonces. And no doubt he was more skilled in football; Coach Zachary loved that. Shaftoe didn't know if Sweet Jillie was aware that athletes from out of state could come to Entonces after putting in the full year of their twelfth grade at their old high school, but still having too few credits to graduate there. And that Zachary recruited them to Entones because the state that Entonces High School was in allowed a non-high school grad to play one year longer.

Some, like Felix Anthony "Skoo" Blanchard, were bigger-muscled, better coordinated, arrogant-appearing, and possessed by a smoking habit.

Yeah, Sweet Jillie didn't know all those details. In fact, better if she didn't. Shaftoe wanted to find out more about that young man, with as few people knowing as possible. His beef with Zachary was personal, man to man. He had to solve it alone.

"Sweet Jillie, you always follow up so well on paperwork without involving me. Let's handle this kid . . . uh, this Blanchard . . . that same way." From what he'd seen, Shaftoe found it hard to think of Skoo Blanchard as a "kid," because he looked like a young adult. "Let Coach Zachary think your call is just another one of those things that you follow up on." Shaftoe looked her in the eye, as if to say, Got it?

"For sure. Just checking on an address for some missing transfer papers. Just between Coach and me."

What a gem she was. But even Sweet Julie said "Coach" with reverence, as if she were saying "the King."

"Don't invite Coach to say anything extra. Especially if he wants to make one of his suggestive remarks to you." They both knew that Zachary was prone to do that. "Make your conversation brief. Don't use my name at all. If Coach wants to talk, please just get off the phone as quick as you can, and then tell me. I can call him back if I decide to. Did I say that clearly, Sweet Jillie?"

"Yes. Clear. Don't use your name at all. Get off the phone. And I'll tell you if he says anything extra to me."

She'd gone straight to the point. Even repeated it. Understood him perfectly.

"Thank you. You're a gem."

Did she blush? Maybe.

Shaftoe walked across more floor space, into his tiny office. As always, specks of something—asbestos?—drifted down between the pulsing fluorescent tubes above his desk, and the nearby trucks on the crumbling Interstate caused his furniture to vibrate. Nothing he could do about the trucks, but he could do something about the damn specks all over the paperwork on his desk. He picked up the wooden chair which faced him, squeezed in between his desk and the wall. He pushed it out through the doorless office door frame, into the empty floor space between his doorway and Sweet Jillie's desk. Now he had space to move his desk so that the menacing airborne specks wouldn't fall on his paperwork. If anyone wanted to sit to talk with him, they'd be sitting just outside his doorway. But at least the specks would fall onto his floor.

Now that summer had given him a more relaxed pace at work, maybe he should phone Borner, his union rep, about the conditions in his tiny office. Workplace conditions—something that Borner might negotiate with the school board—would be a good excuse for the phone call, and he could try again to get Borner to commit to be a character witness for him if Zachary's child abuse bluff went to court. But Shaftoe still didn't see a way to put leverage on Borner to make him help with that.

He turned his attention to what he was paid for in summer, and put in a few hours making his computer try several possible schedules of classes for the fall. Shuffling kids around each time, to see which schedule would give the most students the classes they needed. Some of the classrooms wouldn't hold enough desks for the large number of kids who needed to be there. Damn!

"Shaftoe, you loafer, what's a nice straight boy like you doing in a dump like this?" With those words, Kent Greef sat down in the chair that Shaftoe had just placed outside his door frame. "And why ya got me all the way out here?" He gave Shaftoe a fake leer. "I'm not gonna sit on your lap. Or maybe ya got a communicable disease? I did, but my doctor gave me a big pill and now I can pee again. So relax, I just came over to check my school mailbox."

"Kent, I thought your probation officer told you to stay away from this place."

Kent laughed. He was wearing a replica professional football jersey, and looked alert, tanned, and buff.

Shaftoe quickly added, "You look great! Does that jersey mean that your tryout with the NFL was perfect?"

Now they both laughed.

"Naw, Bobby. Didn't make it. Again. Dang. But I just yesterday got back from teaching my seminars aboard the ships. Spare time, I worked out in the ships' gyms and lounged around their pools. Great for the biceps. And the tan." He flexed his tan arms. "Ya know, the better I look, the more . . ." he let his wrist go limp in an exaggerated way, "*nice men . . .*" he batted his eyes way too long, as if to make sure that Shaftoe got the implication, ". . . the more really nice men I meet."

"I don't wanna hear about it." Greef would know Shaftoe was kidding. All the students and faculty liked and respected Kent so much, it was hard for Shaftoe to bear a grudge for Kent's declining to be his prospective character witness. Anyway, Kent, in turning him down earlier, had made a point that he should have thought of first—about the unsophisticated citizens of Entonces. Shaftoe felt the same chill he had felt at the time. In the public eye, perception was reality. Misperception too. Shaftoe wanted to keep his job.

"Anyway, Kent—how's the name change going— from Mr. Greef to Mr. Sunshine?"

"I dunno, Bobby, maybe it's not necessary. With that shipboard popularity, I was so busy responding to men, I hardly thought about the name change. But it would be more positive in students' eyes: *Mr. Sunshine.*" He sighed. "Whatever. I can always get back to it later."

Shaftoe wanted to keep the conversation going. He and Kent always had good ones. He knew that Kent was the football trivia king. "So what's going to happen in the NFL pre-season?"

"Can't tell you yet. I might put some money down, on the games. I don't want you placing big bets on my longshots and spoiling the odds for me." Greef paused. Then, "How's it look for Coach Zachary—the asshole—without Chip?"

At the sound of "the asshole" Shaftoe caught Greef's eye, and rolled his own eyes toward Sweet Jillie at her desk across the room. Greef looked toward her, nodded at Shaftoe, and silently moved his lips as if to say Sorry.

"As I was saying, Bobby, how's the upcoming season look for Coach Zachary—his Majesty the Emperor—without his son Chip at quarterback? Who's Chip's replacement?"

"Some overage transfer named . . ." Shaftoe paused, he might never find out more about Zachary's recruit unless he used Skoo's full name. ". . . Felix Anthony Blanchard."

Greef roared. For a man who burlesqued his own gayness, Greef always had a genuinely uninhibited masculine guffaw. Now he couldn't seem to stop his freight train of a laugh.

Sweet Jillie, surprised by the uproar, glanced at them. Had she never heard a teacher laugh?

Shaftoe said, "Is that your laugh or a nuclear explosion! Not a giggle, that's for sure. What happened to the limp-wristed act, Kent?"

"I took a macho pill this morning. It just kicked in."

Now Shaftoe laughed too. Whatever Greef had found uproarious about Blanchard's name, his laugh was winding down.

"*Felix Anthony Blanchard,* Bobby? Did the kid arrive in a casket?"

"What? I don't get it." Greef must be jerking him around. Everyone knew that Kent Greef knew more about football than anyone, maybe more than Zachary. Shaftoe had sometimes wondered how Kent would do if, magically, he was made coach in place of Zachary. It would have to be by magic; Principal Fluke would never appoint a self-acknowledged gay man to be varsity football coach.

"Okay. Okay. Sorry to laugh at you, Bobby." Greef tried to return to a respectful face. Shaftoe appreciated that.

"Well? Goddamn it, Kent." Enough of this. He saw Sweet Jillie's face redden.

"Well. The one and only Felix Anthony Blanchard, a great football player, was born in 1924. He died in 2009, eighty-five years old. You never heard of Doc Blanchard?"

Shaftoe didn't like Greef's rubbing it in. "Kent, you're the football trivia authority, not me."

"Yeah. I forget that. I know what plays to send in, too."

"We all know you do. You should be a coach in the pro's. Now, who was Doc Blanchard?"

"Okay. Ready to take notes, Bobby? Listen and learn. Here goes: Felix Anthony "Doc" Blanchard, born in 1924 . . ."

"You already said that."

Greef gave Shaftoe a fake stern look, ". . . born in 1924 in McColl, South Carolina, was a fullback. He was the first-ever college junior to win the Heisman Trophy. He was a three-time All America. He was originally nicknamed "Little Doc" because his father was a doctor. He played college ball for the U of North Carolina Tar Heels, where the coach was his mother's cousin."

"Okay, Kent, you can stop now. I'm friggin' impressed."

"No. No. Here comes the best part. Later he went to West Point; he played three years there and his team was undefeated. His nickname on the Army team was 'Mr. Inside,' he was such a terrific rusher: 38 touchdowns. Glenn Davis was a teammate. Davis, "Mr. Outside," was a terrific runner too. In November 1945 they were both on the cover of Time magazine."

Shaftoe made sure that Greef saw him look at his watch.

"Okay. Okay. Blanchard was a first-round pick of the Pittsburgh Steelers. So he could have played pro ball, but instead he enlisted in the U S Air Force, became a fighter pilot, and in Vietnam he flew 113 missions from Thailand, 84 of them over North Vietnam, and retired as a Colonel. Whatta guy."

Shaftoe jumped in, "And, Kent, I'll bet he even has a highway interchange named after him!" Would Kent catch the sarcasm?

Greef didn't laugh, his eyes got big. "Right! Interstate 20 at U S Route 15, in South Carolina. Howja know that?"

"Lucky guess."

Greef went on, "So, with Zachary's new quarterback, it might have been some relative who named him Felix Anthony."

Now Shaftoe recalled Zachary's verbal stumble when introducing the over-age transfer. It involved the kid's nickname, *Skoo*. Did that mean that Zachary had come up with the nickname Skoo? Or—wait a minute—maybe Zachary had made up an entire phony name for the kid—Felix Anthony Blanchard. Because of Zachary's life-long devotion to football, Zachary would have known about Felix Anthony "Doc" Blanchard. My office has been waiting for transfer papers for a Felix Anthony Blanchard, and getting no response from whatever high school Zachary told us the kid was coming from. And why have the transfer papers arrived for all the other ringers that Zachary recruited, but not for Blanchard? I gotta look into this. For starters I gotta find out what Sweet Jillie hears from Zachary today in her phone call to him.

Shaftoe chose not to tell Greef what he was thinking. He deliberately hadn't told him about the nickname "Skoo." He wanted to handle this on his own. Did the kid have some other, real, name? Shaftoe thought of a counselee from last year where getting transfer papers had been a problem; she was listed at her former school under the name she'd had before the federal witness protection program gave everyone in her family a new name. It had been a bitch for him to discover her secret, keep the secret, and get her records.

Shaftoe thought, Was Skoo in the same situation as that girl? The witness protection program? Was that the reason, at the back-to-school meeting, for the strange look from Zachary after he said "Skoo"?

Zachary then regrouped and introduced the kid as "Felix Anthony Blanchard." What other reasons might there be for a name that now seemed suspicious? There was a possibility—or am I just being paranoid about Zachary?—that there was some sinister reason for the delay in transfer papers. Were the missing papers a glitch that Coach hadn't foreseen? Maybe finding out more about the glitch would reveal why Zachary is threatening to frame me with a phony child abuse report.

Shaftoe let Greef terminate the conversation and leave. Shaftoe wanted to dig into the mystery of the missing transfer papers.

And now Shaftoe's workday was over. It was 4:00, time for him to make an important phone call. On his way out, he needed to ask Sweet Jillie what transpired in her phone call to Zachary.

chapter thirty two

One last thing before he left the office. Shaftoe looked up the phone number of a local business. With the first pen he could find, a red one—why were there no black pens and note paper around when he wanted them?—he copied the phone number onto his wrist. Then he pulled a student's file up onto his computer screen and copied the student's home address onto his wrist.

He walked to Sweet Jillie's desk. "Sweet Jillie, I'm leaving for the day. What did Coach Zachary say to you when you phoned him about Blanchard's transfer papers?"

"Oh. I read him the address he gave me of that student's out-of-state high school, and he said it was correct. He sounded nervous. I'd never heard him sound nervous before. Then he swore." Sweet Jillie's cheeks reddened. "He said that I must have done something wrong when I sent for the papers, and to send for them again. But I know I did it right, Mr. Shaftoe."

"I'm sure you did it right, Sweet Jillie." What the hell was Zachary up to?

"Shall I send for the papers again, Mr. Shaftoe?"

"Yeah, go ahead."

"I don't think we'll get anything this time either."

"Well, let's keep Zachary happy." Shaftoe silently agreed that they would again get nothing in return, but he didn't want to tip his hand. He wanted to handle this alone.

"Then Coach asked me if I was wearing my yellow swimsuit with the polka dots. He must have seen me at the lake."

Shaftoe tightened his lips and shook his head from side to side.

"And?"

"And I said, 'Don't talk to me that way. Thanks for the information about Blanchard,' and hung up."

"Thanks. You did good. Sorry about what Coach said to you."

"Everybody knows he's a jerk." She said it rather pleasantly. Still, Shaftoe knew that, coming from Jillie, "jerk" was very strong language.

"Shall I phone that boy's school, Mr. Shaftoe?"

"Not yet. Give me another day or two. I want to try something else first."

"Try something? Can I do it for you?"

"Not this time, thanks. I gotta do it myself."

Sweet Jillie looked at him quizzically.

Shaftoe headed for the front door. "Well, see you tomorrow. I'm outta here."

"Bye, Mr. Shaftoe, have a nice evening."

If only I could, Shaftoe thought. He forced his concerns about Blanchard and Zachary out of his mind. He'd been eager all day for 4:00 to arrive so he could take his longshot chance at finding Natalie.

In the high school parking lot, inside his car, Shaftoe checked his watch, 4:10, looked at the writing in red ink on his wrist, and entered a number into his phone. His anxiety skyrocketed as he listened to the ringing. He knew he was about to lie, and he wasn't used to lying.

After what seemed like incessant ringing, he heard, "Entonces Feed and Grain."

Damn. Wrong number. Shaftoe disconnected, looked again at his wrist, and entered the phone number more carefully.

Again, incessant ringing.

Finally, an adult male voice, "Gotcha Security Services. We will spy, the law will fry."

"Hi, may I talk with the owner?"

A rueful laugh. "Go ahead. I'm the owner, the manager, the bookkeeper, and the chief cook and bottle washer."

Shaftoe thought, I'll try to humor this small-town businessman. But he wanted to keep his call short. "Wow. You're a busy guy."

"Yep. How can I help you?" Apparently the guy at the other end of the line wanted to keep the call short, too. Good.

Now the lies. "My name is Carl Rogers. I like your town, and I'm looking into starting a business in Entonces . . ."

A chuckle, "Just so it isn't another security service. I don't want any competition."

". . . and I may be needing security cameras serviced late in the business day. Just before 5:00 p.m. Before I ask you any other questions, do you have someone who can do that on some kind of schedule, to come by every time I would need a new disc for a security camera?"

"Do we? Oh yeah. You bet. You know how smart the kids are these days about anything electronic." It wasn't a question.

Then the background noises became muffled, as if the business owner had his hand over the phone. "Hey, fucking Boy Genius . . . Hey, you . . . Come here JEE-sus." Shaftoe could barely make out the words.

"Just call me Zeus, please, sir."

Shaftoe gave a victory fist-pump and covered his

mouth to suppress a cheer. So far, so good! Better than so far, so good! So far, super!

Still muffled, "Whatever, fucking Boy Genius. How late do you service the cameras on your route?"

"I go home at five o'clock, sir"

"Great."

Exactly what Shaftoe had been hoping for. Thank you, God!

Now the owner's voice came back full volume. "Mr. Rogers?"

Who the hell was Mr. Rogers? Oh yeah, dumb ass, it was the fake name you just gave the owner. ". . . Yes? Mr. Rogers here." Lying was getting easier.

"Thanks for waiting. We have a f . . ." Shaftoe wondered if the owner was about to say "a fucking Boy Genius." The owner started over. "I'm happy to tell you that we have a state-of-the-art expert, absolutely up-to-date on electronics. Very reliable. He can do what you asked for, right up to 5:00 o'clock."

That's all Shaftoe wanted to know. "Thanks for the information. I may be getting back in touch with you."

"Mr. Rogers, what number or address may I . . ."

Now Shaftoe disconnected, glanced at his watch, and started his engine. He hoped his plan for the rest of the afternoon would work. His watch said 4:20. He checked the residential address he'd written with red pen on his wrist, and began driving a circuitous route.

Using streets that were farthest from the office of Gotcha Security Services, he approached a block of aging single-family homes. He pulled to the curb on a cross street almost out of sight of the address he wanted, and edged forward on the driver's seat to peer around the corner. He shut off his engine. The drive had taken ten minutes. He was early for what he had to do, but that was okay, he didn't want to miss the opportunity. He could stay in his car, peek around the corner, and barely see the street that Zeus the Boy Genius was most likely to come home on.

chapter thirty three

As Shaftoe surveilled Zeus's parents' house from
behind his steering wheel, his body trembled. He'd set
himself a crucial task. What he was about to do gave
him a guilty conscience. And even if it produced the
information he wanted, could he stand the truth? He felt
the need for something to calm him. Yes, the need for
a cigarette. Strange—he'd stopped smoking years ago.
He looked at his watch again, 5:02 p.m. When would
the kid show up?

Then there the kid was! Zeus. Pedaling a fenderless
old bicycle toward his parents' house. Is that how he
made his rounds to service Gotcha's security cameras—
by bicycle? The kid was eating ice cream on a stick,
guiding his bike with one hand. Pumping savagely, then
coasting. Weaving a little, and smiling. He looked like
his nerdish teenage self, pens and pencils protruding
from his shirt pocket. He'd grown a little during the

summer. Unfortunately, the growth had been outward, at the hips, giving him a slight bottle-shape. The sight made Shaftoe remember a hand-written poem that had slipped out of a girl counselee's notebook as she was leaving his office. She'd titled it "What Is So Useless as a Ninth Grade Boy." Bless your heart, Zeus, you're gonna need some help to ever get a date.

As Zeus rode out of sight into his parents' driveway, Shaftoe stepped out of his car and covered the short distance to the front corner of the weather-beaten house. He wondered what counselor code of ethics he was violating by stalking a kid and sneaking up on him like this. Well, any violation was worth it to find out what happened to Natalie. He peeked into the driveway. There was Zeus, with his fingers wiping vanilla ice cream off the fly of his pants, and heading toward the back door.

"Zeus, how ya doin'? Wait a minute."

Now that the ice cream was mostly off his fly, Zeus was trying to shake it off his fingers. "Mr. Shaftoe, Sir, what are you doing here? This white gooey stuff . . ." Zeus held up his ice cream covered fingers, ". . . it's not what it looks like, Mr. Shaftoe. It's just vanilla ice cream."

Shaftoe almost couldn't resist toying with this unfortunate soul. He thought of saying, Yeah, Zeus. Vanilla ice cream; that's what they all say. Jacking off again, huh?

But that would be cruel. And too easy. Shaftoe had something more sophisticated in mind for Zeus. Zeus didn't know what he was in for.

"It's okay, Zeus. I saw you riding up with the ice cream bar. Ya know, you oughta keep both hands on the handlebars."

"Okay, okay, Mr. Shaftoe, it won't happen again. Will this affect my grades?"

Jesus Christ, what planet was this kid from? Zeus looked completely serious.

Shaftoe put on what he hoped was a thoughtful look. Play the cards you've been dealt. If you do it right, you might get the information you want about Natalie. "Well, Zeus, I'll have to check on the Entonces High School Code of Conduct for Ninth Grade Boys next time I'm in my office. It might say, Not Keeping Both Hands On Handlebars: lower the student's marks in Work Habits." He put his hand to his chin, and rubbed it as if trying to remember the nonexistent punishment in the nonexistent code of conduct.

"A lower mark in Work Habits, Mr. Shaftoe?"

"Yep. Maybe." Shaftoe made his eyes big, and stared unblinking at Zeus.

"Just this one time, can you let me slide, Mr. Shaftoe? Please," Zeus pleaded in a whine that sounded like a distressed puppy dog. He stood in the driveway, looking bottle-shaped, with his bicycle dumped on its side and white gooey stuff still on his fly and fingers. Pathetic.

Shaftoe knew that right now he had a bad attitude for a counselor, but Natalie's safety was at stake. Pour it on. "Zeus, you've been nothing but trouble for me since I came to work at the high school, trailing me around with your video camera, taking unauthorized footage of me, acting like you've got a crush on me." Shaftoe knew the crush part wasn't true. Zeus's filming of him was more like hero-worship. He hated to jerk the kid around like this, but a greater good was at stake.

Zeus looked panic-stricken. "Crush, Mr. Shaftoe! Oh no, Sir, it isn't like that. I'm not like that."

Shaftoe said nothing. Let Zeus stew. He had every reason to suspect that Zeus had no sexual experience whatsoever. And he assumed that Zeus had the homophobia so common among boys in their early teens. Now, blast through the kid's defensive thoughts and take the kid by surprise, "Zeus, I know you have an item that you shouldn't have. I want it. And you can restore my trust in you by giving it to me."

A real shot in the dark. Shaftoe was lying big time, and manipulating the kid unmercifully. He felt bad about that, but he had to do it for Natalie.

Zeus's eyes blinked rapidly, a flush spread over his face. Shaftoe wondered if the kid was going to cry. He looked like he would do anything Shaftoe asked, to get back into the good graces of his counselor. Time to bluff.

"Look Zeus, I know you have the disc from the security camera at the Entonces Motel. The camera that was filming on the night I rescued Ms. Barney." Shaftoe still liked the word *rescued.* He suspected that Zeus had the disc and had watched it. "It doesn't belong to you, I could have you charged with theft, but I haven't decided to do that—yet."

Shaftoe was aware that his anxiety—first, about Natalie disappearing the month after he'd rescued her, and now about having to intimidate Zeus—was causing his voice to quaver and his body to tremble. Had Natalie dumped him? Had she been kidnapped? By Zachary? By Charlie, whoever he was? Was she in danger right now? Being beaten up again? He had to find her—soon. If Zeus has the Gotcha security camera disc from the night I rescued Natalie, clues may be on it. There might even be an image of Charlie. And a license plate number to give law enforcement. But right now Shaftoe was afraid he looked weak, and that his bluff would collapse.

Then, Thank you, God. The apprehensive look in Zeus's eyes signaled that he was mistaking his counselor's quavering voice and shaking body for rage. Go for it! "Zeus, I want that disc. Go get it NOW."

Now the teenager's face and body regrouped. A quizzical expression came onto Zeus's face and he leaned forward, as if to see into Shaftoe's mind. Shaftoe saw the light of hope in Zeus's eyes. Zeus's body language as much as said that he must be thinking, My chance to atone: one-handed bike riding, semen-looking stuff on my fly and fingers, stolen security camera disc. If I give Mr. Shaftoe the disc, that's my path to redemption.

Zeus looked at his fingers as if criminal evidence was on them. He awkwardly bent over a patch of dead grass in the middle of the driveway and wiped the remaining ice cream off. Then he headed for the garage. Shaftoe followed close behind.

Once inside the garage, Zeus glanced at Shaftoe, cringed, drew a ring of keys from his pocket, and unlocked a tall steel cabinet. Inside, Shaftoe saw dozens of video discs, each in a plastic case.

"Give it to me, NOW"

"The . . . one from the night you rescued . . . ?"

The kid was stalling. "Yes! That one, damn it! Now!"

As Zeus reached toward the top shelf, Shaftoe caught a glimpse of a plastic DVD case with a full-color cover of a young woman smiling enticingly over her shoulder. She was wearing very high heels and bending over a very low kitchen sink, her back to the camera. She wore a tiny apron which did nothing to cover her bare bottom. The title on the case, Debbie Dunks Dishes, was not hand-lettered as were the other discs in the cabinet. Debbie Dunks Dishes was professionally-done porn. Well at least the kid was in the mainstream in his sexual preference; that might make life easier for him. The case looked old, maybe from the stash of the kid's dad—or of his granddad; kids today got their porn over the internet. But forget about that, he needed to concentrate on the security camera disc Zeus was getting for him, not on Debbie's elegant ass.

"Here's the disc, Mr. Shaftoe, Sir. I'm sorry I stole it."

Zeus handed over the Gotcha security camera disc. Shaftoe almost hugged him. His risky bluff had worked. He saw the hand-lettered title, *Counselor Shaftoe Rescues Ms. Barney*. Then he became aware of a familiar scent. What was it? Christ, it was Ancient Mariner aftershave. Shaftoe's brand. What the hell was a kid too young to shave doing with aftershave? Then he saw the nearly empty bottle in the steel cabinet, and knew. The kid had taken a souvenir, a remembrance of Counselor Shaftoe, the man Zeus wanted to grow up to be like. The kid had probably been spraying it on like a magic potion to transport himself to manhood.

"God damn it, Zeus. You stole my aftershave, too— off of the sink counter in the locker room at school."

Wait a minute! That must mean . . . "It went missing the evening . . ." Shaftoe decided to backtrack. *I'm this kid's hero; he doesn't need to know that Zachary's trying to frame me with a phony suspected child abuse report of me and that little girl.* ". . . My aftershave went missing the night of the back-to-school meeting."

And if that were true, that might mean . . . what? Shaftoe saw that Zeus looked absolutely terrified. Tears might flow at any second. *Bear down. Bluff again.* "Zeus, you've got a second disc. The one you made with your video camera when you sneaked into the school locker room the night of the back-to-school meeting. That's the night you also stole my aftershave. I'm gonna have your ass thrown in prison if you don't hand it over NOW."

"Hand over your aftershave, Mr. Shaftoe?"

"No, dammit. Hand over the video you made in the school locker room."

Now Zeus's face turned pale. His breath came in gasps. He looked as if he needed help from 911. He reached into another shelf and placed a second encased disc in Shaftoe's hand. The hand-lettered label read *Counselor Shaftoe Directs Lost Toddler To Safety.* Two discs. Two birds with one stone!

Zeus began breathing more normally. His shoulders and jaw relaxed. Shaftoe also saw a flash of compassion. What was that about? Compassion for whom? Zeus was staring at Shaftoe's wrist.

"Mr. Shaftoe, Mr. Shaftoe . . . your wrist! I know you're upset about me, but those red scars . . . the blood! You didn't . . . you didn't try to . . . off yourself . . . did you?"

"What?!" Shaftoe looked toward his hand which held the disc from the motel security camera and also the locker room disc from Zeus's video camera. He saw the red ink marks on his wrist where he'd written the Gotcha Security Services phone number and Zeus's home address. Shaftoe's nervous sweat had made the red ink run.

Go with the flow. "Yeah, Zeus, that's blood. I slit my wrist. To end it all. Thank God I didn't cut deep enough. Take a lesson from that. Always remember . . . ," Christ, now what do I say? Shaftoe raised his index finger wisely, "Always remember . . . suicide is a mistake, a permanent solution to a temporary problem. Don't make the mistake I almost made."

Zeus's mouth dropped open. He looked at Shaftoe with admiration. After a bit, the teenager pursed his lips and—eyes still fixed on his counselor—nodded his head slowly and reverently. Wisdom received.

Fuck it. What a day. Let me outta here. The kid can keep the aftershave.

As Shaftoe exited the garage with the two discs that he hoped would restore his life, Zeus's puppy dog voice followed him, "Mr. Shaftoe, I'm so glad you didn't die."

Shaftoe was halfway back to his car when he heard, "Now that things are okay between us, when school starts again, can you get me a date with that cheerleader, Sheryl Wagner?"

chapter thirty four

Shaftoe drove away normally until he was certain that no one was watching him, then he floored it to his apartment. He knew his heart was beating faster than a politician who was about to win an election.

Once inside his quarters, he thought, First things first. The motel's Gotcha security camera disc might show who drove Natalie to the motel, beat her up when she wouldn't agree to a sex act he wanted, and stranded her. I'd had to pry it out of her that his name was Charlie.

But that isn't enough! I want to see an image of Charlie's face, or maybe a license plate number. Is Natalie being tortured by Charlie right now, whoever he is, wherever they are?

Yes, Shaftoe had to play that motel disc before he played Zeus's locker room video. The disc from the motel was the important one! It might let him identify Charlie. He slipped it into his video player.

Shit, no picture on the TV screen. I'll try to play it on my computer. Again, no luck. Incompatible with my equipment.

Shaftoe felt a spasm of inadequacy. Damn, why haven't I upgraded to state of the art. But wait—I saw Principal Fluke play one of the school's security discs on a device in his office. This *Counselor Shaftoe Rescues Ms. Barney* motel security disc, whatever might be on it, will have to wait until tomorrow, when school will be open and I can get to Fluke's playback equipment. Or not. Dammit, I'm authorized to be in that building any time, it's how I catch up on my work, evenings and weekends. I have a key to the building's front door, and I know how to shut off the alarm system just inside. From there, I can go through the counseling center, and get to Fluke's office and his playback device. I'll go there now. No! Put it off until dark. After dark, there'll be less chance anyone will see me and ask questions.

Shaftoe looked at his watch, 7:00 p.m. Right now, right here at home, while I wait for darkness, I can try the other disc, the locker room footage made by Zeus's video cam. I bet it will play on my TV screen, through my video player.

Shaftoe fed the locker room disc into his video player, picked up his remote, and sat expectantly on the front edge of his couch. Click, click, whirr, click, a picture of the inside of the Entonces High School locker room, time-stamped and dated, appeared on his TV screen. A slow pan showed the shower stalls and their curtains, opposite the sinks and mirrors. It was a damn clear picture. Zeus was expert. Before long, Shaftoe saw himself naked, walking toward a shower stall. A stark view of his backside. For no reason, he felt a guilty complicity in the making of this intimate footage.

I still have some visible muscle from my college wrestling days. I'm glad I've kept working out. Why is my ass so ugly, when the woman's ass on the Debbie Dunks Dishes box was so attractive?

Then Shaftoe saw himself step into the shower and close the shower curtain. Now nothing happened on screen for a while. Shower curtains! A foolish indulgence that Zachary installed in the palatial new field house named after him. Was Zachary nuts? How long did Coach think the curtains would last under the onslaught of teen age males? Well, for years, Coach's mind had focused on only one thing—How can I stock my football team with enough seasoned players to keep my string of championships going.

Suddenly, on the TV screen playback, the action was picking up. A toddler came into view, the laughing pre-school girl in that pink party dress, towing the yellow balloon with the cartoon of a cute puppy. In the video she delightedly shrieked and ran back and forth just outside Shaftoe's shower stall. He saw himself peek out through the gap he'd created near the top of the shower curtain, every part of his body concealed except his face; he paused the disc to make sure, then did a slow reverse search, to double check. Yep, he was completely covered by the shower curtain except for his face. He resumed Play. Then the little girl, her back to the camera, faced the shower stalls, saw his face, and covered her eyes with her hands as if she thought he wanted to play peekaboo. Next, she began spinning—fast—on the shiny tile floor, arms out, skirt swirling, balloon jerking at the end of its string. Shaftoe saw himself curl his arm around the shower curtain, and with his mouth moving, motion her toward the exit. He hit the Pause button, then reverse Search slow, and Pause. He hit Play and the disc advanced again. Again, on the TV screen, his mouth moved. He remembered saying, "Go back. Go back" to the little girl that day. Yep, he saw that those were the words his lips were forming. Eyes on his TV screen, he tensed at what he knew was coming. The girl, again spinning and shrieking with joy, became dizzy and fell on her hip, hard.

As Shaftoe sat at his TV, tears came to his eyes as the girl sobbed in pain, staggered up, hand rubbing her hip, and ran toward the exit to the hall, the way she had come in. Again, he switched the video between reverse and forward several times to make sure there had not been any interaction between the girl and him that could be construed as child abuse.

Then he shut off the video, slumped back into his couch, and exhaled.

The video had shown Shaftoe exactly what had happened, just as he remembered it. And he remembered also what had come next—Zachary's voice from the hall saying, "Oh my goodness, lady. We got a pedal-file in there!" Shaftoe cringed at the memory. But now he was a happy man. Giddy, in fact. Bless your heart, Zeus, you fucking electronic genius. You've saved my bacon, you little sneak, even if you did steal my aftershave that evening. I'd forgive you even if you might have a third disc titled Counselor Shaftoe Tries to Get into Ms. Barney's Pants. Now I have a defense if Zachary follows through with his phony child abuse report on me. Now I've got proof of my innocence, time-stamped and dated, signed, sealed, and delivered. The disc doesn't tell me why Zachary continues to harass me even after he has his replacement quarterback, Felix Anthony "Skoo," Blanchard—that nickname still makes no sense. But now that I'll be in the clear it doesn't matter whether I understand all of Zachary's motivations.

Switching back and forth on the locker room video had taken time. It was 9:00 p.m. now, late enough to go to Entonces High School unobserved and try to view the motel's Gotcha security camera disk on the playback device in Fluke's office.

Shaftoe left the locker room disc in his video player. On his way out of his apartment he grabbed the motel security disc. At his car, he took a flashlight out of his trunk, checked it, and laid the motel disc on the front passenger seat. He started his car and headed for Entonces High School.

At the school, all buildings were dark. He parked his car in the faculty lot, across the highway from the school. As he got out, flashlight turned off, and motel disc in hand, Shaftoe felt guilty. He thought, But why? I work here. I've come here on many evenings and weekends and let myself in, to keep up with the workload. But this is different; I didn't go into the principal's office during off-hours before. On the other hand, the whole damn place is public property, isn't it. My salary, the buildings, the utilities, the equipment— all paid for by the public's taxes, including my taxes. I have every right to use school equipment, including Fluke's security disc player. Go for it. Cut to the chase. Find out who Charlie is. Find Natalie.

chapter thirty five

With apprehension, Shaftoe dodged across the truck-laden highway and took the short sidewalk leading to Entonces High School's classroom building. He carried his flashlight, turned off, in one hand. The disc, *Counselor Shaftoe Rescues Ms. Barney*, from the motel's security camera was in the other. It was a humid summer night, no moon or stars, and unexpected rain was beginning to fall. Even though he'd been on campus before at night, the wet pitch darkness accompanied by the constant growling of diesel engines, whining of tires, and stuttering of truck brakes made him shiver. He felt like he was in a dark rainy woods full of dangerous creatures.

He unlocked the front door. Its hardware was almost silent. From working evenings and weekends, he knew the layout of the school's security system keypad. He stepped quickly to it. No need to turn on any lights. He punched in the code to disarm the system. So far so good.

Christ, it was dark in here. Hands outstretched to sense where he was, he took the familiar route into the counseling center, past his tiny office and down the hall to Principal Fluke's. He stepped inside, clicked his flashlight on, and pointed it toward the area where he expected to see the school's security disc player. Yep, there it was. It even had a Gotcha sticker on it, same as the Gotcha sticker on the camera at the Entonces Motel. Terrific. Now, could he figure out how to operate it?

Shaftoe thought, Does this clunky-looking piece of industrial equipment have the same push buttons as my home video player? He crouched down and pointed his flashlight at the many buttons, knobs, dials, and switches on the face of the black box, trying to locate the few he needed. Fluke's office furniture cast strange disturbing shadows from the moving flashlight beam. Okay, I think I got this monster figured out, at least well enough for my needs. Why do I feel like a burglar?

He flipped a toggle switch labeled "off/on." On the face of the playback machine nothing changed. Nothing lighted up, needles didn't move, and no sounds came from the device. Was it plugged in? Was it controlled by a wall switch that was off? This was going to take longer than he wanted. He stood up and stared out of

Fluke's office window. A lightning flash revealed no movement on the dark rainy campus. Good.

Crouching again, he located a button beside the abbreviation PWR. Of course. Power. He pushed it, dials lighted up, and needles quivered then settled. He hoped the damned machine wasn't recording sounds in Fluke's office, but it might not matter, he didn't plan on making any noise that might reveal he was there. Just to check, he tapped his knuckles on a shelf—knock on wood, a good idea anyway. No needle moved. Okay.

A monitor was sitting on a stand with rollers. But why was its screen not lighting up? Maybe it has its own power switch. He stood up, took a few steps to the monitor, and looked for a power switch on its cabinet. He saw no such switch. What's this sitting on top of the monitor? Shaftoe, you fool, it's a hand-held remote control with a Gotcha sticker on it. With luck, all these electronics were still set from the last time Fluke watched a disc from one of the high school's security cameras. Just push the button marked Power on this remote and see what happens. Shaftoe wanted to cross his fingers, but he had the remote in one hand and was now carrying the flashlight and the disc from the motel in his other. He pushed the Power button on the remote.

Nothing. Then, as he cursed all electronics in the universe, the screen on the monitor flickered and a message appeared: No Disc Is Inserted.

Easy to fix that. He carefully inserted the *Counselor Shaftoe Rescues Ms. Barney* disc into the playback device. Time was wasting. Fluke's office was creepy. He wanted to get out of there.

Still no picture on the monitor screen. He pressed Fast Forward. A blur of images flashed by. Stop. Start again at normal speed.

Now he saw on the monitor a shot of the motel's driveway, and at the far end of it, the motel's small parking lot, and a row of rooms. After a few seconds he recognized the back of his car, going up the driveway, slowing as he looked for Natalie's room number, and finally stopping in the lot. He remembered the clash of emotions he'd felt that night, when Natalie phoned him to save her. Concern, apprehension . . . and pride that he was the one she phoned.

On the monitor, he saw himself jump from his car, run to the door of her motel room, and tap on her window. Finally her door opened a crack, and her bloodied face peered out. He watched himself stand outside her door and exchange a few words with her.

Now, time crawled. Apparently Zeus hadn't edited the disc. Good. Finally, Shaftoe saw two people leave the motel room door and head to his car. Him and a smaller person leaning again him and walking unsteadily. Natalie of course. He remembered his original concern, pride, and the exciting closeness of her body pressing against his.

The two got into his car, it began moving swiftly, and it stayed in focus on the monitor as he drove it toward the street. Shaftoe slowed down the images. He saw the grim set of his mouth. And Natalie's disheveled clothing and wounded face. Now Shaftoe's car disappeared from the monitor. Only an empty driveway.

The disc reached its end. The monitor screen turned blank. Damn, there'd been no sign of Charlie.

Shaftoe thought, Well of course not. Charlie, whoever he is, had escaped in his own car before I arrived. Leaving Natalie helpless and bloodied, stranded in the motel room.

Shaftoe crouched in the darkness of Fluke's office, shaking. The shakes weren't only from fear of being discovered there. They were also from self-reproach at not finding an image of Charlie that might lead him to Natalie.

This was taking way too long. He glanced again out Fluke's window—nothing but rain and darkness—and then focused on the closer darkness in the principal's office, squeezing in against him from all sides. Yes, no one else was around. Why didn't that help him relax?

He'd gone through all this for nothing. Wait! Hang on. Hang on. Could there be more images on this disc? Did I start it too far into it? I gotta find out—now!

Reverse it. Reverse it. Where is the damn reverse button? Here it is! But will it get me what I want to see—Charlie?

He held the reverse button down. The monitor now showed what he had just watched, but moving backward. He didn't want to be caught here, he wouldn't be able to explain. He speeded up the disc, hoping he could stop it in time whenever a body on foot, or a car that might be Charlie's, flashed into view. There shouldn't be many such images, it had been the middle of the night at the motel.

Waiting. Waiting. Eyes straining in the darkness. Nothing significant. Then, finally, on the monitor, Natalie's motel room door was thrown open from the inside. Shaftoe felt bone-rattling anticipation. Whoops—too fast, missed something. He hit Pause, and returned the disc to the part he'd barely glimpsed. He hit slow forward and again saw Natalie's motel room door thrown open. That must have been just after Charlie gave up trying to pressure her into some sex act, beat her up, and decided on a fast exit. The motel room door jolted to a stop as a figure, grainy, ghost-like, and head down, flew out, ran to a late model-car, and peeled toward the street. Shaftoe slowed the images. Now he could make out Charlie's face, behind the steering wheel. Shaftoe stared. He leaned toward the monitor. His eyes ached, his brows arched, his mouth dropped open. He knew that face! That professional attire, that scarf. Charlie was . . . a woman! Charlie, who'd beaten up Natalie for a sex act she wouldn't accede to . . . was . . . Dr. Juliet Mallard, his psychotherapist!

Shaftoe had to get away from that image. He jumped up and ran, to escape it. Out of Fluke's office, back toward his own office, through the counseling center, out of the building, onto the rain-slicked sidewalk. He heard footsteps. Oh, my God! And then . . . and then . . . What? All sensations left his body.

chapter thirty six

"Feeling better, Mr. Shaftoe?"

"What?"

"How do you feel, Mr. Shaftoe?"

"Destroyed."

Crisp sheets. He was on a bed, not his own. His eyes slowly focused. He saw a young woman standing next to him, wearing hospital scrubs, holding a clipboard. Just behind her, a sturdy white curtain hanging from a shiny silver rod. The young woman reached to pull it closed. The curtain rings made a little screeching sound. The noise assaulted his ears. He smelled an antiseptic; it stung his nostrils. Things looked blurry, he began blinking. Then he knew—he was in a hospital.

Now, in Shaftoe's imagination a horrible image of Juliet Mallard battering Natalie flickered. Then— Fluke's office, a security disc player, himself running away from it, through the rain. Footsteps near him. Then . . . nothing.

He heard himself mumble, "I heard footsteps."

The scream of a siren rattled his bed. It was very close. Its horrible warning groaned slowly to a stop. His eyes weren't focusing right. Spinning red light reflected on the ceiling above him, then stopped moving. He knew he was on an emergency room bed. "Still feeling anxious, Mr. Shaftoe? You can rest here for a while. This is a safe place. I'm Rosalie. I'm an RN." She smiled. "Do you have a psychotherapist?"

Psychotherapist? Shaftoe's stomach seized. He thought he was going to puke.

"I used to. Not any fuckin' more." In his ears, his voice sounded loud and distorted. Like the scream of the ambulance siren.

What was he seeing in Rosalie's eyes? Fear? Pity? Compassion? All of that?

She seemed to be composing herself. Now she was holding up a prescription pill bottle like pharmacists give people. "Mr. Shaftoe, as soon as you can, call a mental health professional. Read him or her the label on this bottle, including 'take no more than one every six hours.' Make an appointment to see him or her as soon as you can. If that's not possible, it's important that you come back here."

What did she mean by "if that's not possible"? Did Rosalie think he was incapable of making an appointment? She seemed to be turning more distant. He hated her. Another heartless professional bitch. Like Mallard.

Now Shaftoe's eyesight and mind were clearing; those were going to be okay. But he knew that his emotions would not be okay—ever.

The nurse handed Shaftoe the bottle of pills. As she began leaving the room, she said, "If you feel steady now, your friend can take you home."

"Friend?"

"Your friend . . ." Rosalie looked at her clipboard, "Your friend. At 10:00 p.m. he brought you here. Kent Greef."

"It's okay, Bobby." Now Shaftoe saw Kent sitting on a metal chair at the foot of his bed. "You slipped in the rain, fell, and hit your head. The footsteps you heard weren't the Grim Reaper, buddy, just me."

"Thank God."

"Yeah, I was coming from Entonces' gay bar. Left early. No action there tonight. Got lost on my way home."

Shaftoe thought, Entonces is too backward to have a gay bar. And too small for any driver to get lost. Kent's putting me on.

"Fuck you, Kent."

"Ooh, nice way to talk to someone who saved your ass. Okay. I'd just bought a gallon of ice cream at Seven-Eleven. I noticed your car by itself in the faculty lot. So I walked over to campus and saw a monitor flicker, and then a flashlight beam going crazy. Shaftoe, for an office invader your stealth skills aren't for shit. Here's your friggin' flashlight. And here's your disc. *Counselor Shaftoe Rescues Ms. Barney*? Some title! Found a way to record your wet dreams, huh? I didn't watch it. And I put everything back like Fluke must have left it. So he can watch porn at work if he wants to."

"Not funny."

"Sorry. But because of you, my ice cream's melting in my car. The important thing is, you're gonna be okay and no one's gonna know you were playing a disc in Fluke's office."

"Thanks." From his bed, Shaftoe looked around. "What about me being here? The pill bottle?"

"Well, when I found you, out cold on the sidewalk, you kept muttering 'Charlie' as if that name were important. That didn't make sense, so when I brought you here, I told the nurse you were the nervous type and might need something to calm you down."

"Nervous type! Bullshit." But Shaftoe knew that Kent had done the right thing. Shaftoe's head was still filled with images from the security disk. "Psych ward would have been next?"

"Maybe." Kent looked as if he were pausing to think. "Emergency room records are confidential, Bobby. But you'll have to pay out of pocket; we don't want the district-sponsored health plan to know about this, do we. Accept the damn pills and let's get outta here."

chapter thirty seven

From the emergency room, Kent drove Shaftoe to the faculty parking lot. From there, Shaftoe drove himself home.

He collapsed onto his bed, and woke up early the next morning in still rain- dampened clothes, feeling as if there were insects moving under his skin and a thunderstorm in his stomach.

A fragment of a funeral march edged into his foggy consciousness.

I'm haunted. You're always with me . . .

In his mind, he labeled his excruciating symptoms of crawling skin and roiling stomach *the heebie-jeebies.* Was he going crazy? He got out of bed, shed his clothing, walked naked to the sofa, picked up his phone, and called Sweet Jillie. He told her he wouldn't be coming to work today—the flu.

"Oh, I heard that was going around, Mr. Shaftoe . . . . "

He wondered if Jillie suspected his excuse was phony and was making things easy for him.

". . . I hope you get well quick. We'll miss you."

He didn't have to fake a feeble tone of voice. "Thanks."

"Oh, Mr. Shaftoe, did you know that Ms. Barney isn't coming back?"

"What?"

"She sent resignation papers to the district office today."

Christ! But he felt too sick to be surprised. Things had been going from bad to worse. At least Natalie was apparently alive.

"She left a forwarding address."

Hope. "What is it?"

"It's in Hawaii . . ."

Too far away. Shaftoe's symptoms worsened.

". . . Maui, Mr. Shaftoe. Wow, what a change. From little old Entonces to glamorous Maui. The address is 'in care of' . . ."

Shaftoe thought he knew what was coming next.

Jillie's sweet voice continued, " . . . in care of? Something . . . Miller? No. Mallard. In care of . . . Juliet Mallard."

Shaftoe felt like a little bear putting up a hopeless fight against a predator. Having his guts ripped out.

Dying despite his best efforts to survive.

"Mr. Shaftoe . . .? Are you still there?"

He disconnected.

I'm haunted . . .

As performed by The Heebie-Jeebies, Shaftoe thought as he shrank back into his sofa.

chapter thirty eight

Shaftoe put on dry boxer shorts and a tee shirt. Now he realized it had been a mistake to call in sick. He was alone with the heebie-jeebies, on the sofa in his apartment, with no activities to distract him. He flipped his TV on. After fifteen minutes he realized he had no memory of what he'd been staring at. He took a paperback novel off his bookshelf. After ten minutes, same realization. He looked at his wall clock, uncapped the prescription bottle the hospital had given him, shook out a pill, walked the few steps to his kitchen sink, and ran some water into a glass. After all, six hours had gone by, it was time. He thought about calling a mental health professional; he felt that he needed a psychotherapist, a replacement for Mallard. He shivered. No, not exactly a replacement. Someone much better, someone he could trust. But who? Not just anyone from the Yellow Pages. He had trouble swallowing the pill. It didn't go down easily, and it left a metallic taste in his mouth. To wash the taste away, he chugged the water remaining in the glass.

Then he glanced at the pills left in the bottle. How long would they last?

Damn! The man of Natalie's dreams had not been him. The man of Natalie's dreams had been a woman. And a cruel and heartless one at that. The clues all added up now. And the Maui *In Care Of* had nailed it.

He was suffocating. He had to get out of his apartment. He needed the company of someone who knew at least part of his devastating story and had accepted it well. Hmm. That might be Kent Greef. He phoned Kent's number. No answer. He left a message, "Kent, thanks for helping me last night. Please call me ASAP."

Shaftoe returned to his sofa, dropped into it and channel-surfed into a documentary about mental illness. Maybe the documentary would give him an answer to the heebie-jeebies that ruled him. Unlike the earlier TV program and the paperback novel, he found it easy to concentrate on this particular documentary. But it revealed no answer to his suffering. Now forty-five minutes had gone by since popping the magic pill, and the heebie-jeebies were at a tolerable level. Shaftoe was starting to feel somewhat normal.

His phone rang.

"Bobby, how ya doin'?"

"Kent, I think I'm rejoining the living. At least once every six hours for the time being."

"Ya call a mental health professional?"

"No."

"Ya better do it. I don't need one. I passed my ink blot test with a perfect score."

"There is no score for an ink blot test, Kent."

"And I never took that test. But you know what I mean. All us football trivia freaks get perfect ink blot scores."

"Even Ed Zachary?"

"Not him."

"This is a horseshit conversation . . ."

Greef affected a French accent. "It is to laugh."

But Shaftoe didn't feel like laughing. "Listen, I want to thank you for hauling me off the campus last night."

"You're welcome. Now . . . you need to reimburse me for my melted ice cream . . ."

"Forget you, Kent."

"Nice talk. You're at it again." Kent sounded relieved.

If Kent thought he could make it through this, maybe he could. "Yeah. And I need a drink. Ya want one? I could meet you at the Wagon Wheel at 7:00 tonight."

A silence.

"Okay. But should you be having alcohol,

considering what must be in those magic mushroom capsules the hospital gave you?"

"I'll risk it."

"Okay, you're a grownup. See you at seven. Wagon Wheel. You need someone to watch over you; you're trouble, counselor. See you at . . ." Kent paused and faked a syrupy voice to finish the sentence, ". . . our special table."

"Fuck you very much, Kent. See you at seven." Shaftoe figured that he'd be taking a pill just before that. A good thing, he suspected. He wondered if a pill every six hours would become a lifestyle.

As time passed in his apartment, Shaftoe reviewed all the clues that should have told him that Juliet Mallard was "Charlie." Why had he been so stupid. He went through them again and again. Would he ever think of anything else?

Later, he forced himself to do some paperwork he'd been keeping at home. It was difficult to concentrate. Memory problems. He had to read each page several times. Then it was time to meet Kent Greef.

That evening, in the midst of a few other patrons, neon beer signs, the smell of alcohol, mournful recorded country music, and a second round of drinks at their table, he and Kent continued their conversation. "So, Bobby, you're telling me that the disc from the motel security camera had to be played on Fluke's hardware? That's why you sneaked into his office in the dark?"

"Yep."

"And on the disc, you saw that 'Charlie' was really your psychotherapist, Juliet Mallard? Jesus!"

"Yeah—the bitch. I thought she was helping me learn to love. And all the while, she was Natalie's sadistic sex partner. Christ!"

"For you, tough day in the office, huh, Bobby?"

"Goddamn right. More specifically, nightmare time in Fluke's office."

Kent said, "Ya know the saying, 'The truth will set you free, but first you will hurt like hell.'"

Shaftoe cringed. After a minute, he waved toward the bartender. Then he walked to the bar to bring fresh drinks back to their table. Shaftoe thought, the bartender still has the same tattoo. A drawing of a cherry with words below it. *Here's mine, where's yours?* Of *course* it's still the same tattoo. Unchanging. Something I can count on? Upon this rock I stand? Upon this cherry I stand? He shuddered. Am I so fucking unstable that I'm finding security in the words, Here's my cherry, where's yours? Damn. He thought of Poe's words, "I became insane, with long intervals of horrible sanity." He decided to keep all that to himself.

"Listen, Kent, I gotta tell you more. If it's too much

to listen to, tell me to shut up." Shaftoe took several deep, slow, calming breaths. Audibly.

"Any reason you're breathing, Bobby?"

"What?" No, Shaftoe couldn't think of any reason he should continue to breathe; his life seemed to have ended. Then he realized that wasn't what Kent had meant.

Kent continued, "So Charlie turned out to be a woman, huh? Christ, you straight people lead complicated lives."

"We straight people? Me and Natalie? Natalie turned out to be bisexual at best!"

"Bisexual is *best?*"

"Not *is* best! '*at* best'! Damn it. I was using a figure of speech."

"Oh . . . You're not giving Natalie the benefit of the doubt? Maybe she's straight again."

Was Kent serious? "No benefit of the doubt. There were too many clues I missed. Or maybe just ignored." Shaftoe felt his anxiety rise despite the recent pill. His next words were almost too intimate to say. "I was in love." He plunged ahead, stuttering, "The . . . the . . . first woman I ever loved."

"I can see how that would hurt." Thank goodness, Kent hadn't ridiculed him. "You said 'clues,' Bobby?"

"Yes. A whole ship load of clues. Listen . . . You want 'em in chronological order?"

"That'd be easier for my feeble mind."

Shaftoe groped into the front pocket of his pants.

"Got an itch, Bobby?"

He extracted a slip of paper on which he'd written all the red flags that should have told him that "Charlie" was Juliet Mallard, and that Natalie was sexually involved with her. He'd hoped that by committing his recollections to paper he could get them off his mind, and his self-blame—for being a fool—out of his heart. It hadn't worked. He was painfully aware of every item, without the list. He tore up the paper and shoved the remnants back into his pocket. Can't let someone find these humiliating shards and piece them together. Lord, am I paranoid? Who would care that much about my life.

"Okay, Kent." Shaftoe looked at both their glasses. Still nearly full. That's important, he thought, I can continue talking without Kent or me having to leave the table to get more drinks. He stared at the garish beer signs, their neon colors penetrating the indoor gloom.

Then a voice screamed out, as if from between clenched teeth, "Okay, Mom, you were always trying to get me out of the house. . . . Well, here I am Mom, out of the house!" It was Shaftoe's own voice! Terrified by his unexpected words, he jumped up. His chair fell over. He yelled at the patrons, "You can run but you can't hide!" They turned and looked at him like he was crazy.

"Christ, Bobby. You want to go home?"

"Not home. That's the worst place."

"No, Bobby, I mean back to your apartment."

"Oh." Shaftoe tried to soothe himself. He was only partially successful. He righted his chair and sat down. "No, Kent. I gotta get this out. Now."

He began what felt like a confession.

chapter thirty nine

"Okay, Kent. Here goes." Shaftoe knew he was stalling. What he had to put into words would hurt. More than hurt.

"You forgot to say, Forgive me Father Greef, for I have sinned."

"Go to hell."

"I may. Too soon to say. But first I want to coach the varsity."

"Never happen."

Somehow, their joking made it easier for Shaftoe to reveal what his agony was pressing him to share.

"Here goes. For starters, when Natalie . . ." It hurt even to say her name. He started again, "When she and I were just getting acquainted she said, 'Maybe someday I'll tell you more. If I have the courage, or the integrity, or whatever.' That was clue number one that Natalie had a secret."

Shaftoe had begun his recital. In his ears his own tense, stilted, delivery sounded like a terrified vocal student beginning to struggle through a song he was scared to death of.

He concentrated on Kent's facial expression and body language. Greef better not show any scorn for my plight, or that'll be the end of my trying to tell anything to anyone.

Kent said nothing. He looked receptive and concerned. As a school counselor, Shaftoe'd looked into the eyes of a lot of people. Kent's eyes had a look of . . . of what? Of . . . understanding. Shaftoe was sure Kent couldn't fake that.

"Then one day in Mallard's office, I was telling her how great . . . the . . . lovemaking was with Natalie." Shaftoe had qualms about making himself so vulnerable, but Kent was still respecting his halting delivery. "And I swear, Mallard was getting turned on—you know, squirming around, lips parted, stroking her legs, kind of panting. Well, I thought she was putting herself in the place of Natalie in bed, feeling aroused. I hadn't given Natalie's name to Mallard at that point—but now I think that Mallard . . . *Charlie* . . . was identifying with *me*, being assertive, putting it to a woman."

Kent moved his head slowly from side to side, then nodded. "I get it."

"Then—the big clue, but I was too slow to see Mallard conning me—Mallard told me I was a lost cause."

"How so?"

"You know—that I'd never learn to really love. That I'd always be too sick. That I was stuck. A hopeless case. To make her point she even followed it up with an inappropriate quote from a holocaust survivor."

"A low blow from a therapist to a vulnerable client. Unprofessional."

"To say the least, but I took it all to heart at the time."

"Of course. She was an expert and you'd put your faith in her."

"You got it. Oh, Christ, I forgot to tell you something. That all happened—the ego-crusher—at the appointment when I first told Mallard that my lover's name was 'Natalie.' Mallard kind of dropped her mouth open and blinked a lot. Then she stuttered 'Nat . . . Natalie?' and in a split second said, 'You've got to give up that . . . that . . . *teacher*!' Kent, how the hell would Mallard know that Natalie was a teacher? I never told her that!"

"She knew because . . ." Kent looked closely at Shaftoe's face as if judging whether to confirm what Shaftoe had finally concluded about Natalie and Juliet Mallard, ". . . because she and Natalie knew each other. They'd already been lovers."

Shaftoe felt his eyes welling up. He felt sadness, anger, and betrayal. He'd been had by Mallard—royally. He pondered whether to say what was now on his mind. It was as if the words would be superfluous. Or maybe he just didn't want to voice the awfulness.

Kent saved him the agony, "Mallard was trying to emotionally wreck you, to get you out of her and Natalie's life! You were a rival in Mallard's erotic life with Natalie."

Shaftoe shuddered and nodded. He took a sip of his drink. As he held the glass in his shaky hand, he watched the liquid slosh. Putting both hands on the glass to steady it, he carefully set it down. "Later, I tried to get in touch with Natalie, I tried everywhere. Then, same thing with Mallard, just a note on her office door, when I finally looked for her there."

"And it said . . . ?"

"It said, Sorry, your therapist is Out of Order. Go to hell, sucker."

"That figures."

"Actually, it said something like, Dr. Mallard is temporarily unavailable. If this is an emergency, call 911."

"Cold. The minimum a therapist can do when dumping a client."

"For sure, and there was a subtler clue on the note, Mallard's signature." Shaftoe moved his hand in small loops, as if writing. "*J. Char* . . . something." He threw both hands into the air, "She was a hell of a sloppy writer."

"J. for Juliet, Bobby, the name she went by professionally. And 'Char"—that must have been her middle name. 'Char' was the beginning four letters of what?"

"Damned if I knew. Charlotte? Charmaine? Charlene? But later it made me think of *Charlie*— the name she went by when she was being sexually aggressive, and sadistic, with Natalie."

"What?"

Shaftoe realized that he'd never told Kent about the night when Natalie, beaten up and abandoned at the motel by Mallard/Charlie, had phoned him. With a remnant of pride, he told Kent how Natalie'd trusted him to rescue her, adding, "But all along, I thought that Charlie was a guy."

"Who wouldn't? How could you know otherwise?"

"Because I should have put it all together!"

"Put it together because when you first met, Natalie suggested she had a secret? Put it together because Mallard seemed to be having an orgasm when you told her how great your yet-to-be-named girlfriend was in bed? You just now told me that you wrongly assumed that Mallard was imagining that she, Mallard, was *getting* the goodies, not giving them out.

And then *Char* on the note, Bobby? That's weak. It could have been a coincidence."

"Coincidence? Oh my God, that's not all. In the middle of everything I've just told you, I saw something by coincidence—a big coincidence! Well, I went into a very dark bar near Mallard's office, in Capitol City and there was this woman on a bar stool, with her back to me, flirting with the bartender. I couldn't see her very well, but she was definitely coming on to him, I could hear that much. I think they'd been bed partners in the past. Then he turned down her offer. The bartender's words didn't make sense to me at the time; he said, 'Charlie kept getting in the way.' And when the woman on the bar stool stomped out, right past me, when light came in the door, I saw her face. It was Mallard! Now I know what 'Charlie kept getting in the way' must have meant. The bartender'd had too many instances of Mallard wanting to be the sadistic aggressor Charlie, as she'd been with Natalie."

"He'd gotten whipsawed too many times, Bobby. He was asking himself 'Is this woman even bed partner material?' He'd seen her wanting to be sadistic Charlie in bed with him."

"Maybe. And maybe he knew that he'd never have her all to himself because she was being Charlie with other people, like with Natalie."

Kent said, "That bartender in Capitol City didn't want to feel like part of a trio: Himself, Mallard, and Charlie. Something like your situation turned out to be, Bobby? Yourself, Natalie, and Mallard. Same cards in the deck, except they were dealt differently to you. The bartender knew who Charlie really was, but you didn't, right? Then later you finally saw it, right?"

"It's too fucking much to think about."

"Good choice of words, Bobby."

"And now they've run off together."

"Mallard and the Capitol City bartender ran off together?"

"No, Kent, you fool. Mallard and Natalie. To nirvana. Maui. Thinking they'll live happily ever after, no doubt."

"Maui? Are you clairvoyant? Otherwise, you're getting carried away by your broken heart."

"No. Natalie resigned from the district. Sweet Jillie has her forwarding address. Maui. Care of Juliet Mallard."

"Double-plus-fuck, Bobby!"

"To say the least. End of story." But Shaftoe knew he was pining for Natalie, and he might be forever.

chapter fourty

Now there'd been a long silence between Shaftoe and Kent. The neon beer signs at the Wagon Wheel were beginning to look creepy. And they seemed to be pulsing in time to the recorded country music. Was that a warning? An aura? Maybe the heebie-jeebies were returning. Time for another pill? Shaftoe looked at his watch. No, not yet, dammit.

The Wagon Wheel bartender signaled as if to say, Want more drinks? Shaftoe waved him off.

Then, "Listen, Bobby, ya gotta get your mind off yourself. First you're threatened by Ed Zachary, then your therapist destroys you, and now your girlfriend's run away with her. It's all about *you* . . ."

"About *me*? Yeah, buddy, it's only my job, my love life, and my soul at stake! Of course it's about me. You'd feel the same, pal."

"Wait a minute! You think I've never been insecure in a job, or worried about myself? And you think I've never had a broken heart?"

Shaftoe felt burning chagrin. I'm thinking of Kent like he's always been some kind of carefree gay playboy. How stupid can I be?

"I'm sorry, Kent. That was really thoughtless of me. I apologize."

"Yeah, Bobby. Being a gay man, I get stereotyped a lot."

Shaftoe knew his face was red. He hoped the darkness of the Wagon Wheel concealed it. There was silence, except for the music and sounds from the bar—a clinking of glasses and a murmur of wry laughter. To give himself something to do, he stared into his drink.

Finally Kent spoke again, "Anyway, as I was saying before I was so rudely characterized as blissful, secure in all my jobs over the years, and never having experienced love and a broken heart . . ."

Shaftoe knew that he deserved that rebuke.

" . . . as I was saying, Bobby ya gotta get your mind off yourself, find a larger purpose. Maybe do some good for society at large."

"Christ, during the school year, I'm an overworked counselor, I do good by helping a ton of kids."

"True, but I mean go beyond that, make an impact not just on individuals, but on a larger scale—something that matters to society at large."

Shaftoe stared at Kent. He thought, Kent's implying that I have a limited capacity for doing good. During my suffering, Kent's overloading me. I've never been a social activist on a large scale. No marches and protests for me. And I don't know how to organize things like that. I don't have leadership skills or charisma.

Now it was Shaftoe's turn to be sarcastic. "Oh, I get it, Kent. 'Something that matters to society at large.' Like, If we can put a man on the moon, why can't we build a men's room partition that a drunk can't kick off the wall? Right?"

Kent's eyes glimmered; he appreciated the gag. "An indestructible men's room partition? No, Bobby, that's too small a scale. Anyway, I don't think you have the mechanical aptitude."

"No mechanical aptitude? Ya got that right." Shaftoe put on a look that he hoped Kent would perceive as thoughtful. After a few seconds, he yelped, "World Peace."

Kent seemed to know that Shaftoe felt pressured by him. "Bobby, you're gonna lead the world to peace? Naw, now you're goin' too *big*." Kent chuckled. "You don't have the global vision or the persuasive skills to round up a few million followers."

"Too small? Too big? Dang! Kent, you make me feel like Goldilocks. . . ."

"Goldilocks? Nothing wrong with that." Kent burlesqued a limp flip of the wrist.

"Now who's stereotyping whom?

"Touche'."

"Kent, you make me feel like that fairy tale . . ."

"Fairy? Watch your tongue."

"Allow me to start over. I mean . . . like that children's story—my building an indestructible men's room partition would be 'too small,' and my leading the world to peace would be 'too big.' Kent, what would be 'just right'?"

Could they really be having this nutty conversation! Maybe it was the drinks talking.

But Kent seemed serious. "Bobby, you've got a good mind, it's just a little slow on the draw. Think about your mission, you'll figure something out."

"Listen, Kent. Don't go all idealistic on me. I've heard it before, 'Do unto others . . .' I've tried that for years. It hasn't worked. First Zachary, then Mallard, and now Natalie."

"Bobby, I'm not talking idealism. I'm talking survival. Find something big enough to get your mind off yourself and save your ass from the psych ward."

"A big challenge? Maybe like improving my disposition? Being more cheery? The kids' parents would like that. But it ain't gonna happen. I was born without the cheeriness gene."

"Right. And that might be a good thing for your job. Unless you've been through some serious stuff yourself, how can you understand what the kids are going through?"

Shaftoe was surprised to hear himself say, "So you and I are on the same page now?"

"Not yet, Bobby. No matter what your disposition, you gotta get your mind off yourself to save your ass from the funny farm, and you gotta save your ass from Zachary. Maybe you can kill those two birds with one stone."

"What? Kill those two birds with one stone? I don't get it."

"Think about it."

chapter fourty one

Shaftoe excused himself to pee. Standing at the urinal in the Wagon Wheel, he stared at the sign on the wall that was inches from his face, Please Do Not Throw Cigarette Butts Into Urinal. Next to it some clown had written, *It maks them sogie and hard to lite.* He noticed that his urine had a new smell, very acrid and disgusting. It must be the residue from those pills the hospital gave him. He glanced at his watch; not time for another pill yet. He looked at the metal partition at his elbow. It was dented and hanging by one bolt. How many of those had he seen. Some drunk must have kicked it off the wall. Figured.

Standing there, Shaftoe was thinking about improving the town of Entonces. What project might he pull off? He didn't want to bite off more than he could chew. Something might be achievable if he could dream up a plan to make it happen.

He finished at the urinal, zipped up, returned to the table, sat down, and said to Kent, "Something for the good of this town?"

"Not *my* words, Bobby."

"But this town is beyond redemption. Look at all its dirty laundry. A newspaper publisher who prints too many pages about the town's championship high school football teams. A weak-kneed school board and principal, all under the thumb of Coach Zachary. Zachary's corrupt. And he pushed his son so hard that the kid cheated his way out of being varsity quarterback. And over-age, out-of-state ringers, brought in every year strictly to continue Zachary's championship run. For example, look at . . ." Shaftoe had almost said "Skoo." Oops, he wanted to solve that mystery himself. He rephrased his last sentence, "Look at Felix Anthony Blanchard, or whatever his real name might be." Shaftoe's gut told him that he needed to do something about all that. And time was running out to get Blanchard's transcript, to make him eligible for the opening game that's coming up next week, the week before classes start. Christ, next week. Time is running out!

Kent was looking at him intently, as if he expected Shaftoe to draw some conclusion from his own words. Finally, Kent asked him, "There's no way to make this town better?"

Shaftoe thought, What do I have the capacity to influence that's larger than myself? Make this town better? That task felt impossible. But he realized that he hadn't agonized over Natalie while trying to solve the koan that Kent had posed for him. He suspected that was a sign of progress.

He was surprised to hear himself say, "Kent, I'll think about it."

He was feeling better now. He decided to skip the next pill.

chapter fourty two

Back at his apartment that night, Shaftoe walked to his sofa and sat down. He clicked the TV on. Then, without looking at the screen, clicked it off. The apartment seemed eerily quiet, and he wondered if he could feel comfortable in this much quiet. Without distractions—like the work he loved, and the coach he hated; and fantasies, like images of Natalie, and getting vengeance on Ed Zachary—could he tolerate having only himself for company? Without his willing it, his foot began a jittery bounce as he sat.

He considered saying the secret mantra that he'd paid a guru to teach him years ago. Sometimes it settled his vague and restless feelings, even allowed him to sleep.

He got up, went to the refrigerator, opened the door, and stared inside. He wondered if he had a little light bulb like that in his head, that lit up when his thinking was productive, and went out when his mind had shut down. Is that what "closed-minded" meant—the light went out when you closed your mind; and then you had no productive thoughts? Shaftoe's brain was beginning to hurt. He was getting nowhere with his thoughts. Damn! He took nothing out of the refrigerator, then slammed its door shut.

What kind of thinking would be productive? How could he advance the development of mankind? Or at least reduce the odds of Zachary destroying him with the coach's latest threat, the false Suspected Child Abuse Report?

A cartoon came to Shaftoe's mind: Two dogs in business suits, at a bar. What the hell. More wasted thought. One was saying to the other, "It's not enough that dogs win. All cats must die." What did that mean in Shaftoe's miserable situation? Well, sometimes the sun does shine on a hound dog's ass, he thought. Was he a dog? Maybe. "Dogs win?" Zachary's child abuse blackmail scheme could be snookered by the proof-of-innocence locker room video that Shaftoe had tricked Zeus into coughing up. Zachary didn't know that the video existed. Was the video a win for Shaftoe? Maybe. "All cats must die?" Was Zachary like a cat? Nine lives? Maybe. How long had Zachary been corrupt and abusive—nine years? And now Shaftoe needed to finish him off?

He knew he felt like killing Zachary's evil influence on him, on the high school, and on the community. But how?

He thought, What's still unexplained about the coach's behavior? Well . . . mystery item one, the continuing lack of transfer papers for Felix Anthony "Skoo" Blanchard, one of Zachary's ringers, who might be the oldest potential high school football player that Shaftoe'd ever seen. Felix Anthony "Skoo" Blanchard— an unlikely name and nickname. Also known as—*whom*?

And mystery item two? Wait. Wait. Was there even a mystery item two? Hmm. Maybe repeating his mantra would work like hypnosis by a detective, to help a witness remember vital facts. *Rama lama ding dong?* No, Bobby, stop joking, that's not your mantra. Is it *Harry Kushner, Harry Ramos?* No those were the fathers of two of his counselees. Ya gotta try to recall mystery item two, it might do some good for society. At least this quest was keeping away the heebie jeebies.

Then his mantra came to him. It was *caveat emptor.* What the hell. *Buyer beware?* Immediately he wondered if he had paid his guru too much for that particular mantra. Nonetheless, he returned to the sofa, closed his eyes, and used the mantra to begin meditating: *caveat emptor, caveat emptor.* It felt good. As he started to empty his mind, some insignificant thoughts crowded in along with his mantra. *Caveat emptor. Dog. Caveat emptor. Cat. Caveat emptor. My karma ran over your dogma. Caveat emptor. Corn flakes. Indy 500.* He let the extraneous words drift away. Ahhh. Ahhh.

Then . . . *Schoolage.* Another word without relevance. Was *Schoolage* even a real word'? Where the hell did *Schoolage* come from? Shaftoe waited. Oh yeah. The word *Schoolage* was hand-written on the computer-printed phony accusation of sodomy—the Zachary-created document that the coach had titled "Encedint Report" and waved around during Shaftoe's meeting with Principal Fluke, Zachary, and the teachers union rep. Shaftoe had grabbed that paper away from Zachary and stuffed it in his shirt pocket. Was it still there?

He opened his eyes, leaped to his feet and dashed to his closet. Ten minutes later, he realized that the document with the computer-printed word *School,* sloppily revised by hand to *Schoolage,* was nowhere to be found. Damn!

chapter fourty three

The next week, back in his cramped office, Shaftoe found that the word *Schoolage* was still stuck in his mind.

Sweet Jillie was standing at the counter of the counseling center, sorting some papers. "Sweet Jillie," Shaftoe said, surprised that his words came out in a throaty whisper, "can you come over here and help me with something strange?" Christ, who would word something that way? He felt like a flasher in a dark alley.

Sweet Jillie, with her usual trusting—if not admiring—expression, walked over to his office. Shaftoe motioned for her to sit in the chair, still just outside his doorway, facing him. It had been a long time—well, the first eight weeks of the nine-week summer vacation—since a counselee had sat in that chair. He looked at Jillie for a few more seconds than was polite. She was wearing a short summer dress that Zachary would have drooled over. Shaftoe could imagine how cute she must have been as a teenager. He smiled. He decided not to tell her what he was thinking.

Jillie looked at him as if she were reading his mind. Her eyes sparkled. "Yes, Mr. Shaftoe?"

Shaftoe wondered what to say next. Had he painted himself into a corner?

"Umm," he would rather have continued enjoying looking at Jillie, "Well . . . Jillie, did you ever get something stuck in your mind, and it wouldn't go away?"

"You mean like a tune, or words to a silly song, Mr. Shaftoe?"

He wished she wouldn't always call him Mr. Shaftoe, it seemed so formal. But that was par for the course at Entonces High. Employees had learned that if students heard them address one another by first names, there would be peals of teenage laughter, or rumors would spread that a male and female employee were having a clandestine romance. Sometimes the rumors were true. He wondered if she was a single mom. He and she had never had time to talk about that. He thought of the book, *The Single Working Mother*, with a phony author's name, Erasmus B. Dragon. What the hell, this wasn't what he wanted to talk about with Sweet Jillie. Then he realized that he didn't remember the words that Jillie had just spoken.

She looked at him curiously. Perhaps a bit concerned. For some reason he liked that look.

"You mean like a tune, or silly words, Mr. Shaftoe? You know what I mean?"

"Exactly, Jillie." Oh good, she'd had the same experience. She totally understood. How gratifying it was to communicate so perfectly. What a profound sense of satisfaction to share the same experience so completely.

"Gosh, no, Mr. Shaftoe. I've heard people talk about that, but it never happened to me."

Dang.

"Well, anyway Jillie, it's happening to me. I have this word 'Schoolage' stuck in my mind. Over and over again." He bobbed his head and rolled his eyes, trying to make his state of mind completely clear to her.

Jillie watched him closely. "You got a crick in your neck, Mr. Shaftoe?"

Shaftoe felt stupid.

"No. It's just that the repeating word is driving me nuts." He wondered if it was okay for a school counselor to use the expression "driving me nuts" with his counseling office clerk. He didn't want to damage his professional image. Did he have a professional image? Custodian of Records? Did that image include a broom and a dustpan?

"Gee, Mr. Shaftoe. That sounds awful."

"Yeah."

"What's the word, Mr. Shaftoe?"

Sweet Jillie was setting a new world's record for saying "Mr. Shaftoe," the most times in two minutes. But he liked the way she said it.

"The word is 'Schoolage.'" He felt like a quiz master giving a baffled contestant the answer to a question.

"What?"

"The word is Schoolage."

"Schoolage, Mr. Shaftoe?"

Shaftoe reflected on this conversation. Had he invested five years of college and countless tuition dollars to become a counselor so that he and another intelligent human being could have this inane dialogue about a nonsense word?

"Yeah, Sweet Jillie, one of our esteemed colleagues used it on a document." Shaftoe was sorry he'd ever brought the subject up.

"Never heard of it . . ."

He didn't wait to see if she was going to add "Mr. Shaftoe."

"Sorry I mentioned it." He wanted to get himself out of this.

"Have you googled it, Mr. Shaftoe?"

"What? Google it? Duh . . . my bad." He tried to burlesque a stupid look. Then he was afraid that Sweet Jillie had seen it exactly like his usual look. "Google it.

That's a good idea, Jillie. I'm gonna take a break, then I'll get right after it. Thanks."

He stood up. He saw Jillie smile as she headed back to the counseling center counter. Shaftoe went to the men's room, sat down in a stall, shut the door, and thought about how ridiculous he must have seemed.

Returning to his office, Shaftoe thought, I'm still embarrassed. Embarrassed that I didn't think to do a computer search for the word *schoolage* until Sweet Jillie suggested it.

Schoolage. The baffling word Zachary hand-printed onto the phony form he concocted to fool Principal Fluke, that false "Encedint Report" that said I'd allowed a student to sodomize me. Damn! Why had Zachary repeatedly replaced "school" with *schoolage*?

But now I've got a bigger problem—Zachary's new threat. He filled in a false Suspected Child Abuse Report on me and he might be withholding it—to blackmail me. But blackmail me into doing *what?* I'll bet to blackmail me into letting Felix "Skoo" Blanchard play football, transfer papers or not.

Skoo. Schoolage. Both weird words. Was there a relationship between them?

Those words could be the key to whatever Zachary was up to with Blanchard. But what does *schoolage* mean?

Shaftoe held his breath and typed "schoolage" into the search box on his computer screen. In an instant, the result was displayed.

Schoolage. The age set by law for children to start school attendance. Or, The period of school attendance required by law.

Shaftoe thought, Damn! That was no help. Nothing sinister about that. Why the hell would Zachary repeatedly cross out "school" and hand-print *schoolage* instead? A misunderstanding of English usage? Not likely from Zachary, no matter how crude he appeared on the surface. A misspelling? I've never seen a six-letter word like "school" misspelled into a nine-letter word like *schoolage.*

Not a misunderstanding of English usage. Not a misspelling. What the hell. Why else might Zachary change the word "school" to *schoolage* on the phony form? Did Zachary have an aversion to the word "school"?

Hmm . . . an aversion. Was Coach phobic about the word "school"? Why would that be?

chapter fourty four

The next week, rushing to schedule students and print slips of paper to guide each student to classes next week, Shaftoe lost track of time. And outside his awareness, Friday rolled around.

He stared at the blank wall next to his desk, where the school district could have put a window, but hadn't. After a while he thought, I don't know what to do next. But I wanna be the sole person to finally get the goods on Zachary. To put the last nail in Zachary's coffin. I gotta get to the bottom of this to save my reputation and save my job. Hell . . . to save my self-respect!

Shaftoe pounded his fist on his desk. His computer bounced. He half expected the screen to go blank, and smoke and flames to arise from the keyboard.

"Is everything alright. Mr. Shaftoe?" Jillie said from her desk across the room.

Shaftoe thought, No, everything is all wrong, Jillie, and I want to get out of here. Without answering, he lurched to his feet, darted across his door sill, strode past Sweet Jillie, slammed through the swinging gate at the end of the counseling center counter, left campus, and walked to lunch.

At Miracle Burger, he ordered the lowest-calorie burger he could find, and told himself that it was still too fattening. He sat at a booth, feeling tense. He'd struck out with his attempt to discover the significance of *schoolage*. He thought, That's only my most recent failure in a lifetime of failures. I was a lonely child, and a mediocre college wrestler, and I've been dumped by my psychotherapist, who beat up Natalie and ran away to Hawaii with her. Natalie, my one and only love, who turned out to be more lesbian than straight. And I'm still in a seedy town, at a seedy high school with a dangerous truck route running through campus. The town's only claim to fame is Zachary's record of championship football teams. Zachary—damn him— the corrupt local hero with a history of recruiting questionable players. Zachary—who's on his way to costing me my career and my freedom from prison. Once a registered sex offender, always a registered sex offender. No one ever gets off that list!

Shaftoe was having trouble swallowing his burger. It didn't taste right. He imagined himself swelling up into the shape of a giant dirigible. On the side of his blimp-self were the words—in flashing lights—Child Abuser. Everyone in the world was staring up at him. He dropped his disgusting food onto the table, ducked his head, and slunk out of Miracle Burger. Was everybody in the place watching him go?

Back on campus, he crept into his office. He thought he'd arrived unnoticed. But that was not to be.

"Mr. Shaftoe, did you have a nice lunch?"

Shaftoe stifled the growl that wanted to escape his throat.

Sweet Jillie looked puzzled at his non-answer. "Mr. Shaftoe, it's almost the end of summer vacation. I'll bet you're eager to see the students again."

Shaftoe felt like he was going to vomit. He knew that he was in horrible emotional condition to face any counselees. He remembered what Dr. Juliet Mallard—AKA "Charlie," that sadistic bitch—had once said: If a man's love life and his job both go down the tubes at the same time, he will be in major emotional trouble. He was living the truth of that. He became aware that his eyes were blinking rapidly.

"What did you say, Jillie?"

"Never mind, Mr. Shaftoe. I can see you're thinking about something else."

God, he hoped she didn't know how he felt. He tried to think back, had he taken a pill from his hospital-provided bottle this morning? He couldn't remember. Could he make it through the rest of the workday without becoming a basket case on the job?

Only half-aware, he began mumbling, "Skoo, Skoolage, Skoo, Schoolage."

"Bobby, pal, how's it goin'? Can you show me my rosters of students for September?"

Shaftoe's heebie jeebies zapped him. Hard. Christ, he'd jumped out of his skin as if he was about to be hit by a semi. But it was only Kent Greef standing in his door frame, and if anyone had understood him recently, it'd been Kent. Shaftoe thought, My goddamn nerves are really shot. "Oh. Ah. Well. Well, Kent, I'm running behind on printing class rosters."

"No prob. Anyway, whadid I hear you mumbling? It sounded like 'School Coolidge'."

Shaftoe thought, I must have been mumbling Skoo, Schoolage, Skoo, Schoolage. This isn't funny. I've really gone over the edge. Maybe I need shock treatments.

"Dammit, Kent. This is a tough time of year for counselors. Nothing's settled." Shaftoe wondered if Kent could tell how troubled he was.

"Sorry, Bobby. My bad. But your mumbling reminded me . . . do you know about a kid named Scott Coolidge? A tragic story. Little known. But maybe you don't have time for it today."

Is Kent about to tell me some obscure sports trivia to try to take my mind off my troubles? Bless his heart. Shaftoe hoped it would work. He sighed. "Okay, Kent, if it's not too long. Speak!"

"Woof. Woof."

Fuck you, Shaftoe thought, but he realized that if he listened, there might be something in it for him. He looked at Kent and said nothing.

"Yeah, Bobby. This high school kid a few years ago, Scott Coolidge. From some podunk crossroads a couple states over. Long story short, he felt so pressured to succeed at quarterback, that he was virtually uncoachable. Too nervous to trust anyone but his teen-age self, I guess. Anyway, despite that he was superb. His high school team went undefeated all three years he was quarterback."

"No. Dammit, Kent! Not 'three years' at quarterback. A kid that good would have played in Ninth, Tenth, Eleventh, and Twelfth grades. That's not three years; it's four!"

Shaftoe saw Kent look at him with concern.

"No, Bobby. He never played in Twelfth Grade. He quit high school. Joined the army. The local recruiter was more than happy to see him. When he got to his army post, they put him on the post football team immediately."

Shaftoe thought, I gotta control myself. Think first. "Oh, sorry. So Scott Coolidge redeemed his football career after all. He played football in the army." Where was this story going?

"Not really, Bobby. He couldn't take orders, not even from the army coach. They discharged him 'unsuited for military service.'"

So the kid was aging. This tale sounded like a dead end. Shaftoe glanced at his watch. He hoped Kent would notice. He felt like going home early and crying. But he didn't think he'd be able to cry. "Discharged? So that's the last anyone ever heard of him?"

"Not exactly. I told you his story is tragic." More?

"Well, Bobby, to wind this up. The last I heard of Scott Coolidge was from some weekly newspaper near his village. Just a paragraph. Something like, On Wednesday, Scott Coolidge was jailed by Constable Brandish—heck of a name for a peace officer, huh, Bobby . . . Brandish?—and charged with impersonating an Eagle Scout soliciting donations door to door."

So much for all that blather. "Yeah, Kent. Former athlete felt too much pressure. Wound up impersonated an Eagle Scout. Jail. Tragic." Shaftoe thought of Zachary's son, Chip. He'd found Chip ineligible to play quarterback for Entonces this season. Another tragic story. But, with his own troubles, he could barely feel sympathy now for Zachary's son, let alone for some out-of-control kid named Coolidge who got what was coming to him. "Eagle Scout? I doubt it, Kent, he must have looked too old by that time."

"What? Oh gosh, Bobby. I forgot to tell you. He'd always looked younger than he was. That's why his nickname was 'Skoo'—"

"Skoo?" Shaftoe stiffened. He couldn't believe this. "Kent—his nickname was 'Skoo'? Fuck!"

"Geez, Bobby, watch your mouth, Jillie's right over there. Anyway . . . did you say 'Skoo'?" Shaftoe saw Kent look at him as if he were indeed crazy. "No one in the history of sports was ever nicknamed 'Skoo,' Bobby. You interrupted me, mid-word. *Mid-word,* dammit! Coolidge's nickname was 'School,' short for 'Schoolboy,' because he'd always looked so young."

Shaftoe's mind exploded. Wait! Kent just now said, "*Mid-word*"! That must have been why, at the back-to-school night in the field house, I heard Zachary start to introduce Blanchard as "Skoo . . ." The coach must have started to say the nickname "School," then caught himself *mid-word.* Shaftoe shuddered with the realization, maybe Felix Anthony Blanchard, a phony-sounding name from the start, was really Scott "School" Coolidge! That could account for why Zachary had crossed out the word "school" on the phonied-up sodomy accusation form. Coach *was* indeed phobic about the word "school." Afraid the word would unveil Scott "School" Coolidge, the overage imposter!

Shaftoe took a cautious breath. "'School' Coolidge, Kent?"

"Yeah, my friend. That's why, when I heard you mumbling something like that . . ."

Oh my God! Shaftoe wanted to hug Kent, but instead he said, "Got it. Got it. Great. Great story, Kent. Tragic. Bye now. Paperwork to do." He tried to smile, then cocked his head in the direction of the building's exit. Kent got the message and left.

Damn, thought Shaftoe, if "School" Coolidge, an imposter, played for Entonces, the state athletic commission could make the team forfeit the entire season.

"School" Coolidge? Superb quarterback? High school dropout? Army washout? Eagle Scout impersonator? Jail? No wonder no transfer records had come through under the phony name Felix Anthony Blanchard! But if Coolidge plays—undetected—all season, the team could win all its games and go to the state championships. The whole town would be proud, Coach will get off my back, and I keep my job, my career, and my freedom from blackmail.

On the other hand, if I expose Coolidge any time after he starts the first game of the season, the team forfeits its entire season, and the town hates me. Coach will file his false Suspected Child Abuse Report to punish me, and if law enforcement believes it, I'll lose my school counselor credential, go to prison, be hated there, and be a registered sex offender for the rest of my life. I'll lose everyone's respect forever, and for sure the respect of any woman. Christ—what a choice!

On my God, today's Friday! The first game is this afternoon.

Shaftoe knew he had to take action—fast!

chapter fourty five

Still in his tiny office, Shaftoe thought, Yes! Zachary had crossed out the word "school" because it hinted that Blanchard's true identity was "Schoolboy" Scott Coolidge. The further nickname, "School" was so distinctive that when Greef had heard Shaftoe mumble "School. Schoolage" it had jogged Greef's encyclopedic memory for football minutiae. And at the back-to-school parent night, Zachary had started to announce the imposter as "School," but partially caught himself, and only "Skoo" escaped his lips. No wonder Zachary was so agitated when, in the men's room that night, he denied saying even that much. "Skoo" Blanchard might really be Scott "School" Coolidge!

Greef had said "jail." Had Zachary sprung a very over-age football player from jail? Where might Shaftoe find conclusive evidence that Zachary had engineered an early release?

Christ, the first football game of the season is in one hour! My mind's been too muddled to remember that, and if Coach uses "School" Coolidge that would cause Entonces's team to forfeit the entire season. For the sake of the innocent players, my counselees, I have to find evidence on Zachary—right away!

So—another long shot. How can I get a look at Zachary's computer screen when it might have an incriminating document on it? Christ, Zachary's field house would have to be on fire before he'd jump up and dash out of there with his office door unlocked and a secret document showing on his screen.

Wait!

Fire? The Ed Zachary Field House on *fire*? Yeah, maybe I can make that happen.

Now, Shaftoe felt something he hadn't felt in a long time. Hope. A spark of anticipated success. He smiled. He glanced through his office doorway and saw Sweet Jillie working at her desk. He could depend on her. So loyal. The perfect unwitting accomplice.

He stood up, walked to Jillie's desk and paused. She looked up at him and smiled.

"How's it going today, Jillie?"

"Going good, Mr. Shaftoe." I see you managed to squeeze all the students into classrooms somehow."

Time was short. He had to rope Jillie in quickly. "Listen, Jillie. I have a question."

"Sure, Mr. Shaftoe." She looked at him expectantly.

"Well, our fire alarms and flashing lights have gone off several times since I came here a year ago. Why haven't the fire engines come to campus?"

"Easy to answer. I'm authorized to stay behind when everyone else evacuates. Then I just shut down the automatic process before it notifies the fire station." She looked proud.

"What?"

"Yes, the display next to Mr. Fluke's desk shows him where the fire or smoke is and he runs over there. If it's a prank trash can fire, he puts it out with an extinguisher, or maybe it's just smoke, like from a science experiment gone wrong. Then he radios me on his walkie-talkie radio. 'No problem.' And I shut the system down before any signal goes to the fire station. That way the fire fighters don't drive their engines over here for nothing and get pissed off . . ." Shaftoe saw red come into her cheeks, but he didn't have time to feel amused, "I mean, get . . . *disgusted* . . . at all our false alarms."

"So everyone has evacuated all the buildings, and they're waiting to see what comes next?"

"Yes, Mr. Shaftoe. Then, because there's no danger after all, I sound the all-clear signal."

"What does the all-clear signal sound like?" Shaftoe couldn't remember.

Jillie laughed. "It sounds like a dog yelping. I call it three yelps, followed by silence, then three more yelps."

"So, if all of that happened today, who would be calling you to tell you to sound the all-clear?" Shaftoe knew, he'd read the procedure in the school's emergency manual. But he wanted to be sure that Jillie knew and would have the process fresh in her mind.

"Why, Principal Fluke, of course."

"Jillie, Mr. Fluke isn't here today. He's taking a vacation day." Shaftoe saw Jillie's eyes blink.

"Oh, that's right, Mr. Shaftoe." She pursed her lips. "So you're next on the organizational chart. *You* would phone me to sound the all-clear."

"Got it. Thanks, Jillie."

That all fit perfectly into Shaftoe's plan. Suddenly he felt lighthearted. Like an innocent man set free.

The football game started in an hour. Now everything was up to him.

chapter forty six

Now Sweet Jillie was at the counseling center counter and Shaftoe was back at his desk. He had to make a telephone call, but he still had no door to close. He hoped Jillie wouldn't overhear him.

If his telephone ruse worked, he had to be ready—right now—to dash to the Ed Zachary Field House, the faster the better.

He turned his head away from Jillie, punched in Zachary's field house office number and spoke softly. "Hi, Coach. We still haven't received transfer papers for Blanchard, and the game's in an hour."

"Is that you, Shaftoe? Why the hell are you whispering, you wimp?"

Shaftoe thought, Shit, already this isn't going well. Could he pull this off? He decided not to respond to Zachary's question.

"Listen, Coach, the high school you told me Blanchard was transferring from . . . ? They still can't find any record of him." Then Shaftoe lied, "They said maybe you gave me the wrong birthdate for him."

"Fuck you. His birthdate is July 4."

At this point, Shaftoe didn't really care what Zachary said. He just needed to get to his own next lie.

"Thanks, Coach. July 4. What year?"

"1776, asshole. July 4, 1776. Dammit, I gotta get to the field for warm-ups."

Shaftoe gritted his teeth, then smiled. Zachary was becoming foolhardy. But it didn't matter now. Shaftoe continued his fakery. He turned his mouth away from his phone, and away from Jillie. "What, Jillie?" he said to his office wall. Then he spoke into his phone, "Coach, Jillie got an email from you. Just a minute . . ." He went on with his ruse, "About what, Jillie? . . . What? A prisoner?" He prayed that Zachary had heard that last word.

He heard the coach mumble under his breath, "What the fuck!"

Yes! Zachary had taken the bait!

"Anyway, Coach, are you sure you didn't send an email to Jillie by mistake?" Quickly, Shaftoe disconnected and grabbed his walkie-talkie. He burst out of his office, sped through the tree-lined walkway, and dashed into the Ed Zachary Field House. He ran directly to a red fire alarm box around a hall corner barely out of sight from Zachary's office.

Shaftoe counted on Ed Zachary to be checking on an email—right now—that had something to do with a prisoner—the formerly incarcerated Scott Coolidge. He wanted to see the email with his own eyes, on the coach's computer screen. The email that would incriminate Zachary. He was hoping that Zachary felt compelled just now to search for an email—any email containing the word "prisoner"—that the coach may have sent to anyone.

As Shaftoe paused at the red fire alarm box, shaking took over his body. He took a deep breath and pulled the lever on the box.

Immediately—pandemonium—lights flashed and sirens wailed. Quickly he peeked around the hall corner and looked toward Zachary's door, just as Zachary exploded out of his office, away from Shaftoe, and headed to the exit that would take him to the football stadium. Excellent! Shaftoe felt a bizarre mixture of success and panic. He leaned around the corner of the wall, ready to run to Zachary's office to see if he'd pulled up onto his computer screen an email about a prisoner.

But wait! Zachary was skidding to a stop in the hallway.

Shit! This wasn't working. Coach scurried back into

his office. Maybe to save some cherished mementos from the fire he thought was coming. Family photos? Oh hell, maybe to clear his computer screen. Damn! Then here he came, out again . . . what was he holding? Maybe some precious gift from a loved one. No, it looked like he was holding a very large white handkerchief. Oh my God, it was the cheerleader's briefs he'd been obscenely waving just before Shaftoe told him his son was ineligible to be quarterback. He watched as Zachary stuffed them down the front of his sweatpants.

Then Zachary was out of the building after all.

Shaftoe rushed into the coach's office. There *was* an email on the computer screen. Lucky! Was it the right one? Yes!

Constable Brandish, you bastard, you told me you would send phony high school transfer papers before you sprung the prisoner.

No time to read the rest or print a copy. No need to. Shaftoe'd seen enough. No more mystery. No more questions. He radioed Jillie, "No fire. No need for firefighters. Sound the all-clear."

"Yes, Mr. Shaftoe."

Immediately he heard the all-clear. Three yelps. A pause. Three yelps again.

Shaftoe needed to exit quickly, in case Zachary came back! He sprinted out of the building. He could just make it to the football stadium before the game started. But what would he do when he got there?

chapter fourty seven

Running full speed, Shaftoe bore down on the football stadium. The game was about to start. He imagined himself a bomb expert desperate to get to a package that was ticking its last few seconds. If Zachary put Coolidge into the game, the team would have to forfeit the entire season. And those other players were his counselees. He couldn't let that happen to them. Unjust! But how to prevent it? Could he get to the field in time? And once there, what the hell would he do to keep Coolidge from playing? Cold sweat drenched him. He hadn't thought that far ahead.

As he neared the stadium, time seemed to crawl. His senses felt bombarded. The smells of popcorn, hot dogs, and cut grass, the sounds of the marching band warming up, the shrieks of cheerleaders, and the afternoon sun in his eyes. Adults in the ticket line, jostling, good-naturedly swearing, laughing, and smelling of pre-game beer. He barreled past the ticket booth and heard Principal Fluke say, "Mr. Shaftoe, all faculty must buy a ticket." It sounded like a plea, rather than a command. He bumped the PTA President taking tickets and she fell. Christ, he'd hear about that. It didn't matter. He felt more alive than he had in months.

Now he'd cleared the crowd at the gate. He saw referees, the band, a news photographer, and flag squad girls on the sidelines, waiting. He had to get to the Entonces players' bench. Right now.

But, damn! The band, on the sidelines, blocked his most direct route. The musicians were his counselees too, but fuck 'em, this was more important now. Zachary was about to betray the whole community. He had to get to the bench, where the coach and Coolidge must be. The band struck up National Emblem March, his favorite, and all the musicians whose mouths weren't occupied with instruments began singing the time-honored words, *"Oh, the monkey wrapped his tail . . ."* He battered into the backs of the woodwind players. He heard, "Hey, asshole!" "What the fuck!" Sour notes squeaked out as he plowed forward, jostling the band members right and left. The ranks ahead of him continued singing, ". . . *around the flagpole . . .*" Now he elbowed through

the percussion section. *". . . to see the grass roll . . ."*
His senses were assaulted by sweaty band uniforms,
shiny tubas, the quick fade of interrupted notes, and the
dangerous footing of his street shoes on slick turf. He
bulled through the saxophones—a sound he loved, but
no time to listen—and into the trumpets. *". . . around
his ass hole."* Now a trombone whacked Shaftoe's
funny bone with its slide. He heard, "Godamn it,
bastard," then "Jesus! Look, it's Mr. Shaftoe!"

Shaftoe staggered forward.

Disoriented, he cleared the band. He saw the school's
flag girls slouch in formation onto the field —the squad
that Fluke had dubbed The Corsairs. "Coarse hairs.
Coarse hairs," male voices in the bleachers cat-called.
The head flag girl gave the spectators the finger. The
girls and the rude voices were his counselees too.
Well, the whole damn student body and town would be
demoralized if the season was forfeited. Why hadn't he
seen the big picture sooner?

He thought, The students rule, and the faculty
can only make a dent in their lives; but today their
counselor will be powerful!

At last he could see the Entonces bench. What the
hell! It was empty. Was he having a nightmare? Where
were the players? Wait. Wait. They must be finishing

warm-ups, calisthenics, on the field. He shifted his focus and saw them. Yep. Maybe he still had enough time to stop the game. But how? The players finished their jumping jacks and started toward their bench. He saw Zachary lumbering alongside them. And Coolidge jogging proudly, chin up, grinning at the home crowd, then doubling over, spoiling his image with a smoker's hacking cough.

As Shaftoe used his remaining energy—Jesus, am I out of shape?—to try to reach the bench, he saw Zachary stop and stare, mouth open, looking at him as if he were Elvis stepping out of a flying saucer. But where was Coolidge? Now Shaftoe couldn't spot him in the crowd of uniforms.

As Shaftoe closed on Zachary, the coach's mouth firmed and he stomped toward him, breathing fire.

Shaftoe thought he tasted blood, and he knew. That's the blood that will be spilled between Zachary and me.

chapter fourty eight

Words, like some displaced TV commercial, flashed through Shaftoe's mind. He yelled at Zachary, "Limited time offer. While supplies last. Act now, Zachary. Pull Coolidge off the field."

Zachary looked astonished, then sneered. "Shaftoe. You candy-assed wimp."

A nuclear hatred threatened to overwhelm Shaftoe. That does it! I'm gonna battle a giant brawler. I gotta focus. See if Zachary telegraphs his next move.

A few feet away now, Zachary shifted his feet. But Shaftoe couldn't tell if the coach was about to ignore him and walk away, or about to rush him. He'd seen Zachary put wrestling holds on Fluke from behind. He told himself, I can't let him get behind me. That could put me in the hospital. If he lunges at me, what I have to do will cost me my career. But Zachary's had this coming for a long time. I have to do this or I can't live with myself!

Speed, technique, agility, Shaftoe thought. Those are my only hope.

He went into a wrestler's crouch. At first, Zachary looked surprised, then his eyes sparkled. Shaftoe saw that the big man was confident that he could meet any physical challenge; in fact he welcomed it. No matter that the coach outweighed him and was still strong; Shaftoe's muscle memory kicked in. No matter that it had been instilled long ago in the college wrestling matches he'd lost. His stomach muscles tightened. He couldn't tell if that was a sign of determination or if he was about to vomit.

"That child abuse report's goin' in, Shaftoe."

"Try it, Coach. I've got proof otherwise. A video. Signed, sealed, and delivered. You can't frame me!"

Shaftoe glimpsed Kent Greef, coming out of the stands and motioning to the players to stay on the bench.

Zachary lunged at Shaftoe. Fans in the bleachers gasped.

Shaftoe'd been here before. In college matches. The anger, the fear, the nausea.

Then courage. Set-up. Head fake.

In response, Zachary shifted to defend one side.

I've got to move the fastest of my life, Shaftoe thought.

Speed. Single-leg lift. He exploded across the potholed sideline turf, rammed his head into Zachary's belly, clamped onto one thigh with both arms, and jerked upward. Off balance, the big man tottered and grunted. Each second was an eternity as the coach tried to muscle his way back down onto both feet.

Then Zachary broke loose.

"You little girl, Shaftoe! I smashed Borner's nuts. You'll be easy." He launched a kick at Shaftoe's genitals. Anticipating, the spectators in the stands groaned.

Shaftoe sidestepped the kick, grabbed the big man's thigh again, and slammed his head into the coach's belly. He breathed deeply to gather his strength and concentration, and gagged from the coach's body odor. Zachary reached for Shaftoe's eyes. His nails raked Shaftoe's cheek. His fingers were hairy and reeked of cigars. Shaftoe thought, Oh—so no holds barred? Well I've got something coming for you.

Then "Ooof! Christ!" THUD. And Zachary fell onto his side. The sound of Zachary's great weight hitting the turf reminded Shaftoe of the few opponents he'd ever dropped onto the mat. But this was much more gratifying than that. Shaftoe, his full weight stretched out on top of the coach's side, head to head, pressed him into the turf.

Technique. Perfect so far. Zachary's on his side and I've got an arm around him. Do I have the strength to hold him down? Shaftoe knew what the coach would instinctively do next; he'd been on the bottom so many times himself. Sure enough, Zachary struggled to get his massive body off the trampled grass. Shaftoe thought, Christ, he's powerful. Oh no! He's rising onto all fours.

"You're a dead man, Shaftoe."

Agility. Now Zachary, with Shaftoe face-down on the coach's back, was pushing upward. Head to head, Shaftoe saw the dirt behind the coach's ears. A voice inside Shaftoe goaded him, Don't let him shake you off!

Speed, technique, agility. Again.

It came back to him like riding a bicycle: He had to break Zachary down—get him off all fours.

Speed. Shift to arm bar, with my left arm immobilizing his. And far arm hook, my other arm reaching over his back. Lever the front of my thighs against the back of his.

Accomplished, it immobilized Zachary and gave Shaftoe a second to think. Now, the bleachers were roaring. Were they his counselees cheering him on, non-athletes despising the coach; or townspeople of all ages, just expressing blood lust?

Technique. I won't try to roll him onto his back for a pin; he's too strong and heavy. I'll jerk his arms from under him. And, with my hips, shove him from behind. That might put him on his belly.

Now things moved in slow motion. Shaftoe jerked and shoved violently, several times. Zachary's arms were like fence posts. Shaftoe kept wrenching them, but the big man was still on all fours. He wouldn't go face down. It was taking forever, draining Shaftoe, but he couldn't afford to have the coach get up and get behind him. With the strength of desperation, he jerked Zachary's arms again, and shoved from behind. At last Zachary skidded onto his face. Blood spurted from his nose. Shaftoe liked that.

Agility. Waist and ankle. In a flash, Shaftoe reversed his own body, put all his weight crosswise on Zachary's back, at the coach's waist, and pressed his chin into the coach's tailbone. Christ, didn't the guy ever bathe? With one hand he pushed Zachary's thigh down into the turf.

"You motherfucker, Shaftoe."

Let actions speak louder than words. Now, my other hand to the coach's other ankle. Look at that bastard's foot flopping to get traction. Grab it. Lift it. Trap him on his belly. You've lost everything if he escapes and gets behind you. You've got to finish him off. No holds barred, right, Zachary? Twist the ankle. Hard!

"Owww! Jesus Christ, you're breaking my leg!"

Twist farther. "Say 'uncle,' Zachary." Shaftoe was surprised at the calmness in his voice.

"Fuck you."

"Ed, are you deaf? I asked for one word, not two."

Shaftoe kept his focus. He had to show Zachary who's boss once and for all. With what strength he had left, he applied more twist to the coach's ankle. He heard Zachary groan, and a hand slapping the ground. Was Zachary signaling he was giving up? Shaftoe didn't trust him.

"Owww . . . owww." Then, "Uncle, goddamit."

"I can't hear you, Coach." The ankle was at its max. But Shaftoe wanted an inch more; could his own cramping muscles keep applying the pressure? Twist!

"Uncle!"

"I still can't hear you, Coach," Shaftoe taunted.

"UNCLE!"

The spectators heard the word signaling defeat, and cheered. There was no question whose side they were on.

"Gotcha, Zachary." The words came out in a hiss. Shaftoe's lungs burned. Every muscle ached. He was completely drained. Victory!

As Shaftoe released his hold on Zachary, the coach seemed too beaten to move. Then he groaned, rolled over, slowly wiped the blood from his face, looked at his blood-stained hand as if he'd never seen blood before, and began to struggle to his wobbly feet.

As he did so, something white dangled from the waistband of his sweatpants. A large handkerchief? News photographers' cameras began clicking. In the stands, hundreds of cell phones pointed at Zachary. As if one-by-one, the crowd in the stands ceased cheering

Shaftoe's victory; and, recognizing the white fabric to be cheerleader panties, began giving Zachary a horselaugh of ridicule.

Shaftoe knew that this panty-humiliation would hurt Zachary even more than losing the struggle on the sidelines.

chapter fourty nine

Shaftoe, standing in victory, knew he had to move quickly to capture Coolidge. That would save the team from disqualification, and silence the Zachary hero-worshipers. Gotta go after Coolidge, he's the point of Zachary's conniving. I'll drag the kid down physically if I have to.

It was time for the referees to call the teams' captains together for the coin toss. Then the game would start. Only seconds left to prevent Coolidge from playing. The head referee seemed determined not to let Shaftoe and Zachary's battle on the sidelines delay the start of his official responsibilities. He sounded his whistle, and the home and visitor's captains headed toward the center of the field to open the game. Had Zachary had the gall to make Coolidge the captain? No. Shaftoe saw that the Entonces player heading for the coin toss wasn't Coolidge. Shaftoe kept looking for him. He yelled, "Coolidge! Coolidge! I know who you are!" But there was no answer and Coolidge was nowhere to be seen.

Where the hell was he!

Christ! There was Coolidge, running toward the stadium exit, which opened onto the insanely dangerous truck route. Had Coolidge figured that the jig was up and was high-tailing it out of the stadium? For sure, Coolidge wouldn't want to go back to jail. Damn! Shaftoe needed Coolidge, to nail Zachary.

Can I catch him before he goes through the exit and escapes?

It was worth a try. Shaftoe ran, trying to kick his afterburner in, but his energy was low from wrestling Zachary. Well, Coolidge, a smoker, wasn't a ball of fire either, loaded down with his weighty football gear. Shaftoe, panting, was slowly closing the gap.

Now he had almost caught up to Coolidge on the gravel path leading to the exit gate.

Shaftoe launched an awkward tackle. Got him!

Coolidge stumbled, coughed, then squirmed free and was off again. Shaftoe tried to recover from crashing his face into the gravel. When he looked up, he saw Coolidge run through the stadium exit and disappear from view.

Then—from the highway beyond the exit—Shaftoe heard a terrifying rat-tat-tat. It was the machine-gun-explosion of engine brakes, from eighteen-wheelers! Then the blast of air horns and the screech of tires. He glimpsed big rigs bounding and skidding sideways. The same as at the start of the summer, when he had leaped toward the curb, lost his shoe, and a furious driver had given him the finger. Now, as he stood up and ran out the gate, he saw a cloud of tire smoke rising from the roadway, and smelled diesel fumes and the stench of shredded treads.

Oh my God! Could this really be happening? On the highway? To Coolidge? Had he been run over?

As Shaftoe reached the near curb, he couldn't see Coolidge anywhere. Only jumbled big rigs and drivers opening the doors of their cabs and scrambling down, one with a first aid kit. Shaftoe zigzagged into the center of the mass of jackknifed trailers. Then he saw it. The worst! Coolidge, in uniform, bloody, body twisted, lying motionless face-up on the cracked pavement. Shaftoe felt guilty; he'd caused this disaster by chasing Coolidge at the last second and failing to tackle him.

Wait! Hoping against hope, Shaftoe wished that the mangled athlete wasn't Coolidge. He knelt beside the ghastly body, in front of the face bars on the football helmet. How could it be anyone else? Well, in this bizarre town, anything was possible. But why even think that way—would my causing the death of a stranger be any less of a sin? A stranger? No way. The face—not so arrogant now—was that of Scott "Schoolboy" Coolidge. "School." "Skoo" for short. A pawn in Zachary's selfish scheme. The eyes were open, but unseeing. No movement of any part of the body. Was he dead?

Now the scene was silent and smelled of . . . Blood?

Shaftoe looked into the unseeing eyes and said, "Coolidge, you're going to be okay." It felt like a lie. Coolidge gave no sign of hearing.

He patted the bloody "22" on the chest of the young man's football jersey. Yeah, 22. Had that been Coolidge's age? What balls Zachary and Coolidge had! Well, it was all over now. Maybe he'd caused involuntary manslaughter. And all the witnesses, to his wrestling match with Zachary and his chasing Coolidge onto the highway, would seal his fate.

He heard sirens.

Then he noticed, for the first time, Principal Fluke standing stiffly beside him. Fluke stared down at Coolidge. Fluke's face turned ashen. He leaned forward with his hand over his mouth and his Adam's apple bobbed. Was the principal about to vomit? He looked as if he wished he were somewhere else, and Shaftoe wished the principal were somewhere else too.

Then, a miracle! Coolidge blinked, and the light of consciousness slowly came into his eyes. He looked first at Fluke, then at Shaftoe. He made some horrible gurgling sounds. Blood came from his mouth. He didn't seem able to speak. He cupped one hand and slowly brought the tips of his thumb and first finger almost together in front of his pursed lips. He looked pleadingly at Shaftoe and exhaled gently.

Principal Fluke saw Coolidge's gesture. "Look, he can't speak, but he's indicating his soul leaving his body, to go to the Afterlife." The principal placed his palms together in front of his chest. He whispered, "Let us pray."

Shaftoe ignored Fluke. He knew that Coolidge was really asking for a cigarette.

chapter fifty

Now, four months after Coolidge was crushed on the highway, the same four months that Shaftoe had stayed away from the town of Entonces and most of its news, he finally drove down from his new home, Capitol City, to have an evening drink with Kent Greef.

The neon beer signs on the walls still flickered through the gloom. From another table came the intermittent sounds of conversations of men in bib overalls. Farmers. Their big Saturday night at the Wagon Wheel.

"Well, Coach Greef, you finished off the Entonces football season. How do you like the big-time so far?"

Kent smiled. "That's Coach *Sunshine* to you, Shaftoe."

"Oh, you finally changed your tacky last name. What's next, a sex change?"

Kent seemed happy that their kidding had resumed. "Listen, Mr. Confused, I'm gay. I'm not transgender —"

Shaftoe faked astonishment, "Oh . . . my bad."

"— and I didn't have a perfect season."

"Yeah, but you did okay, right? And now you're Varsity Football Coach?"

Recorded music suffused the Wagon Wheel's alcohol-and-peanuts smell. It was an ancient tune, *All by myself . . .*

"Bobby, they're playing our song."

"Go to hell, Kent."

They both laughed.

Shaftoe signaled the bartender to make more drinks for them. He knew he would have to walk over to get them.

"Anyway, Shaftoe, where the hell you been? No one in Entonces ever saw you after the wreck on the highway. Good thing Coolidge recovered completely."

"He did?"

"Yeah, and now he's back in his home state, finishing the jail time that Ed Zachary sprung him out of."

Shaftoe smiled ruefully. "Seems fair."

"You won't believe it. He was 22 years old . . ."

Shaftoe silently congratulated himself for guessing that the number 22 on Coolidge's blood-soaked jersey hadn't been a coincidence.

Kent continued, ". . . with a wife and two kids. Yeah, he was in jail for impersonating an Eagle Scout. Soliciting money. He came by his nickname, 'Schoolboy,' naturally. His youthful looks, you know."

"Christ. Got it. And Zachary?"

"No investigation. And nobody really stopped their hero worship. The school board president and newspaper publisher —"

"Harley Huntington, Zachary's buddy."

"— hushed up all the dirt. But you cooked Zachary's goose, Bobby. Trounced him on the sidelines, in front of everyone."

"And Zachary's cheerleader-briefs-humiliation topped it off. That panty fetish was the icing on the cake."

"Panties are *icing on the cake*? That's a strange application of that saying, Bobby. I'd like to see your ink-blot test."

They both guffawed. Hearing their laughter, the bartender, washing glasses, looked at them. Shaftoe noticed that it was not the same bartender who had insulted Kent at the start of the summer. Things *were* getting better.

Kent went on, "So even Huntington gave up boosting Zachary. Zachary could see the handwriting on the wall, and he made up a lame excuse."

"Excuse? What the hell?"

"Yeah. He told the community that somebody'd slipped him a mickey just before you wrestled him down, and that the cheerleader white panties were planted on him. He implied it was a Communist conspiracy."

"And the community bought that bullshit." Shaftoe knew he was making a statement, not asking a question.

"Yep. Most of them. Zachary knew his fans. Once a football hero, always a football hero."

"Christ, I'm glad I'm outta Entonces. What about the little lost girl in the men's locker room, and her grandmother just outside the door? Did Zachary plant them?"

Greef set his half-empty drink down. "What?"

". . . and her grandmother just outside the door? Did Zachary plant them?"

"Shaftoe, have you been hallucinating?" Greef paused as if scanning his memory bank.

Shaftoe realized that he hadn't told anyone about the little girl or about Zachary's threatened phony Suspected Child Abuse Report on him. "You haven't been listening closely, Bobby. I said there *was no investigation.* Nothing about . . . about, what did you say? . . . a little girl? . . . ever came to light."

Shaftoe exhaled a long-held breath. So maybe Zachary never filled in, nor phoned in, the false Suspected Child Abuse Report, let alone mailed it. He thought, Let sleeping dogs lie. He sipped his drink. He overheard one of the farmers telling a dirty story. Something about a pig waiting in a wheelbarrow.

"So, Bobby, where'd you disappear to? People were asking 'Who was that masked man?'"

"Nothing that heroic, Kent."

A western tune was playing. . . . *walk away* . . .

"Well, Kent, you might say I knew when to walk away —"

Kent interrupted, "Did you hear that Harley Huntington and the board decided to clean house at Entonces High? They kicked Fluke upstairs, made him Assistant Superintendent for Curriculum, K-12."

"In that job, no one except the unfortunate teachers below him will know if he's doing things right or not."

"Excellent analysis, Bobby. And with Fluke out of the way, the board appointed Ethan Borner to be principal."

Shaftoe felt happy for the veteran teacher and union rep. He knew Kent could see the happiness on his face. Kent was telling him what he'd missed in the last four months, and Shaftoe wanted to hear more.

Kent continued, "Yeah, the board finally got smart. Who would have guessed it."

"And you, Kent? The board got cured of its homophobia?"

"Not exactly. Long story short—you put Zachary on the disabled list, Bobby. When you slammed him down on his face, you gave him an eyesight problem. So, combined with his lingerie display, that made the board happy to give him a medical leave for an indefinite time. Right away they opened his coaching job to all applicants."

"So you'd been acting coach, and you applied."

"Sure, it was now or never."

"Without a perfect season?"

"Well, I didn't do bad, even so. For that opening game, I ran out of the stands and down to the bench and took over as coach. You'd incapacitated Zachary, and you—or rather those eighteen-wheelers —took Coolidge out of the equation."

Shaftoe felt his stomach churn at the memory of Coolidge lying bloody on the highway.

"So, Bobby, I played Refugio as quarterback in that game."

"Who the hell is Refugio?"

Kent laughed. He looked proud. "Ya might say Refugio was a sleeper. He's a quiet skinny kid, never called attention to himself. Zachary probably considered him a wimp. He would have stayed a bench warmer under Zachary."

"But?"

"But I'd been watching him develop for years. In club football—Pop Warner League. I knew he would improve with my coaching. Anyway, who else could I turn to? Zachary's son was ineligible, then he lost Coolidge; he'd never thought to prepare a backup. Too arrogant. So, we lost that first game big time, but we steadily improved through the rest of the season. Harley Huntington in particular noticed that. His newspaper's advertisers stayed with him."

"And Huntington and the rest of the board overcame their homophobia and replaced Zachary with you?"

"Not so fast, Bobby. It wasn't as easy as that."

Shaftoe lifted his chin and raised his eyebrows. Go on.

Kent took the cue. "Well, the board used a formal application process. First, a paper screening, with anonymous application papers. Ya know, I understand football tactics and strategy better than Zachary ever did. And I placed first in that paper chase."

"The paper applications were anonymous. The Entonces school board didn't have a clue it was you."

"Right."

"So?"

"Well, Bobby, they had to give me an interview. And when they saw that I was as masculine as an Olympic decathlon champ . . ."

"Maybe that's not the best example, Kent."

"Just jerking your chain, Shaftoe. Anyway, at the interview I told them I'm gay. Self-protection, you know. They couldn't trot out a phony concern that I might be outed. Everyone knew I was gay anyway, except a few on the board."

"And they made you Zachary's replacement at the close of your interview."

"Again, not that simple, Bobby. I think they saw by the look in my eye, that I might play the *gay card* if they turned me down. You know, I might say,

'You only turned me down for varsity coach because you're prejudiced against gays.' Damn it, I was showing effective coaching skills under emergency conditions, and I deserved due consideration."

"Congratulations, Coach Greef— er, sorry—Coach *Sunshine*."

"Thanks. No reason not to go ahead with the name change, right? As John F. Kennedy paraphrased, *If not me, who? If not now, when?*"

"I don't think that JFK was talking about your name change. And I wouldn't quote a liberal in front of the Entonces school board."

"You're right. That would be pushing my luck."

They both chuckled. Laughter from the table of farmers sounded as if another animal story had hit the bull's-eye. *Bull's* eye? *Bulls?* Well, there was no limit to the different kinds of farm animals, was there. Shaftoe wondered if he should stop drinking for the evening.

Both men became silent.

More recorded music played. Then Shaftoe broke the silence.

"What's Zachary doing now?"

"My god, Bobby, you hadn't heard? The bastard used his medical leave to run for sheriff."

"What!"

"Yeah. Got elected in a landslide. Once a football hero, always a football hero. New sheriff in town."

Shaftoe shook his head from side to side in disbelief. Anything could happen in the town of Entonces.

Kent said, "What about you, masked man? Where the hell have you been for the last four months?"

"Well, I was lying low. Gentlemen's agreement between me and the school board. Sort of."

"Sort of?"

"The board didn't know what to do with me. They were busy trying to keep a lid on the football scandal. My presence in town would have been an embarrassing reminder. So right away they went on a fishing expedition—phoned my previous district and found out about my tackling the flaky kid who was about to crash the line for diplomas at graduation. They called me to a confidential meeting and said I had *a history of violence.* I had to get out of Dodge."

"They held all the cards. As a first-year employee, you had no job rights."

"You got it, Sherlock."

"That's *Head Coach* Sherlock to you, Bobby."

"Whatever. But for sure, the board didn't want me to go public by contesting anything. That would be another reminder of the Zachary fiasco. So I bargained for the best deal I could get."

"Which was?"

"The board got me a position at the State

Department of Education. That's why I moved to Capitol City. I'm now on the State Civil Rights Commission. Compared to Entonces High it's cushy. Quiet. Carpets in the halls, offices with doors and windows, people smiling at each other and taking time to chat. Smart, fascinating people of all ethnicities, genders, and sexual preferences, trying to swing their weight for their particular group."

Greef chuckled. "No deathly truck route? No diesel fumes, noise, and vibrations? No asbestos falling from the ceilings? No Flukes and Zacharys?"

"That's for sure. That's for damn sure. On the Commission our actions are civil and right —"

Kent groaned. "Civil and right because it's the *Civil Rights* Commission. Bad joke, Shaftoe."

"— But I miss the students. After a year of this glory, I may look for a counscling job again. I miss the kids."

Then Shaftoe began thinking about all the ways Kent had helped him. Saved his bacon, really. And he'd never properly thanked Kent.

"Listen, Kent. I want to tell you what a good friend you've been. After I collapsed, you pulled me away from Fluke's office in the middle of the night. And when you saw that I'd gone off the deep end you took me to the emergency room." Then Shaftoe remembered his search through Natalie's sinister apartment building when he thought Ed Zachary had kidnapped her, maybe worse. And the anti-anxiety meds which he no longer needed.

"No thanks are needed. You would have done the same for me."

Shaftoe wasn't at all sure of that. He signaled for more drinks, went to the bar, picked them up, and brought them back to the table.

Then it was as if Kent knew what Shaftoe had begun thinking.

"By the way, Bobby. Do you want to hear an update on Natalie?"

Shaftoe felt his heart begin to thump, and his eyes blink. "Maybe."

"Yes or no, Shaftoe."

"Okay. Yes." Shaftoe tried to conceal his trepidation, taking deep, slow, calming breaths.

"Well, here goes. Natalie's still living in Hawaii. As is her sadistic lover, your ex-psychotherapist, Juliet Mallard."

"Different strokes for different folks." Shaftoe bit his tongue not to say more.

"Strokes? Maybe too many strokes of Mallard's fist to Natalie's face. In Hawaii, last month, Natalie took out a restraining order on Mallard."

"Mallard has a history of violence, Kent."

"Different than your 'history of violence.'"

Shaftoe paused. He was aware that despite   or

maybe because of—his travails, he had a new strength of confidence. Had his defeat of Zachary, his surviving his busted romance, and his salvaging his career, built his confidence? Maybe.

He decided to get back into the conversation.

"Kent, you people get all the gossip, don't you. Even all the way from Hawaii." Immediately he saw that he'd put his foot in his mouth.

"What do you mean—*you people*—straight guy? You gotta get over casting those aspersions, Shaftoe."

"Sorry, Kent. My bad."

"Anyway, it was Sweet Jillie who told me. I guess she's still forwarding mail. And Jillie ain't one of *my people;* she's straight." Kent seemed tense.

Shaftoe hung his head. He decided to shut up.

Then he remembered something. "Kent, maybe I thanked you in a practical way. You know, the Entonces School Board sent me packing to Capitol City real fast. I was already up there and on the Civil Rights Commission, when the Board contacted me because you'd listed me as a reference for the varsity coaching job. I gave you a great one. You know everything about football."

Kent's face lit up. He seemed to relax.

"And, Kent, I signed my letter, Member, State Department of Education Civil Rights Commission."

"The school board must have thought you were

going to sic every LGBTQ+ organization in the world onto them if they didn't make me varsity coach." Kent smiled. "Thanks, Bobby. I'll dedicate a game to you next season."

"Make sure you win that one," Shaftoe said.

Kent reflected, "So the board hustled you onto the Civil Rights Commission, and then you backed me for Zachary's job."

"Yep."

"The board was hoist by its own petard."

Shaftoe faked an uncomprehending expression and stared at Kent. "Hoist? Petard? I don't know what that means. You talk like a college graduate." He gave Kent the finger.

Coach Sunshine laughed his freight train roar. The new bartender looked over as if he knew he'd missed a joke.

Suddenly Shaftoe felt drained. A good time to wind up the evening. "That about wraps it up for tonight, doesn't it."

But Kent looked as if a light bulb had lit up his brain. "Oh, wait. Something bizarre happened. Some kid who called himself Zeus got on the internet. I guess he was some kind of ninth grade fuckin' electronic genius. Anyway he posted a message. It was, *Ed Zachary Disease: A disease that makes your face look ed zachary like your ass.* Typical of the town, right?—corny, rude, and immature. The board made up a new term: electronic disrespect. But they were afraid to punish this Zeus kid, it would have revived the Zachary embarrassment."

Shaftoe smiled and inwardly rejoiced. Zeus had distinguished himself. Maybe that would even get Zeus a date with some geek girl.

He and Kent finished their drinks. They shook hands at the table. Shaftoe watched Kent walk out the door and disappear into the blackness of the parking lot.

Shaftoe heard approaching thunder.

chapter fifty one

Sitting alone in the gloom of the Wagon Wheel, Shaftoe overheard the farmers winding down a debate about whether the quack of a duck makes no echo.

Soon he saw that all the farmers were leaving. Late for them. He would be the only patron in the Wagon Wheel. With threatening weather, and no customers except him, the bartender could decide when to lock up. Shaftoe watched him shut off the buzzing neon beer signs, one by one. Then from behind the bar, he shut off the music. All was quiet except for the sound of rain beginning. In the lonely darkness, Shaftoe stared at the top of his table. He thought about his life. Win a few, lose a few. The bartender picked up a cowbell and rang it. It echoed.

Shaftoe wondered if the quack of a duck really does leave no echo. The bartender said, as if to no one in particular, "Last call."

Acknowledgements

Thanks to all the following:

My mother, who made her baby eat healthy. My father, whose subscription to Writer's Digest allowed me to begin reading it at age ten. James V. Smith Jr. of Writer's Digest Books, whose You Can Write a Novel, 1st and 2nd editions, were consulted often. All the school clerks and secretaries, teachers, administrators, students and parents who showed me the inner workings of schools. Ben Fonseca, for tips on how a wrestler might grapple with a larger opponent. "Doc" Murdock, leader of the Ojai Writing Workshop; its members, and Zoe Murdock, whose insights were especially helpful. As important as any of the above, were: Donna Loyd, interior layout and cover designer; and Martin and Nicolas, of Computer Idiot computer repair. This is a work of fiction. Any errors are those of the author.

About the Author

Wendell H. Jones is a former teacher and school counselor.

He lives with his wife, a theatre educator, in Ojai, California